LOVING AMANDA

"Amanda, tell me what's going on."

Her breath grew ragged and she buried her face in her palms, trying not to think how close Philip had come to dying, how close she had come to losing him. She stiffened at the feel of Jack's hands on her shoulders, but her protests were halfhearted when he turned her round and drew her into his embrace.

His palm eased down her spine in a gesture so tender and comforting that she was helpless to resist, and Amanda wept in his arms.

At last she quieted and, weak from vented emotion, let her head rest against his shoulder. Suddenly, she realized the picture she made—a sobbing, hysterical female—and she bristled, desperate to regain her composure. Jack gathered her closer when she would have pulled away, and she glanced up to search his face for dismay or chagrin.

Instead, she found understanding and longing.

His thumb traced the line of her face, wiping away the tears, and she shivered at the feel of his breath on her damp cheek. He lowered his mouth to hers, and the feel of his lips moving over hers caused her to shudder. She leaned forward, clutching at his shoulders to keep from slumping against him.

His hand still lingered against her face, and he held her firmly as he deepened the kiss . . .

—from "Philip's Mother" by Lisa Higdon

<u>BOOK YOUR PLACE ON OUR WEBSITE</u>
<u>AND MAKE THE</u>
<u>READING CONNECTION!</u>

We've created a customized website just for our very special readers, where you can get the inside scoop on everything that's going on with Zebra, Pinnacle and Kensington books.

When you come online, you'll have the exciting opportunity to:

- View covers of upcoming books
- Read sample chapters
- Learn about our future publishing schedule (listed by publication month *and author*)
- Find out when your favorite authors will be visiting a city near you
- Search for and order backlist books from our online catalog
- Check out author bios and background information
- Send e-mail to your favorite authors
- Meet the Kensington staff online
- Join us in weekly chats with authors, readers and other guests
- Get writing guidelines
- AND MUCH MORE!

Visit our website at
http://www.zebrabooks.com

DARLING MAMA

Joyce Carlow
Lisa Higdon
Maggie James

Zebra Books
Kensington Publishing Corp.
http://www.zebrabooks.com

ZEBRA BOOKS are published by

Kensington Publishing Corp.
850 Third Avenue
New York, NY 10022

First Printing: May, 1999
10 9 8 7 6 5 4 3 2 1

Printed in the United States of America

CONTENTS

ERIN'S BABY

Joyce Carlow

Chapter One

The house on Berkeley Square was one of the most elegant in all of Mayfair. It was also a special house in the eyes of Erin Connors because it was the home of Lady Georgiana Montague, a woman of beguiling charm, intellect, and renown. People of great importance came and went from this house, and they came to see Lady Montague, a woman who had made her own mark on literary life in London. That Erin worked for Lady Montague was a source of great pride, since she had moved to London only a year before from Belfast.

In one sense, leaving Belfast had been extremely difficult, for she had known no other home. In other ways, it was easier for her to move than it was for many of her countrymen. Those with families who had to forsake their homeland in order to find work

were always horribly homesick. But Erin was an
orphan, raised in a strict Church of England orphanage and only recently discharged from the institution.
When she sailed for London, she left no weeping
family on the docks. In fact, she left no relatives at
all, so in that sense her departure had been uncompli-
cated. Now she counted herself fortunate indeed. She
had steady work in an unusually stimulating atmosphere, she had made friends, and she had her Jack.

She looked around the sitting room and smiled.
The other servants were like the family she had never
had. They were a diverse lot and had a potpourri of
accents from all over England and beyond the British
Isles.

The butler, who headed the household staff, was
a most proper Englishman in his late fifties named
Mr. Franklin Hardy. He made all the decisions concerning the household, except of course those made
by Lady Montague. He set the work schedules, hired
staff, and got rid of those who did not please him.
He acted, in Erin's opinion, rather like the captain
of a ship or the strict father of a most diverse family.

Miss Martha George, the housekeeper, was as strict
as Mr. Hardy. It was she who planned the menus in
conjunction with Pierre Boudreau, the cook Lady
Montague had hired. Between Miss George and
Pierre there was little communication, for theirs was
an often stormy working relationship. When Miss
George and Pierre fought, Miss George immersed
herself in her other duties, those of assigning the
shopping and seeing to the cleaning both upstairs
and down. The other maids were Leticia Gordon
and Millicent Warder. Leticia was from Scotland and
Millicent from the West Country.

John Findley drove the carriage, and his son, her

very own Jack, took care of the horses and did all manner of repair work in and around the house and grounds.

There was also a groundskeeper from Italy, but he and his family did not live in the servants' quarters and Erin hardly knew them.

Erin smiled to herself as she went about her chores. When she left Belfast, she had never in her wildest dreams thought things would turn out so well.

An ever-so-slight shiver of pleasure went up her spine whenever she thought of Jack. He was a bit wild, but he surely loved her and she knew she loved him. It was true that there were facets of his personality that were still a mystery to her, and it was also true that he had known other women before her. But what man had not sown his wild oats? He was dashing! He loved a good time and he made her feel wonderful! In her heart, she did not believe Jack different from other men. As soon as they married, Jack would settle down and make a fine husband. Certainly Jack's father was a wonderful man, a man known for his integrity and sense of responsibility.

Erin polished the silver teapot as hard as she could. In its round surface she saw her own face reflected back at her, a distorted image that made her look as if her face were plate-shaped with small blue eyes and bulging, rosy cheeks. She laughed and put the teapot down.

"You'd better hurry," Leticia said a bit anxiously. "We've a lot to do before the Literary Ladies arrive."

The Literary Ladies was the name given to the women who gathered weekly at the Montague house. The Literary Ladies had all given up the more usual pastimes of cards and gossip in order to discuss literature and to write. They invited famous men of letters to their parties so they might enjoy lectures and stimulating conversation, and learn about the latest books. They immersed themselves in all the arts, but primarily in literature. Their meetings were the talk of London.

Erin tossed back her red-gold hair and put down the teapot. "Miss George asked me to go down to the greengrocer to get some fresh cucumbers to put between the bread."

"Then you had best hurry, or that handsome grocer will have retreated to the back room and sent his wife to work in the front."

"I like his wife. She and I often talk."

Leticia giggled. "I should rather talk to him," she said, dusting the sideboard furiously.

Erin hurried out of the dining room, down the long hallway, and into the kitchen.

Pierre, dressed in his immaculate white uniform, was already busy making scones and petite pastries. High tea was an important affair in the home of Lady Montague and it became all the more important when the Literary Ladies were expected.

"I'll need that produce," Pierre said in his still-thick French accent.

In spite of his accent, Erin felt close to Pierre because she knew they shared a heritage of sorts. Although she was an orphan, those who ran the institution in which she had been reared had seen fit to give her as much information as they could about her background. Just before she left, the superintendent had called her into his office, and there she learned that her mother had been a French Huguenot whose family had come as refugees to Belfast to work in the growing linen industry. "A hundred years ago," he told her, "the French outlawed the Huguenots because they were Protestants, and after the Edict of Nantes, thousands sought refuge in England and parts of Ireland controlled by the English. Many were brought here to Belfast where they could practice their religion freely. According to our records, your mother was the second generation of Huguenots born here. Your father was a man named Connors. Frankly, we have no information about him."

For a time, Erin had tried to find out more about her father, but she learned almost nothing save the fact that, like her, he had red hair and blue eyes.

It was her Huguenot heritage she shared with Pierre who was himself a Huguenot, though he had left France much later, when new persecutions had begun. According to Pierre, his family had practiced their religion secretly for several generations.

Certain areas of London had large Huguenot settlements and Pierre had lived for some time in a district called Soho. He knew about her heritage, and she assumed that was why he liked her.

"I have many little English hors d'oeuvres to make," Pierre muttered. His words came quickly out of his mouth, and Erin could tell he was agitated.

"I'll leave right away," she replied as she reached for her cloak, which hung on the hook by the back door. Pierre didn't look up, but she knew that was because he had once again become engrossed in his cooking. Pierre was more than a cook, he was a culinary artist with a temperamental nature. Erin knew when to engage him in conversation, when to compliment him, and when to just remain silent and do his bidding. He did not get along with the others, especially with the housekeeper, Miss George. In fact, he had once ranted on for nearly an hour and finally laid down the ruling that he wanted no one about when he was cooking except for Erin. "You, out!" he had shouted with petulance. And then, turning toward her, he added with a flick of his wrist, "She can stay. She makes Pierre smile."

As a result, Miss George communicated with the temperamental Pierre through her, and nearly every morning Miss George presented Erin with a list of things to tell Pierre.

As Erin opened the door, Pierre looked up. "I want the firm cucumbers. They must not be soggy or they will not do for these miserable little English tidbits."

He made a little face, and Erin gave him a knowing glance. He loved making pastries, exotic sauces, game, and all manner of foods. But the little tidbits that the Literary Ladies so liked, and which were indeed a staple at teatime in the Montague residence, were quite beyond his understanding. He thought them disgusting and entirely without substance or even artistic merit. *"Pâté de foie gras,* perhaps, but the cucumber, eh!" he exclaimed with disdain.

Erin pulled her cloak together and opened the door to step outside into the March drizzle.

"No wasting time with Jack," Pierre called after her, shaking his finger. "You should stay away from that one. I, Pierre, know he is up to the no good business."

Erin did not answer. She was all too well aware of the fact that Pierre did not like Jack.

Erin sped out of the door and down the lane that ran behind all the houses on the square. Once she reached Charles, she walked on toward Lawson's, the shop which Pierre preferred to all others. It was run by Philip Lawson and his wife Adelle.

There were many other shops, but Pierre insisted that Mr. Lawson was scrupulously clean and personally selected what he sold in his store. "Each and every morning he goes to the large market at Covent Garden. He has fresher produce and far better cheeses," Pierre had told her. "So you must always go there."

In fact, Erin had her own reasons for liking to make her purchases at the Lawson shop. She was very fond of Mr. Lawson's wife, Adelle, and they often chatted while Erin selected what was needed. In truth, she did not know Mr. Lawson, though now and again she saw him. He was usually in the back room and with rare exception, all she saw of him was his profile as he sat at his desk. She did, however, know that Leticia was right. Mr. Lawson was handsome.

It was Adelle who worked in the front of the store, and it was Adelle who had become her friend. At first, Adelle talked with her about the weather, about the other servants, and about the other families who lived on Berkeley Square. In time, Adelle shared with Erin the more intimate details of her life.

Poor Adelle. She was a tiny woman who seemed shy and often ill. Her skin was like tissue paper, and her large brown eyes were always filled with unhappiness. And yet Erin knew Adelle Lawson to be happily married to a handsome man who, according to Adelle, was gentle and kind as well. Her sadness had to do with her inability to carry a child to full term. Each time she conceived, she lost the child within a few months.

"But as far as a good husband goes," Adelle confided, "Philip is a fine man, a good man. Our marriage was arranged by my father, of course, but I could ask for no one kinder or more responsible."

In turn, Erin confided in Adelle and told her all about Jack. "He's funny and carefree and I adore him," she told Adelle, "even though he doesn't want to settle down."

Adelle, as did everyone who knew Jack, cautioned her. "He's a wild one. You must take care. Jack has something of a reputation."

"But no one knows him as I do," Erin said to herself as she hurried along. She looked forward to talking with Adelle and to hearing all the neighborhood gossip.

Erin reached the shop and ducked under its large green awning. There, protected from the elements, the produce was neatly displayed.

"Good morning to you," Erin sang out.

"And good morning to you," Adelle returned, although she looked weary. Erin could tell that she had been crying.

"Are you all right?" Erin asked, leaning close to Adelle.

Adelle shook her head. "I lost my baby," she said in a near whisper.

"I'm so sorry. I didn't know you were pregnant," Erin replied softly.

"I wasn't very far along. I always lose them in the first few months." Tears filled her eyes at once, and she shrugged her shoulders in bewilderment. "I don't know what to do. I want a baby so much."

Erin touched Adelle's hand. "I'm sure you'll have one."

Adelle shook her head. "I'm not as young as you. I fear I'll never have a child. The doctor says I'm too sickly to carry a child."

Erin bit her lip and then, covering Adelle's hand with hers, she whispered, "You could adopt a wee baby. I know you, in just a little while you would love it just as if it were your own."

"Wherever would I find a child to adopt?" Adelle asked.

"Perhaps from the Gardner Home in Croydon. I've heard they help find homes for infants whose mothers are unwed or who cannot support their children. There are other such places as well."

Adelle nodded. "I'll talk to Philip about it. Perhaps it is the only way for us. Still, I am not ready to give up yet. I want to try for as long as I can."

Erin gave her friend a big hug. Adelle wanted children so much that Erin knew she would go on trying to have her own even though each failure brought her new heartbreak.

She glanced toward Philip, Adelle's husband. As usual, he was at his desk in the back room working on the books. Adelle had a good husband, and she was glad of that because Adelle was not physically strong. She needed someone who was willing to look after her, and Philip Lawson was known to be that kind of man.

Erin picked out the cucumbers and a few other greens and then put them in her basket and charged them to Lady Montague's account.

"I must hurry," Erin said, squeezing Adelle's hand. "Pierre has much to do before tea."

"Please come back when you have more time. I enjoy talking with you," Adelle told her. "But I'm being unfair—I know Pierre will get angry if you don't hurry."

Erin smiled. Everyone in the neighborhood knew about Pierre's famed temperament. She headed for home and hoped she would see Jack as soon as high tea was over. Then, she thought happily, they would have the rest of the evening together.

* * *

Jack's father, John Findley, lived in the carriage house, a small cottage to the left of the main house, but Jack did not live with him. Quite by choice, Jack lived in a small room over the stables. It was an open secret among the servants in the neighborhood that John Findley did not always approve of his son's ways, though he did approve of Erin very much and hoped his son's interest in her meant that he would settle down. Still, in the beginning, he had seen fit to caution her about his son. She was a splendid girl, an innocent girl whom he did not want to get hurt. Jack had a "love them and leave them" reputation.

John Findley was brushing his favorite mare as he thought about his son and Erin. He daydreamed that one day soon Jack would marry Erin and he might become a grandfather. He grinned. Any child of Erin's was bound to be not only a beauty but as sharp as a tack.

Erin was lovely! She had waist-length, thick, curly, red-gold hair, huge blue eyes, a heart-shaped face, and a thin line of light freckles right across her nose. She also had a nice figure and the humor and good health of a fine Irish lass. He loved to listen to her speak; her lilt was musical and once he had caught her singing. Ah, she had the voice of an angel! He could not help thinking how nice it would be when she sang his grandchildren to sleep.

He finished brushing the mare and straightened up. Through the open door, he saw Erin heading toward the stables, and he waved at her.

"Have you seen Jack?" she called out.

"He's grooming the other horses, round back," John Findley called to her.

She waved back and fairly skipped on. Jack was a fortunate young man, John thought. But he hoped his son was also honorable.

"Jack?" Erin called out as she rounded the stables. They were divided in half and separated by a solid wood partition. Half the horses were kept in the front, where John Findley was brushing his mare, and the other half were housed in the back.

Erin stepped inside. It was never really light in the stables unless the doors were wide open. There were no windows, and the only light came from an opening in the roof and from the lantern that hung from a hook on the side of the wall.

Erin made her way through the shadows. "Jack? Where are you?"

Suddenly, she shrieked with surprise as two strong arms seized her from behind. "You were looking for me, my pretty?" he asked in his deep voice as he nuzzled her neck.

She relaxed in his grip. "Oh, you startled me, Jack Findley."

"And does your presence mean the tea party is over?"

"That it does. It was an exciting party, though. Dr. Johnson was there and so was Mr. Fielding."

"Stuffed shirts, I call them."

"Oh, no, they're really not. I think Dr. Johnson is quite a sensible sort. Do you know what he told Lady Montague?"

"That he likes the swing of her hips?"

"Of course not. Oh, you are terrible!"

"No lectures. So what did he tell her?"

"He told her that anyone who wrote for any reason other than to make money was a fool."

Jack laughed and spun her around in his arms. "Well, I can agree with him on that, but surely writing is not the way to one's fortune."

"And what way do you choose?" she asked, looking into his devilish brown eyes.

"The horses, my love. I want to raise the best horses in all of England and Ireland. And I want to win all the races too. That's where the money is, my girl— in breeding fine horses, racing them, and winning."

It was hardly the first time he had expressed his desire to breed horses. She knew how he felt about it and she leaned against him, letting him run his hands over her back as he daydreamed aloud.

Then, quite suddenly, he drew her back and kissed her lips. She shivered in his strong arms, but when he tried to touch her breast, she pulled away. "None of that now. Not till we're properly married, Jack Findley."

He looked at her and his eyes were penetrating. A smile curved around his lips. "Then let's get married, Erin. I can't wait forever. I have needs."

Erin's eyes grew large. "A very good idea, if you mean it," she answered.

"I mean it."

Erin laughed happily. "It'll be great fun, Jack. We'll live together in your little room. I know it's not big, but we'll have our privacy."

"Ah, privacy is what I want! I want to be alone with you." He kissed her again. "Yes, privacy to ravish my beautiful wife."

"Mind you, Jack Findley, I'll want to be redecorating that room. It needs a whitewash and some new curtains. It needs a woman's touch."

Jack lifted her off the ground and whirled her about. "It needs a woman's touch! I need a woman's touch!"

"You're a shameful man!"

He laughed. "And you love me."

She looked evenly into his dancing eyes. "And I love you," she repeated.

John Findley sat in his chair by the hearth in the central room of the carriage house. It was his custom to smoke one pipe full of tobacco a day, and he almost always chose to take this small pleasure after he had finished his dinner.

He felt quite relaxed as he watched the orange flames flicker and listened to the fire as it crackled. His eyes were half closed, his thoughts on the past, a past long gone but not forgotten. He had almost convinced himself that his wife was in the kitchen and that he was relaxing after the supper she had prepared for him. A faint smile crossed his lips as his thoughts filled with dreamy nostalgia. He was about to doze off into a light sleep when he heard the knock on his door. His eyes opened and he pulled himself up and went to the door.

Jack and Erin stood on the steps. Her cheeks were rosy from the cold night air, and Jack looked flushed and happy. He was holding Erin's arm.

"Come along in before that March wind cools off the house," John urged.

They both stepped in, and Erin took off her cloak. "We've come to talk to you," she said cheerfully.

"Come in and sit down by the fire."

Jack sat down on a bench, and Erin sat next to him. There was only one chair.

"What brings you two here?" he asked. "Not that I'm ever unhappy to see Erin."

"We've decided to get married," Jack said forthrightly.

John Findley was sure his expression revealed his apprehension. As much as he liked Erin, and as much as he daydreamed of grandchildren, he was not at all certain his son was mature enough to take on a wife. And yet, Jack had settled down since he'd known Erin; she was most certainly a good influence on him.

"You're not pleased?" Erin asked.

John quickly smiled. "I am pleased, very pleased."

"We want to get married right away," Jack said quickly. "Maybe next week."

John Findley looked seriously at his son. "Are you sure you're ready to take on the responsibility of caring for a wife?"

"As ready as I'll ever be," Jack replied.

It was not entirely the answer John Findley had hoped to hear.

"What I meant was, you don't earn a very good living yet."

"Good enough. After all, Erin works too."

Again, his son's answer was not the answer he had hoped to hear. Didn't Jack realize that with marriage there would also be children? A stable hand and handyman did not earn as much as a driver.

"We're going to move into the room over the stable." Erin's voice was filled with enthusiasm, and her blue eyes danced with happiness. "I'm going to redecorate it. I'll sew new curtains and make it clean and cheerful."

He felt a pang of disappointment that they would not live with him, but he knew it was for the best that they be alone.

"Are you sure you want to get married so quickly?"

"Very sure," Erin answered before Jack could say a word.

"Then I'll make the arrangements for next Saturday," John said. He reached down and took Erin's hand. "I'll be pleased to welcome you to our family."

Erin blushed; then, standing on her tiptoes, she kissed him on the cheek. "I've never had any family, so this will be a new experience for me."

As they left, John watched them. Jack's arm was around her small waist. He shook his head. How he wished his son was as interested in Erin's other attributes as he was in her curvaceous figure. She was a lively, bright young girl. He hoped she would not be saddled with too much too soon.

"You are getting married!" Pierre boomed. His voice filled the kitchen and reverberated off the pots and pans, which hung from the ceiling to the side of his large cooking stove.

"On Saturday," Erin said. "Please come. I have no family and I want my friends to come."

Pierre scowled. "Pierre will come, but Pierre does not approve. He is not good enough for you. He is an impudent puppy. He is loving you only for your body."

Erin could not but smile at his accent and use of English. He seemed to frighten the others when he got mad or was loud, but she could only see the humor in him. He was, of course, capable of giving anyone with whom he did not agree a good tongue-lashing, but he did not mean it. When his bad temper had passed, he forgot everything. "No, Jack really loves me," Erin said confidently. "I know he does."

"I suppose you will ask Madame George," Pierre muttered, a pouty expression covering his face.

"I'm going to ask everyone, and I'll ask Lady Montague if they can all attend. It won't take long."

"She is very generous. I'm sure she will say yes."

Pierre came close to her. "You be careful," he warned. Then he kissed her gently on the cheek. "Very careful."

Franklin Hardy, the butler and chief of the household staff, wore his uniform. It always made Erin smile because his collar was high and extremely stiff, giving the impression that it held up his head. Miss George appeared wearing a woolen suit with a prim white collar that was almost as stiff as Mr. Hardy's. Leticia Gordon came wearing a plain dress with a plaid sash, and Millicent wore a slightly faded gown she had borrowed from a friend.

Erin herself wore a frothy white dress bestowed upon her by none other than Lady Montague herself. "I wore it once to a party, my dear. Of course that was some time ago—I could not begin to get into anything so frivolous these days."

But Erin was grateful. It was white, and it had ruffles and lace. She had removed some of the lace from the overskirt and fashioned it into a little veil. In the end, when she had stood before the mirror in the dressing room of the little chapel, she felt as much a bride as any woman could, and she thought she looked like one as well.

Reluctantly, Pierre agreed to walk her to the altar, but he muttered over and over that Jack had better take proper care of her.

When she met Jack at the altar, his eyes glazed over

with such admiration that it made her feel warm and expectant inside. He smiled at her, that wonderful crooked smile he had. And he raised one brow too, a sure sign that he was impressed with her appearance.

The ceremony was short, and then Jack lifted her veil and kissed her. It was a far too passionate kiss to have occurred in front of others, and she knew her face turned the color of her hair.

"A good thing Lady Montague gave us two days off," he whispered in her ear. "We're going to be worn out with our lovemaking."

His whispered words made her blush even more, as did his arms around her waist. But she was overwhelmed with happiness and thought, *Tonight I will become a woman.*

Chapter Two

April, 1752

Erin walked slowly across the expanse of grass between the main house and the carriage house, taking care not to trip or spill the rich, thick soup she carried. The soup was left over from the noon meal, and Pierre had ordained that it should be taken to her father-in-law, who had not been feeling well and appeared to be suffering from a lingering fever. He had been taken ill in February and worked on in spite of everyone's advice that he should take to his bed and rest. But John Findley was a stubborn man, he continued to work, and then in March he became so ill that Lady Montague herself ordered him to bed.

Now it was the first of April, and he seemed little better. His cough was acute, his wheezing was continual, and he rambled on, making little sense when he spoke. Erin tried to spend as much time caring for him as possible, but her household duties were rigorous, and she had little time except in the evenings. "Surely he'll get better soon," she said to herself. Rows of daffodils filled the beds that bordered the green lawn. There was no doubt that spring was here. "Yes, you'll get better now," Erin said, trying to convince herself.

The rains of March had caused a spurt of growth, and everywhere bulbous flowers were bursting into riotous colors. As beautiful as Ireland was in the spring, the gardens of London were far more elegant. And that, Erin thought wistfully, reflected in some way the temperaments of the two peoples. In Ireland, it was the wild untamed quality of the place that made it so pleasing. But here in England, the gardens were all quite proper, all meticulously laid out and well planned. The hedges were trimmed, the flowers planted so that the colors would blend with one another to create a living painting. When there were wild gardens, they were intended to be so, rather than having sprung spontaneously into being. Gardening in England was a profession, and to some a way of life. Even the small gardens of the working class were well tended and not allowed to meander. In Ireland, by contrast, flowers grew among the rocks on hilly, uneven ground and among the hedges and in the fields. It was as if the landscape were the result of random scattering. Hills, rocks, and plants appeared to have been thrown from the heavens as a child might toss out a handful of jackstones.

Ireland was as undisciplined as England was disciplined. And that thought brought Jack to the forefront of Erin's mind. Her husband was wild and undisciplined, and she feared that their marriage had not changed him one whit. She bit her lower lip as she thought about their year together. In all ways their relationship was far less than she had dreamed it would be. Jack was gone a great deal, and when she asked him where he went, he was harsh with her and told her not to ask questions or pry into his business. In their year together, they had argued more than once. Jack was quick of temper, and Erin side-stepped his outbursts as well as she could, but sometimes he angered her, and then she fought back, trying to make him realize that he was being selfish. In her mind, Jack was not just selfish in his relationship with her, he was also self-absorbed where his father was concerned. She had wanted them to move in with Jack's father so that she could better look after the elderly man. But Jack would not hear of it.

Erin reached the carriage house and knocked on the door. She waited for a few minutes and when there was no answer, she knocked again. "I brought some soup," she called out to John Findley. As she waited for a response, she wondered, not for the first time, how father and son could be so different. She was quite certain that Jack's father had not treated his wife as Jack treated her. John Findley was a man whose reputation was one of steadfastness, honesty, and decency. He was said by everyone to be a responsible man. If only Jack were responsible, she thought sadly.

Jack's father was always glad to see her, and he was very grateful when she brought him food, as he disliked cooking for himself. He was a very lonely man.

When no one answered the door or called out to her, Erin glanced around, craning her neck to see if the carriage was there. It was parked in its place to one side of the house, so John could not be out driving

Lady Montague about. Not that Lady Montague had asked him of late. She had engaged a part-time driver until John recovered.

Erin set the soup down and opened the unlocked door. Then she picked up the soup and walked into the house.

It was odd. It was nearly two in the afternoon, but the house was in darkness and it was still, as if Jack's father had never gotten up from his night's sleep. It was at that moment that a strange foreboding came over Erin.

"Mr. Findley!" Erin called out. She set the soup down near the hearth. "Mr. Findley!" she called again more anxiously.

Not a sound. Her foreboding turned to a strong feeling of discomfort. She walked hurriedly toward the bedroom and carefully opened the door. She peeked into the darkened room. There, on the bed, John Findley lay—a great still lump beneath the covers.

Erin tiptoed softly to the bed. She laid her hand on his hulking shoulder and jostled him gently. "Mr. Findley? Mr. Findley?"

There was no movement of any kind. "Oh, dear God," Erin whispered. She moved her warm hand across John Findley's cold forehead. There was no doubt about it. Her father-in-law was dead and had almost assuredly died in his sleep.

She stood for a long moment and looked at his tranquil expression. It was certainly not the worst way to die. "I'm so sorry," she whispered. "If you'd lived a little longer, you'd have known your grandchild." Erin touched her stomach. She hadn't told Jack yet, but she was quite certain she was pregnant.

She sat down on the edge of the bed, her head

filled with jumbled thoughts and her heart filled with apprehension. Mr. Findley had been a good man, a dependable man who had worked hard all of his life. He had wanted a grandchild desperately.

"Not that I intended to get pregnant so soon," she said aloud. But truly, what bothered her was neither her pregnancy nor the fact that Mr. Findley had not lived to know his grandchild. It was Jack's reaction to her pregnancy she feared.

She closed her eyes and touched the quilt on the bed. Like a blind person, she felt its texture with her fingers, and somehow the movement clarified her thoughts. She shook her head. Things were not as they should be. She had tried to put everything aside, tried not even to consider the realities of her life. But the emotion she now felt in the face of Mr. Findley's death combined with the knowledge of her pregnancy to make her doubly aware of Jack's shortcomings. "No, things aren't right," she said aloud. Jack had not been a good son, there was no denying it, and she feared he would not be a good father either.

Tears began to well in her blue eyes—tears for Mr. Findley and tears for the future of her unborn child. She tried to recall her own thoughts of a year ago. What had she expected?

Jack had been so loving. She had daydreamed endlessly about how it would be when they lived together. But nothing was as she had imagined. She had painted and decorated their little room above the stables by herself. Her days were spent working in the big house, her evenings alone because Jack was either tending his beloved horses or at the pub. He left early in the morning and came home late at night. He made love to her, but that too was not as she had anticipated. He was quick and perfunctory, taking his own pleasure and ignoring hers. It was true enough, she thought, that she had no one to tell her what married life would be like. But she had heard the other maids talking, and often they confided secrets about their love lives. She had thought there would be more to it, but there was not. Jack was a bit rough too, and though she said nothing, she wondered why he could not be a bit slower and more loving when he desired her.

But even more than their love life, his long absences both upset and mystified her. He was gone before she left for the big house in the morning, and when she came back after supper he was nowhere about. She usually ate alone, spent the evening alone, and then went to bed. More often than not, he would return just after she had fallen asleep. Then he would wake her and satisfy himself before dropping into a deep and sometimes drunken sleep.

Erin let out her breath and then stood up. She was filled with sadness as she walked downstairs, out of the carriage house, and toward the big house. She could not tell Jack right away about his father because he was already gone. She would tell Mr. Hardy. He would know what to do.

As it was still only early spring, there was no summer produce to fill the bins at Lawson's. Instead, rows of cabbages were front and center, and behind those potatoes and carrots. Beyond the bins were rows of containers filled with dried produce and parched cereals, while assorted dried herbs and spices hung from the rafters.

In order to expand their business, Philip and Adelle

Lawson stocked baked specialties and candies. The aroma of the freshly baked bread made Erin's mouth water as she inspected the cabbages.

When she had selected two, Erin looked about for Adelle and saw her talking to her husband in the back room. She waited a minute, and then Adelle emerged. As slender and frail as she was, Adelle looked radiant. Her long brown hair was tied with a ribbon, and she wore a new flowered apron over her plain dress.

"You look wonderful," Erin said, leaning close.

Adelle took Erin's hand. "I'm with child again and I feel wonderful. Oh, Erin, I think I'm going to carry this one. I'm quite certain we're going to have a child at last."

"How far along are you?" Erin asked.

"Two months, but I lost the others earlier. This time I've missed two bloods, so I think it will be all right."

"Oh, Adelle, I'm so happy for you." Erin leaned over and kissed her friend's cheek. But she decided she would not yet tell Adelle of her own pregnancy. She had, after all, only missed one blood so far, and she thought it might yet come. And more important, she had not yet told Jack. In fact, she admitted, she did not know quite how to tell him, especially now that he was so preoccupied.

"You look troubled," Adelle said, leaning close. "Is everything all right, Erin?"

"It's a minor trouble," Erin answered. She shook her head. "You know Jack's father died only a week ago, and of course Lady Montague had to hire a new driver immediately. His name is Frederick Walmsley."

"I wouldn't suppose she could go without a driver for very long," Adelle answered.

"Oh, of course not," Erin said quickly. "Anyway, Mr. Walmsley moved into the carriage house right away and took over full responsibility for the driving and the horses. The trouble is, he doesn't get on with Jack very well."

Adelle frowned. "Erin, is Jack doing his job? I don't mean to pry, but you know I've heard that Jack has a reputation for not working very hard. Everyone thought that when he married you, he would settle down. Hasn't he?"

Erin did not know how to answer. Adelle was well-meaning and only wanted to comfort her. But it didn't seem right to talk about one's husband even if there were something wrong. "He's a good husband," Erin answered a bit too defensively.

At that moment, Philip Lawson came out of the back room.

"Good morning," he said warmly.

Erin nodded shyly. He was a good-looking man, even better looking than she had first thought. He had soft gray eyes and thick, dark brown hair. He was tall and muscular and looked more of an athlete than a shopkeeper. He slipped his arm around his wife's waist protectively. "I was sorry to hear about your father-in-law," he said sincerely.

"He was a fine man," Erin said softly. Even as she said the words, she wondered if they sounded like a criticism of Jack.

She turned her attention back toward the produce. "I have a few more things to purchase," she said. Vaguely, she wondered how much they knew about her and about her life. The neighborhood was small, and everyone knew everyone else's business. All the other servants gossiped and talked. News spread like wildfire. She decided to say no more at the moment.

Jack had enough problems with Mr. Walmsley without her letting it be known that she was troubled by his actions.

"I think these will be enough," she said, charging the items she had gathered to Lady Montague.

Erin made her way home. A full day's work lay ahead. It was once again Lady Montague's turn to host the Literary Ladies. It would be another long evening and, Erin hoped, full of dazzling conversation. If one listened carefully, being in the same room with the ladies and the likes of Dr. Johnson and Mr. Fielding was almost as good as going to school and being taught. She felt that each time the ladies met, she learned something new. She had to serve all evening, of course, but that did not matter. The time sped by, and she was able to eavesdrop on fascinating conversations. Her evenings spent serving the Literary Ladies gave her the opportunity to learn, and she knew learning was important. If only Jack felt the same! She had once said something to him about learning and indeed, she had offered to teach him to read. But he had shrugged and said, "What a waste of time!"

Erin climbed the narrow steps to the room over the stables. She kicked off her shoes, removed her uniform, and threw herself across the bed, exhausted. It had been a wonderful evening, physically and mentally exhausting, but nonetheless wonderful. She closed her eyes and in a moment had dropped off into a dreamless sleep.

She sat up sleepily at the sound of voices coming from downstairs in the stables. Erin instantly recognized one voice as that of Jack. The other, she was quite certain, belonged to Mr. Walmsley. She couldn't make out the words, but she could certainly tell they were both angry. She strained to make out the words, but then she heard the slamming of a door and Jack's footsteps on the wooden stairs.

Erin stood up and walked hurriedly toward the door, but before she reached it, Jack threw it open and stomped angrily into the room. She frowned, smelling the whiskey on his breath.

"What the hell are you scowling at, woman?" he shouted at her. She stepped back. Never before had he frightened her, but the odor of whiskey, the tone of his voice, and his expression combined to make her feel threatened.

"I'm not scowling," she protested without raising her voice.

"Well, I call it a scowl. Fine thing when a man can't even come home without criticism."

Erin said nothing.

"Don't waste your time with lectures. Pack our things. We're leaving here! Right now! Tonight!"

Erin opened her mouth, not just in surprise, but in deep shock.

He suddenly walked toward her. He reached out and put his arm around her waist, pulling her close to him. "I will say, I do like to come home and find you in your little chemise lying across the bed."

He kissed her roughly and pressed her breast hard. She pulled away and out of his reach.

"Jack, we have to talk! I don't understand. What do you mean, pack? Why are we leaving?"

Jack ignored her question. "We have time for a quick romp, my darling."

Again, she eluded his grasp. "Jack, we can't leave here. Where will we go?"

He grimaced back at her. "I said we're leaving, and we are."

"What happened downstairs?" she demanded.

"I had a fight with that old bastard, Walmsley. He gave me some orders I didn't like, so I told him I quit! And I told him to go to hell!"

Erin blinked disbelievingly at him. How could he do such a thing? In her heart, she knew that all Walmsley had demanded was that Jack be at work on time and do his job.

"I still have a job here," she said in a near whisper. In her wildest dreams, she could not imagine leaving now. These people were like family to her; she had no one else. "I have obligations," she murmured.

"The hell with your obligations! I'm going and so are you."

Tears began to fill her eyes. Not because she wanted to cry, but because she was so frightened. "We can't go," she said even more softly. "We can't go, not now."

He looked at her harshly. "What the hell are you blubbering about?"

"I'm pregnant. We need our jobs. Please, Jack, go to Mr. Walmsley and apologize. I know he'll take you back. I know he'll give you another chance."

But it was as if he only heard part of what she said. "Pregnant! How the hell did you let that happen? That's just what I need, a blubbering wife and a screaming kid!" He kicked the side of the bed, then looked into her eyes. "You stay here and have the bloody baby. I'm leaving!"

He kicked the side of the bed again for emphasis, and while Erin watched in stunned silence, he threw his things together and tied them into an untidy pack.

"Please," Erin murmured. She held out her hand toward him, but he did not respond.

She was beyond crying. She trembled violently. Why was he behaving this way? Perhaps all the things people had said about him were true.

He picked up his pack, turned, and without looking back, slammed the door behind him.

Erin sat on the side of the bed. Perhaps when the effects of the drink wore off, when he had time to think about it clearly, perhaps then he would come back. She fell back across the bed and tried to think. If he did not come back, what would become of her? What would become of their child?

After a long time she got up off the bed and went to her secret hiding place behind the loose board in the wall. There she had saved some money in a small wooden box. It was money given to her by Jack's father and some extra money given to her for helping one of Lady Montague's friends on her day off. She lifted the box and opened it carefully. Her mouth opened in surprise. It was empty! Only Jack could have taken it! She let the box drop from her hands. Now there was nothing! She didn't have even one extra farthing. What was she going to do?

The morning light filtered through the window of the kitchen. Pierre was already at work chopping herbs and preparing for his day's cooking when Erin came in. He turned to smile at her, and the smile faded from his face. He looked down his long French nose at her. "And what is the matter with my little *champignon* today?"

There was deep concern in his face. What could

she say to him? "I don't know where to begin," she
answered in a near whisper.

"Begin with that Jack, that miserable little cock-
roach! Pierre knows he has done something horrible!
Pierre can tell to look at you. *Mon Dieu!* You've been
crying all night! What is it?"

She sat down on one of the wooden chairs and
Pierre quickly poured her some coffee. "Ah, *ma petite
amie!* Drink this and tell Pierre what has happened."

"He had a terrible fight with Mr. Walmsley."

"Ah, I knew that was coming! Monsieur Walmsley
said Jack did not work and spent all of his time gambling and drinking. He told Mr. Hardy yesterday, and
Mr. Hardy told Walmsley to have a talk with Jack."

Erin nodded. "Jack lost his temper."

"*Chèrie,* Jack is no good. He drinks too much and
gambles too much. I know you think you love him,
but he is the same as he was before you two were
married. If he is gone, I say good riddance!"

Pierre didn't have an inkling that she was pregnant,
and she did not know if she should tell him, at least
just yet. Still, of all those on the staff, she trusted
Pierre the most.

He leaned close to her face. "There is more. I
know there is more."

"I'm pregnant." She said it so softly, she was uncertain whether he understood, but he suddenly put his
pudgy arms around her. "Oh, *mon petit chou!* He is a
wretch indeed."

Then Pierre drew back and looked her in the eyes.
"You did tell him this, did you not?"

"Of course."

"Ah, he is more than a wretch, a cad, a *diable! Mon
Dieu,* whatever shall we do!"

"I hope he will come back."

"I never want to see his face again, but for you, I too shall hope he comes back."

She nodded and sipped some of the coffee he had given her. Pierre took her hands. *"Ma chèrie,* if he does not come back, we will think of something together. Please, do not worry. Pierre knows that you will survive this. You are a strong, beautiful young woman."

She nodded and squeezed his hands in return. He was her friend, and although she could not immediately think just how he could be of help, she knew he would help if he could.

Erin finished her coffee and dried her eyes. There was work to be done, and certainly she could not afford to lose her position too.

Weeks went by and, feeling great sadness, Erin moved back into the servants' quarters. Her room there was tiny, but she saw the others at meals and often played cards with them in the evening. It was better, she thought, than being alone. There was less time to think about Jack, less time to wonder where he was, and if indeed he would come back. Weeks went by and she missed her third blood and then her fourth. It was nearly the middle of July, and the sun was warmer, the days longer.

Erin was in the library, carefully dusting the books on what Lady Montague called "my precious shelf." These were books all personally autographed by their authors to Lady Montague.

Leticia opened the door and proffered a letter. "It's for you," she said almost excitedly. It was rare indeed that anyone on the staff received a letter.

Erin looked at the envelope curiously. The handwriting was neat and careful, but it was not a hand with which she was familiar. But then, she reminded herself, Jack could not write, so if it were from him, it had no doubt been written by one of those professional writers who specialized in selling their skill to those without the education to write for themselves.

Erin sat down in a nearby chair and opened the letter, unfolding it carefully. It was indeed from Jack, but it was not what she had prayed for. It was not an announcement that he was returning to her.

> *Dear Erin,*
>   *As you might guess, I am having this letter written for me. I have decided to go to America. I will be leaving from Portsmouth on the fifteenth of July aboard the* HMS Willis. *I will work off my passage when I arrive. I'm going to the Virginia Colony to raise horses. I hope things won't be too hard for you.*
>
>   *Jack*

Hard? She read the letter again. Did his marriage vows mean nothing to him? There wasn't a single word about sending for her later, about caring for their child; there wasn't even so much as an "I love you." Hard? Yes, she suspected it would be very hard. Miss George already wanted to speak to her. They all knew she was pregnant because when she began to show, her uniform became too tight. She had told everyone. They were all sympathetic, but that would not help. In the end, she had to face having a child alone and rearing it with no money. She had to work, and working meant she could not care for a baby.

"Are you all right?" Leticia asked.

"Oh, yes," Erin answered. "Jack's going to America."

Leticia went on dusting. "There's lots of opportunity there. He'll send for you, Erin. You'll have a new life."

Erin pulled herself out of the chair. "Perhaps," she said, turning away, knowing it would never happen. She picked up her dust cloth and went back to work. That afternoon she would meet with Miss George. Then perhaps she would know what to do.

"I've heard that those who work hard in America can own their own land in no time." Leticia was chattering, and Erin could only think that the key to success in America was hard work. But Jack was not a hard worker.

Chapter Three

Philip Lawson was in his late twenties. His gray eyes twinkled when he laughed, his smile was easy, and when he was younger, he had been immensely popular with his father's customers.

Like many tradesmen, Philip's father had held certain ambitions for his son. He had engaged a tutor for him when he was a boy and then sent him to a good grammar school. Philip was quick mentally, and he enjoyed learning, which pleased his father immensely. But there were other aspects to his personality. He was good at sports and he excelled at all those commonly played. Then, unexpectedly, just as he was about to go away to university and fulfill his father's dreams by joining a respected profession, his father died.

Philip knew immediately that there was no choice; university had to be given up. He was his father's only son, and his mother and sister could not run the business alone. He went to work in his father's store in order to support his mother and sister. It was hard work, both physically and mentally, but he did not mind. He knew the business, and he vowed to improve it and see it grow. He spent hours gathering merchandise, arranging it, doing the books, and delivering merchandise to those who for one reason or another could not manage to go shopping on their own.

Three years before, after his mother died, he had gone to see a banker about obtaining a loan to expand his business. The banker seemed to like him and invited him home to dinner to meet his daughter, Adelle. She was a pretty little woman with a good disposition and a friendly way about her. Though their relationship lacked passion, he knew she would make a good wife and helpmate. Adelle's father encouraged their relationship, and they were married. The business flourished, and Philip felt satisfied and contented.

Both he and Adelle wanted children desperately, but thus far parenthood had eluded them. Adelle lost one child after another, and as a result her health suffered badly. Philip worried about her, knowing she was not a strong woman.

It was a warm day in late July, and Philip sat in his worn but comfortable blue chair in the central room of the little apartment above their store. He leaned back, his eyes closed. He often napped before dinner, although tonight he did not drop off into a deep sleep. Instead, thoughts moved across his mind in slow motion. He was half dreaming, half thinking. Adelle was pregnant again, and this time she had carried the baby longer than usual. "Let this be it," he murmured to himself. If she lost the baby now, she would be deeply affected; in fact, he was certain that her heart would break. She talked of nothing but the coming child. Still, as he watched her daily, he grew more and more apprehensive. She was so frail, so terribly drained by her previous miscarriages.

Adelle opened the door and came in. Her hair was mussed from the wind, and her tissue-paper white skin was pale. He could hardly believe she was the same age as he. She looked older, drawn, and her appearance frightened him.

"Did you have a good walk?" he asked, trying to hide his own anxieties.

"Yes, it's still very warm out."

"Adelle, I've been thinking. I believe you ought not to work in the store anymore. At least not until after the baby is born."

"I love working in the store," she protested weakly.

He suspected she was secretly relieved because he knew she was weary. "I know you love it, but it's tiring. You must rest. You must stay off your feet," he urged.

He stood up and walked over to her. He brushed the loose strands of hair off her forehead. She was so tiny that the child protruded like a round ball sitting on her abdomen. "Please, I want you to rest, I want this child to be born, and I want you to save all your energy for the birth and for motherhood."

Adelle smiled up at him. He was thoughtful and good. She nodded. "I hate leaving you with all the work."

"I'll manage," he replied, even though he was not sure how. Having her wait on customers was invaluable. He himself arose before dawn to go to Covent Garden Market. He returned to arrange the goods, and then he set about keeping the books and ordering various items for delivery. Before noon and after three, he delivered things that had been ordered by various customers. It would be far more difficult alone, and he knew he would have to curtail some of the services he offered, thus risking a loss of customers. Still, it had to be. She just was not strong enough. He wrapped his arms around her and held her. "I'll manage," he repeated.

Erin walked through the back garden that stretched out behind the house. Lady Montague was a most progressive employer. She allowed her servants two half days off a week and full use of the grounds, unless of course she was hosting a garden party. But that was not the case today, so Erin walked through the formal gardens, admiring the multicolored flowers and stopping now and again to study a piece of statuary. Lady Montague's garden was a beautiful and restful place.

But try as she might, Erin could not forget that more than a week had passed since Jack had sailed away. In her heart, she knew it was over between them. He would not send for her when he got settled in the Virginia Colony. Indeed, he had not even mentioned such an idea in his letter. No, his letter was a mere courtesy to let her know he would be gone from her life forever, to let her know there was no hope he might return. Her friends, hoping to cheer her, insisted that once he got to the Virginia Colony he might well change his mind, save his money, and decide to send for her. But she discarded their predictions as mere wishful thinking, or words spoken to her in kindness so she would not feel so bad. Pierre alone was realistic. He never told her Jack would come back. Indeed, he told her she was better off without him. "No good, no good," he muttered whenever the subject of Jack came up. "Jack is no good."

Erin walked to the far end of the garden, then turned and walked back, finally taking a seat in the warm sunshine.

She once again reviewed her conversation with Miss George. The woman who had such a reputation as a harridan had been nothing less than kind to her. She had agreed to keep her on until her seventh month, and then to take her back a week after the child was born. "But you cannot keep a child with you in the servants' quarters," she warned. "You must find someone to care for it or perhaps offer it for adoption since you cannot afford to rear it alone."

It was an agreement that gave her time to think of what to do; it gave her time to plan. But thus far, no plan had come to mind, although she had saved a bit of money. Jack's father had left a few things, and since Jack was gone, they were given to her. Erin had sadly sold them all and put the money away. It wasn't much, but it was a start.

Not that she had made any plans yet. She admitted to herself that for a time, she had been preoccupied with the date of Jack's departure. She supposed that in some corner of her mind, she had hoped he might change his mind. But now she knew the departure was final. "I can fool myself no longer," she said aloud.

She was utterly lost in thought when she heard Leticia's voice calling her. She looked up and saw Leticia's curly brown hair blowing wildly in the wind as she ran toward her.

Erin stood up and walked briskly. Leticia was carrying a newspaper, and as she drew closer, Erin could see that her face was filled with anguish.

"What is it?" she asked.

Leticia's face was ashen, and she seemed unable to speak. Instead, she held out the newspaper, which Erin took. She could not read quickly, but she had learned to read and she practiced often, trying always to learn new words. She did not need anyone to help her with the newspaper story. It was in large bold print, and the dark black letters seemed to stare at her from the page. The words were accompanied by a drawing of a ship, and underneath was the name of a vessel, the ship Jack had said he would take in his letter, *HMS Willis*.

The print danced on the page, "British ship sunk off the coast of Spain! Most lost at sea!"

For more than a few moments, she was unable to move her eyes off the headline.

"Lady Montague herself said I should bring you this. She said you could have time off to find out if—" Leticia's voice stopped in mid-sentence. She was unable to even say the words. She cleared her throat and finally added, "Lady Montague said they have lists of passengers and some recovered bodies in Portsmouth. You have to go there to find out if Jack—if Jack was drowned."

Erin felt her hand tremble. Even Lady Montague knew of her condition. Doubtless Miss George had consulted with her. It was kind of Lady Montague to give her time off—but how would she get to Portsmouth? Her mouth felt dry as she forced her eyes down the page to read the remainder of the terrible story. Men, women, and children on their way to the Virginia Colony had perished. There had been a terrible summer storm and the vessel had crashed on the rocks in high winds. Only a few had managed to make it ashore, and still a few others had been plucked from the water by passing fishermen.

"Dear God," Erin whispered. Surely Jack was dead, but she had to know. She had to know because she carried his child.

"Thank you, Leticia," Erin managed. Then she lifted her skirts and ran across the lawn toward the house. She had to go to Portsmouth! She had to find out if Jack had been saved.

Pierre was in the kitchen, and as if he had been waiting for her, he opened the door. "Oh, *ma petite amie!* This is too much!"

His arms encircled her, and he gave her a great bear hug.

For a moment, she leaned against him. "I must go to Portsmouth to find out if Jack is among the dead," Erin said. "I have some money saved. I think it is enough for the coach fare."

"No, no, no! Pierre is not rich. Indeed, Pierre has little money because he is so frivolous. But he has enough for you to go to Portsmouth and you shall go! You must know if you are a widow or not. How can you have any life if you do not know?"

Erin did not want to go to Portsmouth to confirm whether or not she was a widow, but simply to know what to tell her child when the time came.

"I can't take money from you."

"You are not taking it, I am giving it, *ma chèrie.* You will go to Portsmouth and find out if Jack is truly dead."

Pierre rubbed his chin thoughtfully. "In fact, I will go with you. You absolutely cannot go alone. It is unsafe."

"Will Lady Montague allow such a thing?"

"I will arrange for a substitute cook. When I return, she will be so glad to have me back, she will never let me go. If she lets me go, she would have to hire an English cook! No sane person would want that! Run along now. Put a few things in a satchel, and we will go on the night coach."

Erin nodded and headed toward her room. Pierre would not be much protection, but he was kind to take her to Portsmouth, and she was glad for his company. She touched her stomach and suddenly thought of Adelle. How fortunate she was to be married to a man like Philip! She wondered if Adelle was all right, and if she was getting stronger. She made a silent vow to visit the Lawsons when she returned.

Pierre dressed in a long black cloak that would have given him a funereal look had the appearance not been counteracted by the red feather in his floppy hat and his comical moustache, which was long and curved at each end. His eyes were very round and large, and he had a long nose that was not quite straight. When he spoke, he always used his hands, as most Frenchmen did. But he was quite clumsy and tended to hit things as he spoke, often sending them to the floor with a resounding crash. Overall, he had a clown-like appearance and except when he was in a temper, his demeanor was genuinely funny and he enjoyed making people laugh. He befriended few people, so Erin felt honored that he seemed to care for her. But theirs was not a usual male-female relationship. She knew full well that Pierre had no interest in her beyond friendship. She smiled to herself. He was not a fop, either. It could honestly be said that his only true love was food, and there was simply no room in his thoughts for anything or anyone else.

"Do cover up your hair and hide it under your bonnet," he urged. "Your hair is very—how shall I say it?—alluring. I like your dress. It is modest. That is good. Travel is difficult enough without being with someone who thinks herself a fashion plate. Such women only attract trouble."

Erin smiled. "Thank you again for going with me."

"It is nothing. Pierre needs to see more of this country. Pierre has hardly ever been out of London."

"But we shall be traveling at night."

"Then Pierre shall learn about the bumps in the road."

"Is that our coach?" Erin pointed to the large coach that was drawn by fourteen horses.

"Yes. Come along so we may obtain a good seat. I want to sit by the window so I can look out."

Erin did not ask at what he would look, but followed as he led her to the coach, which was quite large and held twelve people.

He quickly took a window seat and she sat beside him. Soon the coach was full, the doors were locked, and they headed off into the dark night.

As they bumped along, Erin's thoughts turned to Adelle and her husband. How frequently she thought of them! How much she hoped all would be well for them and that this time Adelle's child would live. For a moment, she thought of Philip Lawson. Erin often daydreamed about how different her life would be if only she had chosen a man like him.

Overhead the sun tried desperately to shine through heavy clouds. The fog had still been thick when they arrived; now it hung in low places and everywhere there was a pervading dampness.

"Even in summer the English seaside is horrid," Pierre muttered.

As they walked toward the shipping office, Erin had to tiptoe over large puddles, and the slippery stone-covered street glistened with droplets of water. It seemed to Erin as if everything in all of Portsmouth was wet.

Outside the shipping office, Pierre stood next to her in a long queue until finally they were admitted.

The clerk who greeted her was small, a nervous sort of man with an abrupt manner. He studied her for just an instant before taking out a large piece of paper and a long pen.

"Name?" he asked officiously.

"Erin Connors Findley."

He wrote her name. "Now I will need your address, employer, and the name of your missing relative."

"Husband," Erin said. "Jack was my husband."

The clerk looked at her bulging stomach and half smiled. "I should hope he was," he muttered sarcastically.

Erin said nothing, but she gave him the answer to each of his questions. When his paper was filled out, he disappeared and returned after some twenty minutes to announce coldly that Jack was not among the survivors.

"You will have to come to the warehouse and look at the belongings we took from the bodies that were recovered from the water and buried."

Erin stood up. She felt weak in the knees and was suddenly truly glad Pierre was there to take her arm.

The clerk led them into a large room with a long table. On the table were small heaps of different items. There were rings and pendants, scarves, shoes, purses, even a doll or two. It was a deeply depressing room.

Erin looked through the items, and her eyes caught sight of the ring—Jack's ring, a silver ring with the Celtic design. She picked it up and turned it in her fingers. There was no doubt. It was Jack's ring.

"Does that belong to your husband?" the man asked.

Erin nodded.

He made a mark on a paper, then handed her the ring and the paper. "Take this inside," he instructed. "You will be given a death certificate."

Erin nodded dumbly as she took the ring and turned it in her fingers. It had been her grandmother's ring, and she had given it to Jack, who wore it on his little finger. She slipped it on her own finger for safekeeping.

"It is better that you know," Pierre said solemnly. "Now you can make a new life for yourself."

Erin nodded, though she was not exactly certain of what kind of life she might look forward to now. Still, she did know Jack's fate, and now she would have to make a plan for herself and her child.

"Tell me your thoughts," Pierre insisted. "I know from your walk that you are thinking terrible things. Your shoulders are all hunched over."

"It's hard to explain," she said slowly, knowing she had to share her inner fears and guilt with someone.

"Try," he insisted.

"I loved Jack, I really did. And I will love the child, I swear it."

"You do not have to convince me. I know what kind of person you are."

She took a deep breath. "He was not the man I

loved, not in reality. Over the months, I thought he would change, but he didn't. Now I feel guilty that he is dead, and yet I cried all my tears the night he left.''

"You did your best, little one. It is good that you realize Jack was not the man you thought he was. You were in love with love, not with Jack. He is dead, and that is sad, but with or without him, life will not be easy for you now that you are going to have a child.''

Erin nodded. "I'm going to the Gardener Home in Croydon. Perhaps they can help me.''

"You will not give up the baby, will you?''

Erin shook her head. "I won't give the baby up to go to an orphanage. I want to keep it, but if I can't, then I want it to have a good home.''

The home was located on the edge of Croydon in a large brick house surrounded by green lawns and tall, graceful old trees.

The superintendent was Catherine Dudley, a kindly old woman of seventy-two. Her second in command was Miss Agnus Atherton. Even the casual observer could see that they were extreme opposites. Mrs. Dudley was concerned and gentle, but Miss Atherton was tight-lipped, strict, and unsmiling.

"You really must not be nervous," Mrs. Dudley said reassuringly, as she leaned across her large oak desk toward Erin.

But it was not Mrs. Dudley who made Erin nervous, it was Miss Atherton, who stood behind and slightly to the right of Mrs. Dudley's desk. Miss Atherton, dressed entirely in black, was tall and angular. She stood in the shadows, her face partially obscured. She was like a hovering black cloud, Erin thought, while dear old Mrs. Dudley was like warm sunshine in her powder-blue dress.

"It's a terrible tragedy," Mrs. Dudley murmured. "To have your husband die so young."

Erin did not tell them that her dilemma might have been the same if Jack had lived.

"What brought you to us?" Miss Atherton asked somewhat sharply.

"I heard that you often help women who are pregnant, women with no family."

"And so we do," Mrs. Dudley said quickly. "It is our mission. So many children are born and end up in terrible workhouses, or they are given to unscrupulous people and become little ragamuffins begging in the streets of London."

"Or thieves," Miss Atherton added.

"Do you want us to find a good home for your child?"

Erin shook her head. "First I need a place to have my child. Then I should like to keep the baby."

"And just how would you support it?" Miss Atherton asked. Even though she stood in the shadows, Erin could see her raised eyebrow.

"I will work. But I need time, time to get settled and time to save some money." She did not say that Jack had run off with all her savings and that all she had in the world to give her child was her ring.

"How long do you estimate that would take?" Mrs. Dudley asked.

"At least a year," Erin said. "I've managed to save a little."

There was a long moment of silence. Miss Atherton scowled, and as if Mrs. Dudley had eyes in the back of her head, she turned toward Miss Atherton. "I know it is not our usual procedure, but a child should be with its mother."

Miss Atherton did not reply except with her revealing stony silence.

Mrs. Dudley turned back toward Erin. "You will have to excuse us. We must speak privately."

"Of course," Erin said in a near whisper. It seemed obvious to her that they were going away to argue.

Mrs. Dudley stood up and eased out from behind her desk, and Miss Atherton, the taller of the two, followed her colleague out of the room. Her hands were folded tightly in front of her and her lips were pressed together.

Erin stretched to relieve her tension when they had gone. Then she sank back into her chair. What if they would not help her? Her head was alive with questions, and her heart felt like a great lump inside her chest.

The longer they were gone, the more apprehensive she became, but after what seemed hours, the heavy oak door opened and Mrs. Dudley came in alone.

Erin looked up expectantly.

"You may come here and live during your last two months. Then you may leave your child with us for a period of no longer than one year. But if you do not return to pay for your room and board during your stay here, and reimburse us what it cost to care for the child, it will be given over for adoption. Is that clear?"

Erin felt relief flood over her. "Oh, yes," she said. "Yes, that is most agreeable." It was really not a solution, but Erin knew it would give her valuable time.

"Even though I am giving you my word that your child will be kept here for one year, I want you to understand that you must sign the usual papers. We are supported by donations from wealthy patrons and our business matters must be run properly. Normally, when the adopting parents pay our fee, those costs I have mentioned are covered."

Erin nodded. "You're very kind."

"Rules should sometimes be bent," Mrs. Dudley said.

Erin walked down Stratton Street, turned a corner, and found herself in front of The Lion's Head, a pub Jack had frequented when they were married.

Women were not allowed in pubs, and even if they had been, Erin would not have wished to go inside. It was quite enough to stand in the doorway. From outside she could smell the stench of whiskey, ale, and the strong odor of tobacco. She glanced about uneasily, hoping no one she knew would pass by.

She stood to one side of the door. It was nearly noon and she looked about expectantly. It was mysterious, but also troubling. She had received a note asking her to come to the pub to meet a Mr. Ferguson. The note said it concerned her late husband. Erin had no idea what it was all about, but she had gone off to meet the stranger and now, as she waited, she wished she had at least told Pierre.

As the moments went by, her feelings of apprehension increased. She was about to leave when a man appeared, not a well-dressed man, but a working-class man with an unkempt beard.

He tipped his hat slightly. "Mrs. Findley, I presume."

Erin nodded. She had never before seen this man and wondered what on earth he wanted.

"You're the widow of Jack Findley?" he asked in a sharp cockney accent.

"I am."

He looked her up and down. "Pretty wench. I wouldn't have thought Jack had one at home like you. He liked the ladies too much."

Revulsion surged through Erin. Jack was a drinker, a slacker, and a gambler, but had there been other women too?

"What do you want?" she managed, only wishing to run away from this man and whatever else he might tell her. Jack was dead; there was no need to hear more ill of him.

"I want me money, that's what I want. Your husband ran off with me blunt and I want it or I'll have the magistrate throw you into debtors' prison. I've got the paper right here. It's all legal."

Erin opened her mouth in surprise and at the same time, she shivered at the prospect of debtors' prison. "I must see this paper," she said.

"You might tear it up," he muttered suspiciously.

"I wouldn't do that, not if it's an honest debt."

The man screwed up his face. "I see you're pregnant. I'm sorry about that, but I got kids of me own and I needs my money."

"I understand," Erin answered. Doubtless Jack had borrowed money for a gambling debt and then not paid it back. It would be like Jack to rob Peter to pay Paul.

"I'll hold the paper and you can look at it," he suggested. He took a rumpled bit of paper out of his pocket and Erin stood beside him and leaned over to read it. The terms of the debt were laid out, and underneath she clearly saw Jack's mark. He could not write, but he had learned to make a mark that was distinctive.

"See, it's all legal. Even the magistrate will think so."

Erin did not doubt for one minute that the man was quite right. The amount was all she had managed to save. Now she would have to use it to pay Jack's debt. She took a deep breath. "Meet me here tomorrow and I'll bring the money."

"Good. I wouldn't want to send a woman with child to debtors' prison."

Erin lifted her skirts and almost ran toward home. She hoped this would really end it. She could only pray Jack had left no other debts for her to pay.

Chapter Four

The November sun was obscured by dark gray clouds that moved in from the sea. It seemed to Erin as if it rained heavily at least every other day, leaving puddles and the ground in a permanent state of sogginess. Equally depressing, the long days of summer had disappeared, and each day grew shorter than the one before. Erin made her way to the grocer's, walking slowly and feeling the weight of her pregnancy as she tried to avoid the puddles that seemed to be everywhere. In another week she would go to the home in Croydon and remain there until after the baby was born.

Erin had not been to Lawson's in many months, and as she walked along she realized that she missed talking with Adelle. She wondered how she was, and if indeed Adelle had managed to keep the child with which she was pregnant. "We'll catch up," she said to herself.

She reached Lawson's and looked around. Adelle was nowhere to be seen but when he saw her, Philip hurried out of the back room.

"Are you looking for something special?" he asked, warmly.

Erin smiled back at him. As often as she had talked to Adelle and as much as she considered Adelle her friend, she had never spoken very much with Philip. He was almost always in the back room and to Erin he had become a profile bent over his books. Seeing him in the store today rather surprised her.

"I just need a few things," Erin said. "But I was looking for Adelle. I hope she's all right."

"Oh," Philip said. "You're Erin—you work for Lady Montague. I know you always talk with Adelle. I remember you. You haven't been here for months."

"I've been kept busy in the house. Pierre has been doing his own shopping."

"Ah, you needn't tell me." Philip laughed. "Pierre is very particular."

"Is Adelle well?" Erin pressed.

"Adelle is quite all right. I've made her give up working in the store, though. She isn't a very strong woman, you know. Her health has always been bad." Unspoken was his thought, "not like you." Erin was the picture of robust health. Her skin glowed, and though she too was heavy with child, there was still an obvious liveliness about her. Moreover, she exuded warmth and cheerfulness. Her red curls and freckles just made him want to grin.

"I'm so glad you've made her stay home to rest. I was quite worried about her. The last time I saw her, she looked very peaked. I told her she needed to stay off her feet."

Erin walked about as they spoke, choosing this and

discarding that until she had every item on Pierre's list.

"When is your child due?" Philip asked as she was putting things into her little crocheted bag.

"Next month. I fear I won't be in again till after the birth. Please tell Adelle I came by and I wish her well."

"I'll do that," he responded. "I know she'll be glad to hear you dropped in to see her."

Then, as if prolonging their conversation, he asked, "Does your husband still work for Lady Montague as well?"

Erin looked down. It was hard for her to talk about Jack, hard for her even to think of him. "No, he drowned. He was going to the Virginia Colony, where he would have worked and then sent for us." It was a lie, but she did not want to say, "he left us."

"In that terrible ship wreck?" Philip asked.

"Yes," Erin replied. "Off the coast of Spain. Many were killed."

He remembered reading the story in the newspaper. Small wonder, the poor girl had not been in for so long. She must have been devastated, especially considering her condition. Yet he knew about Jack Findley's reputation. Surely everyone knew about his death too. That he did not served to remind him how isolated he had been for the past year.

"I am sorry. I do hope you and the child will be all right."

Erin looked up at him, and for a moment their eyes locked. In that moment, Erin could not describe the sensation that swept over her. Somehow, she knew he must have had the same sensation.

"We'll be fine," she said quickly. Then she picked up her parcel and turned about. "Thank you," she said without looking back. The sensation lingered, and she felt somewhat uncomfortable. Not that a single thing had happened. Philip had said or done nothing improper. But she was aware of having some vague feeling for him, a feeling that was beyond admiration. *I'm just lonely,* she told herself, putting it out of her mind.

The short, gray days of December were even more depressing than those of November. Erin found the Gardener Home in Croydon to be colder and far less cheerful than Lady Montague's house on Berkeley Square. She was not alone, but Erin found little in common with the other girls who were in various stages of pregnancy. None of them was or had been married. All of them intended to give their babies up.

In spite of her advanced pregnancy, Erin was assigned chores around the house. They were not arduous chores, and she found they made the time pass more quickly. After the first week, she realized that what she missed most was the mental stimulation she so enjoyed at Lady Montague's. She missed the witty comments and discussions, and most of all she missed the knowledge she gleaned from borrowing books from the shelves of Lady Montague's library. She also missed Pierre, who always encouraged her and who taught her about cooking. Most of all, she missed her walks and shopping for groceries. She wondered how Adelle was, and more than once she wondered if Adelle had finally had her child.

Erin was dusting the reception room and paused to look outside. Snowflakes had begun to fall from the gray skies. Not ordinary snowflakes, but huge flakes, some as large as a penny.

She turned to continue working when she felt the first pain, and it took her breath away. She waited for a moment and then continued working. Soon there was another pain, and then another and another. She left the reception room and hurried to find Sister Claire, the midwife in residence.

Sister Claire maintained a small infirmary on the third floor of the house. It was neat, clean, and smelled heavily of vinegar, with which she scrubbed everything down.

She had Erin lie down in the birthing bed. There she examined her carefully, prodding and feeling about. "Yes," she said needlessly, "you are most definitely in labor, and I don't think you will be very long with this birth either."

Erin could feel the perspiration on her forehead, and she bit her lip when the next pain started.

"You won't be long," Sister Claire said again, then added, "Good Irish stock, you are. Built to have children."

At the moment, Erin felt nothing but pain combined with the knowledge of the terrible responsibility of rearing a child on her own. Still, she told herself, she would have time. She would go back to work and at the end of the year, she would return and take her child home with her. She already loved her baby, already knew it was part of her.

She closed her eyes and listened as Sister Claire's soft voice directed her. She took deep breaths when told, and in spite of the pain, she pushed.

Erin felt an incredibly strong, long, and intense pain and then heard Sister Claire say, "Push now!"

Almost before the other pain had ceased, another began, and again Sister Claire directed her to push.

Again, and then Erin heard Sister Claire say, "It's a little boy. You have a son, Erin."

A faint smile crossed Erin's lips. She felt another pain, and Sister Claire said, "Just the afterbirth."

All the pain soon subsided, and Erin marveled at how quickly she felt herself again, albeit weary and damp with the exertion of the birth.

"Is he all right?" Erin asked anxiously.

"He's quite perfect, a fine young man."

Erin smiled. "Quite perfect," she repeated happily, feeling almost drunk with weariness.

"Well, there is a wee birthmark on his little bottom, but I think it's quite nice."

Sister Claire had washed and swaddled the child and now she handed him to Erin.

His little face was perfectly round, and his mouth was puckered up as he moved his head, seeking her breast.

"You won't have milk for a few days," Sister Claire told her, "but the liquid that comes out is nourishing and the child will be satisfied."

Erin cuddled the baby and smiled down on it. Her heart was full, and she wondered how she would be able to leave her son even though she knew she would return. But she didn't have to leave right away. She held to that thought, telling herself over and over that all would be well.

Pierre's kitchen was the warmest room in all of Lady Montague's house. It was the meanest day of the winter thus far, and outside, a light snow swirled about in cold northern winds.

Erin opened the huge side oven next to the stone fireplace and withdrew a tray filled with loaves of crusty bread. The smell was wonderful, and she inhaled, hoping that the coziness of the kitchen and the aroma of the bread would somehow lessen the terrible feeling of emptiness that filled her.

"Ma chèrie, you look so sad you will make Pierre cry."

Erin tried to force a smile, but she could not. "I know he is in good care, it's just so hard being separated. I keep feeling as if there is something I must do."

"Feed your child," Pierre said authoritatively. "You were on a schedule, and now you keep thinking there is something you must do."

"Yes, of course, that's it. I hated leaving him, but what choice did I have, Pierre? I can't keep him here and I have to work in order to save money."

"You had no choice, little one, none at all. You did the right thing, and now you must just count the days. You must wait patiently until you can be reunited with your baby."

She nodded. "If only the weather were better. It's so difficult to get to Croydon now. I won't be able to see him for weeks."

Pierre put his pudgy arms about her, "You're a strong girl. Pierre thinks it will all turn out well."

Erin pulled back and dried her eyes. The tears came now unexpectedly; sometimes she was not aware of crying. "I won't even have this job if I don't get to work," she said, hurrying off. But inside, questions filled her head. How could she save enough money working for Lady Montague? Perhaps, she thought,

I'll have to look for another kind of job. The most difficult thing was that it would take nearly all her spare money to travel to see the baby and that would prevent her from saving. She vowed to stay away for as long as possible, but she knew it would not be an easy promise to keep.

By mid-February, the snow and wind of January had given way to a cold persistent rain. Erin, her cloak drawn about her, hurried down the street toward the grocer's. She thought about Adelle. Doubtless, she would not be there. She must have given birth in December too, so she was probably home with her infant, unless, of course, she brought it to the store with her. That, Erin thought, was entirely possible since they owned the shop. But then, Adelle might still be unwell, and if that were the case, her husband would not want her back at the shop. *But I hope you are there,* Erin thought. *And I hope you have your baby there as well.* She wondered if it would make her happy or sad to see a child so close to the age of her own. Again, the now-familiar feeling of emptiness combined with guilt and swept over her. She had not been able to go to Croydon since she had left in January. She had not seen her child for nearly two months, and she yearned to hold him, yearned to feel his warm little body against her own, yearned to look into his clear eyes. And yet she could no longer feed him from her breast; her milk had dried up within two weeks of her leaving the home.

Erin reached Lawson's, but even before she got there, she saw that the awning was rolled up. She felt a quick jolt of premonition. She stared at the grocer's, and a frown covered her face. The shutters were drawn over the windows, and the door was locked. A handwritten sign in bold letters read, "Temporarily Closed."

Erin walked round the side and between two buildings to the back alley. There she climbed the stairs to the apartment above the store where she knew that Philip and Adelle lived. But why was the store closed?

When she reached the apartment, she knocked on the door, but no one answered. She waited, then knocked again. There was still no answer. She felt mystified and apprehensive as well. Had something happened? How silly, she told herself. They had just had a child and since Adelle was not well, perhaps Philip had taken them both to the country. Surely that was it. They had gone away for a short time on a holiday. Erin went back down the steps. She looked about. There was another grocer farther down the street. She sighed; she had wanted to see her friends, but they were gone. She headed for the other store still wondering about Philip and Adelle.

Erin sat on the chair in front of the large oak desk. But Miss Agnus Atherton did not sit behind the desk; instead she hovered beside her chair like a giant crow. Her expression was somewhat cross and Erin felt suddenly uncomfortable, sensing something was very wrong even before either of them had said a word.

"Where is Mrs. Dudley?" Erin ventured, unable to bear the stony silence of Miss Atherton for another second.

"The Lord saw fit to take her from us," Miss Atherton intoned without any emotion at all.

Erin felt a sense of loss. Mrs. Dudley, old though she was, had always been kind to her. And during the two months she had lived in the home, it was Mrs. Dudley who had come often to see her and who encouraged her to continue reading and learning.

"I've come to see my baby," Erin said. Words could not describe how anxious she was to hold her child, to see how he had changed, to kiss him, to hug him. She ached to see her baby, but in order to save money, she had waited for over two months before making this journey. She had asked as soon as she had come in to see the baby, but she had been sent to see Miss Atherton instead.

Miss Atherton did not look at her. Instead, she studied the pattern in the rug that covered the floor.

Silence so filled the room that Erin shivered. Something was wrong. She could feel it. "What is it?" she insisted. "Where is my baby?"

"He's not here," Miss Atherton said coldly. "He's been given over for adoption."

Erin felt as if the breath had been sucked out of her. "Adoption? No! That can't be. Mrs. Dudley promised—"

Miss Atherton lifted her face and looked icily at Erin. "And in so promising broke our rules. We do have rules. Our rules are that when we help a woman with child and care for her, the child must be given up for adoption."

"She promised to give me a chance! She promised to keep my child for a year!"

"Far too long. We simply cannot afford that sort of thing. I had the opportunity to find a wonderful home for your child—a home with two loving parents. Your child is most fortunate, most fortunate indeed. And of course, as you did not even come to visit, I assumed you realized how hopeless your situation was. I mean, how could a girl like you possibly save enough money to make a home for your child?"

Miss Atherton's voice was filled with disdain.

Erin's eyes swam with tears, and she felt herself flushed with a kind of hopeless anger. "I would have! I didn't come to visit in order to save money! I want my child!"

"That is quite impossible. The family took it over a month ago. It is all quite legal. It is our obligation to find good homes, and we found one for your child. And if you recall, you did sign the proper papers."

"Where is my child? Who has him?" Erin demanded.

"You know I will not tell you. The child was abandoned to us, and the adoption is quite legal."

Erin could hardly speak. Her hands were trembling, but she knew there was little she could do. Everything in her wanted to show Miss Atherton just how angry she really was, but her own good sense kept her from violence. Mrs. Dudley had been willing to bend the rules, but Miss Atherton was not at all willing, and she was now obviously in charge.

"How could you do this terrible thing?" Erin said, her voice quivering.

"I spoke with the Lord, and I'm confident I did what was right for the child. Now you must leave or I will call the police."

Erin stood up and, clenching her fists, whirled about and fled the room. She was so filled with emotion that she grabbed her cloak and ran down the hall, nearly knocking down another of the women who worked around the home. She fled through the front door and ran down the street, tears running down her cheeks, her heart still pounding. She ran and ran until she nearly collapsed beside a building.

Her breath came in short pants, her tears had dried, but streaks where they had run down her face were still evident. She trembled uncontrollably and was aware of passersby staring at her. She leaned against the side of a building on legs that felt like rubber. Over and over a voice inside her told her she would never again see the only human being in the world that she truly loved. "Not ever again," she gasped.

The past blurred in her memory. Her parents had been taken away before she ever knew them and she had been reared by an ever-changing parade of stoic women. She had thought she loved Jack, only to discover that she was in love with love and Jack was no good. But she truly loved her child. She had felt it inside of her for nine long months; she had held her precious bundle and fed him from her own breast. It was the greatest pleasure she had ever known, and now it was gone, taken away forever by the cruel nature of an ungiving, uncaring woman. Erin moaned. She felt ill, and it was as if the gray clouds that swirled above in the sky had all come down to earth and were surrounding her. She felt dizzy and her legs gave out as she crumpled to the ground.

Chapter Five

October, 1753

Erin wrung out the washrag in the warm water and surveyed the damp, newly washed floor. She rested on her knees for a moment, then pulled herself up and, carrying the bucket, headed for the kitchen where Pierre would have her lunch prepared.

It had been six long months since she fainted on the street a few blocks from the Gardner Home in Croydon, six months since her child had been taken from her. They had been long, lonely, difficult months.

After she fainted, Erin was taken to a nearby hospital. Pierre had come to fetch her, and it was he who had brought her home. He made her get up each day and work so she would not lose her job. He stuffed food down her even when she was not hungry because he insisted she needed to build her strength. He helped her to survive each day, but he could do nothing about her troubled dreams or about her deep and haunting loneliness.

"There you are," Pierre said as she entered the kitchen. "You work too hard. None of the others work as hard as you do."

"That's because you were right. Hard work helps me to forget."

"Autumn is here, and the shops are full of fine produce. What will make you forget even more than work is to get out of this house and walk. I want you to go shopping for some fall delights. It's time to make some preserves."

At the very thought of going out, fear gripped her. She felt safe within the confines of the house, but afraid as soon as she stepped onto the street. "I couldn't do that," she said, looking down.

"This is not the Erin I once knew," Pierre said, shaking his finger. "You haven't been out for a very long while, Erin—what are you afraid of?"

She shook her head sadly. "I'm not sure."

"Pierre knows what makes you afraid. You are afraid of seeing women with babies on the street, afraid of seeing small children. You are afraid that you will wonder if every baby you see is really yours."

She stared at him and nodded. She had not really thought of it herself, but now that he said it, she knew he was right. It was more than that too. She did not know how she could stand to see other mothers happy with their children.

"You must go out and you must keep busy as well. You are not the only one in this world with troubles."

Again he shook his finger at her, admonishing her. He almost made her smile when he scolded her. "I'll try," she relented.

"You will not try! You will do it! You will eat your lunch and you will go! Right now! Today! You have to stay healthy. Think, if you found your child you would have to be able to care for him. That is reason enough to get well."

She sat down at the table, and he put a bowl of thick soup in front of her. He was right. She knew she had to do as he told her.

"The grocer you used to go to has reopened," Pierre said matter-of-factly. "Please go there. Pierre likes his produce much better than the others. It is of a higher standard."

Panic flooded over her all over again. Adelle's child would be the same age as her own son. What if she had him in the store? How would she react? But she said nothing. She had to fight this fear, this terrible anxiety. "All right," Erin answered, then out of sheer curiosity asked, "Why was it closed for so long?"

"Pierre does not know. Perhaps some family difficulty. But no matter, Lawson's has reopened and I would like you to go there."

Erin did not answer. Pierre had no way of knowing it, but the store of Philip Lawson was the most difficult of destinations he could send her to. Even if the child were not there, Adelle would most certainly have returned to work. She wondered if she could bear hearing Adelle talk about the joys of mother-hood—joys which she had been denied. But then, she thought, Adelle deserved those joys because she had lost so many children and because she had waited so long. Erin suddenly felt quite selfish, and she vowed she would go and see Adelle, that she would listen to her stories, no matter how difficult it was for her to do so. Pierre was right—she had to rejoin life, and her new reality would begin at Lawson's.

Erin finished her soup and bread. She stood up and stretched, and then she reached for her cloak.

Pierre said nothing more; he simply handed her the list of things she was to buy.

Erin opened the door and stepped out into the pleasant afternoon sunshine. It was still warm, and most of the heartier flowers were still in bloom.

"Take your time," Pierre called after her.

As the door closed behind her, Pierre let a smile of satisfaction cross his face. "Pierre will solve this problem," he said aloud to himself. "Pierre thinks that Mr. Lawson can help Erin."

Erin stood outside the shop and tried to prepare herself for the conversation she was quite certain she would have with Adelle. Then she forced herself to go through the door. The bell that rang as she came in seemed loud indeed, but she knew it was her nerves.

It was not Adelle who greeted her. It was Philip Lawson who was moving about the store, putting various items on the shelf and straightening things out.

He turned at the sound of the bell and gave a wonderful warm smile when he saw her. "Erin! I was not sure you would ever come back to my store."

Erin could not help but return his smile. "I only just learned you had reopened."

"Yes, it's been difficult, but I've returned to work. Sometimes there is no other answer—work is a healer."

Erin was puzzled. It was as if he were talking about her rather than about himself. How long had his store been closed? She had assumed he had simply taken Adelle on holiday, but now that she thought of Pierre's words about the store being reopened, she realized it must have been closed for other reasons. She knew that for many, many months she had been lost in her own dilemma. She wondered what had happened; she wondered how even to ask her questions.

"I've been away," she said in desperation. And she supposed it was not a total lie. She had been emotionally lost, which had resulted in her isolation.

The smiled faded from his face. "Oh, I didn't know."

Erin struggled for words. "I came here once— many months ago. I found the store closed and thought you and Adelle had gone on a holiday because when I went upstairs to your rooms, no one was there."

He looked down. "Adelle died a few months ago."

Erin was so taken aback, she could not speak for a minute. "I'm so sorry," she managed in a near whisper. She knew that no words would be adequate, and she felt at a total loss. She had dreaded coming here because of her own problems; now she felt guilty that she had not even considered the fact that Philip might have more serious problems. "I didn't know," she said again.

He looked at her and nodded. "I know. It's hard for me to talk about it. She was sick for a very long time."

"I knew she was unwell," Erin said. "She always seemed frail."

"Yes. For a time, I did take her away. I thought she might recover. But she did not. I know you lost your husband. I know you understand how terrible it can be."

He was not looking directly at her now, but off to

one side, and it was almost as if he were talking to himself.

"How is your baby?" he asked her.

"I lost him," she said vaguely. It was much too difficult to explain.

"It seems we have both had a terrible tragedy," Philip said, meeting her eyes. "But I do have my son."

Erin had assumed that Adelle had died in childbirth. She had not asked about the child because she was afraid to. "I'm glad you have the child," she said. "But it must be difficult for you."

He forced a half smile. "Very. But I manage."

"For me only time will help. That is what Pierre says."

"Ah, yes, Pierre. How is he?"

"He's fine."

"Well, I'm glad he's turned the shopping back over to you." Philip smiled. "You are just as particular, but much prettier and more pleasant."

Erin blushed. In spite of all his troubles, Philip could still smile and laugh. He was a most engaging man, and just talking to him made her realize how caught up she had been in herself.

"Thank you," she replied. "I'm afraid the housekeeper, Miss George, feels the same way about him. But I think I might not still have my job were it not for Pierre. He has always been very good to me."

"He says you are his little carrottop."

"I probably would not like that comment from anyone else."

Philip looked directly into her eyes. "I believe that people are brought into our lives for a reason."

Erin felt another little blush cover her face. His comment seemed somehow to be directed at her rather than at Pierre. She shyly turned away. "I had better do my shopping or Pierre will be angry with me."

"You will come back, won't you?"

"Of course. I'm sure Pierre will be sending me here several times a week. It's good to get out, he says. It's not as difficult as I had feared. I know I can't hide anymore."

"Neither of us can," Philip said.

Erin looked back at him and for a moment, it seemed as if they were talking without words. He made her feel—she wasn't sure how he made her feel—or perhaps she could just not define the feeling yet.

Philip watched as Erin left his shop and walked rapidly away toward Berkeley Square. And he found the image of her remained long after she was gone. Her blue eyes were the most intense blue he had ever seen, and her red curls were bright and framed her very pretty face. She had a fine figure too. Her breasts were full and her hips rounded, yet she was not in the least fat. She was a very pretty Irish colleen with a lilt in her voice and a bright smile. She was a soft looking woman, the kind of woman a man wanted to protect even though he could clearly see she had spirit of her own. She was a woman he knew had suffered as much as he, perhaps more so. And yet there was a twinkle in those blue eyes, a promise.

Then he shook his head. Surely it wasn't right to be thinking of another woman so soon after Adelle's death. Moreover, he reminded himself, he had responsibilities.

Pierre flitted about the kitchen while Erin watched. His movements were rapid and somewhat agitated.

Then he turned to her, hands on his hips. "I must send you back to Lawson's today. I have forgotten a vital ingredient. You must go right away, this afternoon."

It was not like Pierre to forget an ingredient. "Of course I'll go," she replied.

"I know I sent you yesterday, but I did forget some things. Important things."

"I thought it was only one thing."

"One thing, two things, it does not matter. As long as you go off at once and fetch them for Pierre."

Erin once again donned her cloak. "Mr. Lawson asked after your health. I didn't know you knew him so well."

"Well, of course I know him. While you were unable to go out, I had to do my own shopping. What a bore! I'm glad you are once again able to take on your duties."

Erin just smiled at him. Now and again, he treated her as he treated others, but she knew the two of them had a very special relationship—a relationship he was reluctant to have the other servants observe for fear they might realize that his prickly, petulant image was just a facade and not the real Pierre.

"I didn't know Mrs. Lawson had died," Erin said. "It's very sad. Adelle was very pleasant."

"Yes, she was a lovely woman. It is a tragedy, but life must go on," Pierre said, turning back to his work. "Now run along."

Erin did not see it, but when she had gone, Pierre laughed pleasantly to himself. He rubbed his hands together. "Pierre is a fine little cupid," he said, grinning foolishly.

* * *

"How very nice to see you again so soon," Philip said as he greeted Erin with his warm smile.

"Pierre is growing forgetful," Erin replied. "This time I made him write his own list."

Philip came around the counter and stood next to her. Erin was vaguely aware of a pleasant sensation when he leaned close to her, taking the list she held and touching her hand gently.

"There's not much on it," he said as he examined it.

"Sometimes I think he is just forcing me to exercise."

Philip laughed. "Let me get these things for you."

Erin stood and watched as he moved about taking items off the shelves and out of the bins till he had everything on the list. "I'm so sorry to bother you again so soon."

He turned quickly. "It's no bother at all. I'm almost never busy this time of day. In the mornings, and when I reopen in the afternoons, it's a madhouse around here, but the rest of the time it's slow but steady."

"It must be very difficult," Erin ventured. "I mean, running the business and caring for your son."

He paused and turned slowly to look at her. "It's very busy, very difficult." He looked down and without looking her in the eyes, added, "And terribly lonely."

"I know," Erin said. "I know loneliness."

He stepped closer and handed her the items he had gathered. Again he touched her hand, though this time he did not withdraw his so quickly, and Erin felt a little chill run down her spine as, with his hand still on hers, he looked into her eyes. At first, she thought he was going to say he liked her, or that she was pretty. But he said neither. He just looked at her, and yet she felt she could read the words in his eyes. She felt her cheeks flush slightly.

"Erin, I hope you won't consider me forward—but I would like to have you join me for tea sometime. Would you consider it?"

Erin nodded. "Tuesday afternoons I'm off work."

"Can you come at two? We'll just have some tea in the little room off the store. I think that would be quite proper."

"That would be very nice," Erin answered. "Will your son be there?"

"No. I've sent him to my sister in the country for a few months, just till I get organized. That makes the loneliness worse, of course. Now I miss him too. And I feel guilty because he ought to be here with me."

Erin thought Philip Lawson a very unusual man. He was strong and masculine, yet she could see that a side of him was also gentle and loving. "I know you're a good father," she said softly. "I'm certain you've done the right thing."

"Thank you," he murmured. Then he turned away quickly as the shop door opened and two women came in.

Erin turned and left, calling out, "Good day," as the shop door closed. She walked down the street quickly, but she could not shake the mental image of Philip Lawson. It was not the first time she had thought about him, but she knew it was the first time she had let herself think about him in that certain way. She looked forward to seeing him again—she wanted to know this man better.

* * *

Lady Montague's main reception room was spacious and meant for entertaining. On one side, floor-to-ceiling windows looked out on the garden, which was now obscured in darkness. The other walls were covered with fine art, and the furniture consisted of elegant inlaid tables, a variety of expensively upholstered chairs, several loveseats, and a huge sideboard with silver candelabra. The sounds of the many conversations going on at once were muted by thick carpets and high ceilings.

The guests, as usual, were London's literati. They stood in small groups of two and three talking intently, stopping now and again to nibble on hors d'oeuvres or sip from crystal glasses of deep red burgundy. A few, including Mr. Henry Fielding, smoked pipes.

Leticia walked about carrying a large tray of tempting hors d'oeuvres while Erin brought wine or, if requested, stronger drinks.

From behind one of the large pillars, Leticia frantically motioned to Erin who came over to her as soon as possible.

"That Mr. Fielding is ever so interesting," she whispered as Erin leaned close. "Here, you take the hors d'oeuvres and I'll take the wine. See if you can hear what they're saying. It was something about a special person—a detective, he calls it. You know Mr. Fielding is a magistrate as well as a writer. He has set up a group of men to find criminals."

"That sounds very interesting," Erin agreed.

"Not just interesting. Erin—if they can find criminals, why can't they find your child?"

"I don't think they would—unless they were paid."

Leticia shrugged. "Take these. Go and listen. Perhaps you'll overhear something useful."

Erin took the heavy silver tray and moved as close as she dared to the group. One thing she had learned while serving at Lady Montague's parties was that servants were practically invisible. No one paid them any mind, and the guests discussed the most intimate of subjects. Not that this discussion was at all intimate.

Mr. Fielding was a tall, debonair man. His voice was deep and she listened intently, though she tried to look as if she were not listening at all.

"Yes, Gattlin is a true detective. I tried to get him to join the force, but he insists on working for himself."

"You and your brother John have done an amazing job," Dr. Johnson said, patting his protruding stomach and reaching for another tiny tidbit from Erin's tray. "London is a far safer place now."

Fielding shrugged. "It isn't just a matter of law enforcement. One day we must have proper detectives, men who can investigate crime and be more than thief-takers."

Erin stood off to the side. She bit her lip and wondered if she dared to ask just where she might find this Mr. Gattlin. She drew in her breath and glanced around. No one was paying much attention, and so she boldly curtsied in front of Mr. Fielding.

"Pardon me, sir. I could not help but overhear you. I have an acquaintance who is much in need of this Mr. Gattlin's services. Could you tell me where to find him?"

Mr. Fielding looked down at her and nodded. "Indeed, he has an office on the third floor of a building near the Thames no more than a stone's throw from Tower Hill. Now let me see, I think it's in that little cul-de-sac. Beeker Lane."

Erin smiled and curtsied again. "Thank you so much, sir."

"My pleasure," Mr. Fielding answered. "But tell your friend that Mr. Gattlin does not work for pleasure. He may be too expensive."

Erin had not expected less. He nodded and she once again passed her tray of treasures to Dr. Johnson, who not only took one, but stuffed three into his rumpled vest pocket. Lady Montague's literati were not usually well dressed or wealthy. Their well being, she had learned, entirely depended on the generosity of their patrons.

Erin felt strong arms around her, and she turned as she responded to gentle, yet firm caresses. It was her wedding night, and she was wearing her white chemise, the one with the pretty blue ribbons. The man in her dream was loosening her ribbons, as once Jack had. But this was not the same. This was gentle yet exciting, and she looked into soft gray eyes as the man in her dream took on form. "Philip," she whispered in her dream. She felt something very special, something very different from that which she had felt when Jack had made her his wife.

Erin's eyes flickered open and she found herself in her own bed, quite alone. Her room was narrow and off the kitchen. The great clock in the hall struck four and she shook her head. She was quite awake now, even though it was a full hour before she was compelled to rise.

She felt her cheeks. They were warm and slightly flushed. "All because of a dream," she thought. And yet her dream had been so real, so delightful, that she had not wanted to awaken. But now that she was

awake, she felt distressed by it. Why was she dreaming
of Philip Lawson? And in this most intimate way? But
it was only a dream. How could she be responsible
for it? She bit her lip. Was her dream an unconscious
wish?

Erin sunk back down under the covers. Her
thoughts were jumbled, and her dream tantalizing.
"He is a most attractive man," she said aloud. Surely,
her thoughts were not improper, at least as long as
she did not act on them.

She thought back, long, long ago before she had
even known he was married. Even then she had
thought of Philip Lawson and wondered about him.
There was no doubt about it; she felt drawn to him.
Perhaps she always had, she thought a little guiltily.

Erin pushed him out of her thoughts and rolled
over on her back. No matter what she felt for Philip
Lawson, and regardless of how much better she felt
mentally and physically, she still had one primary
goal. That goal was to get her child back, and in spite
of Miss Atherton's refusal to tell her anything, she
had not given up. Only this morning Leticia had
reminded her about Mr. Fielding's friend, about the
gentleman who investigated such matters. She knew
he would be costly, but even so, she decided to go
and see him. "I must try," she vowed. "I must try
everything."

Erin wore a blue woolen dress with a stiff white
collar. It was tight fitting on top with long, white
cuffed sleeves. The bottom of the dress was full and
fell in folds to the floor. The truth was, she owned
only three dresses and this one had been a gift from
Lady Montague, who often gave the girls who worked

in her household clothes she no longer intended wearing. It was a far more expensive dress than Erin could herself have afforded, and she knew she looked well in it. Erin felt this dress was both demure and yet somehow alluring. The color was the color of her eyes, and the white collar and cuffs set off the red-gold of her hair.

When she reached Lawson's, the "Closed" sign was hung on the front door. She knocked and Philip opened the door and stood looking at her. "Please, come in," he said after a moment.

Erin followed him into the back room of the shop. There he had covered a small round table with a white cloth and in the center was a teapot. At each of two places, there was a delicate china cup and a silver spoon. He had even arranged some little cakes on a plate.

He stepped behind her and removed her cloak. Erin felt a now familiar chill pass through her. It was a polite gesture, but far too reminiscent of the times when Jack would stand behind her and remove her clothes. She moved away quickly and when she turned, she saw that his face was flushed. There was some kind of magic between them—about that there was no question in her mind. But there were other things between them too. She had not told him about her child; she had said only that she lost her son. He did not know it had been given away and that she was obsessed with finding him, if only to know he was safe and well and in a good home.

"Please sit down, Erin." He pulled out the chair for her and Erin sat down, hardly daring to lean back.

He sat down opposite her and poured some tea. His hand trembled slightly. "Adelle and I used to have tea every day when we closed the shop for lunch. We'd talk, then rest a bit before our noon meal.''

Erin sipped some of her hot tea. ''I know it's difficult for you. Have you gone to see your son?''

''I can't go as often as I want,'' Philip confessed. ''I will go to the country this weekend and see him. But then I might not get back again for several weeks. There aren't enough hours in each day.''

Erin wanted to say that her day had far too many hours, empty hours. But she did not. ''My days seem short too,'' she told him.

''I imagine Pierre keeps you busy.''

''Very, and he does not like Miss George so I must be their go-between.''

He watched her as she spoke. It was only natural that they would make small talk, but it was not what he wanted to do. He wanted to get to know her, really get to know her. He wanted to know what she was thinking and if there was another man in her life. She was, at the moment, a mystery, an enigma. For a young lady from Belfast who worked as a maid, she seemed very well spoken. Moreover, he had noted that she could read, or at least it appeared she could read. He wondered where she had learned, and if she had many secrets. Silently, he admitted that though he had told her he desired company, he had meant something quite different. The fact was, he was beginning to desire her. It was too soon, but he could not deny how he felt whenever he saw her.

''Will you come again?'' he said suddenly.

Erin blushed. ''I should be pleased to come again.''

Chapter Six

A short distance to the south of Beeker Lane, the Thames wound its stately way through London. This area, near the docks, was easily the busiest part of London. A never-ending parade of coaches, wagons, and carriages came to fetch merchandise. Daily, hundreds of vessels arrived from as far away as China bearing all manner of goods for sale in the markets of London. It was an area which was also not far from Newgate Prison and the Tower. It seemed to Erin as if there was a pub on every corner, and beggars and prostitutes in every doorway.

Erin stopped long enough to check the address, then she went in the door and climbed the winding staircase to the third floor. She paused outside the door before she knocked. A thousand questions ran through her head. "Please let him be able to help me," she whispered to herself. Then she gathered up her courage and knocked on the door.

"Come in!" a male voice shouted.

Cautiously, Erin opened the door and stood poised on the threshold.

"Well, don't just stand there like a frightened sparrow! I haven't time for coy women. Either come in or go away," the man behind the ancient desk shouted gruffly.

In spite of her misgivings and a sudden feeling that she wanted to run away, Erin forced herself to step inside. She jumped as a draft caused the door to slam shut behind her. She turned in panic.

"Stop acting like a frightened deer. I'm not going to bite you. It would be bad for business."

Erin turned toward him again. His tone had changed, and his comment made her laugh.

"I assume you are here on business." He looked her up and down.

"Are you Mr. Frederick Gattlin?" Erin asked.

"One and the same. If it's lost, I'll find it for you. That's my business."

"I want you to find someone, not something," Erin said, hesitating. "But first I must know what it will cost."

He stared hard at her, taking her measure. "Whom have you lost? Your husband? Did he run away?"

Erin shook her head. "No, my husband drowned in a shipwreck."

"I didn't suppose any man in his right mind would leave you," he said. "No offense."

Erin felt her face flush.

"Don't look so embarrassed. You're a pretty girl. I'm sure you know that. That's the trouble with women. The pretty ones are either in love with themselves, flaunting their wares, or so shy they turn crimson when you look at them. Now sit down and tell me whom you have lost, if indeed lost is the right word."

Erin sat down on the edge of the straight-backed chair. "It's my child."

"Your child was kidnapped?" Mr. Gattlin lifted bushy eyebrows and leaned forward. "How unusual." He shook his head. "I've never heard of a poor girl's child being kidnapped. Now if you were wealthy . . ."

"He wasn't exactly kidnapped. It's more complicated than that."

"Well, I can't possibly tell you how much this might cost if I don't know the whole story. Tell me everything."

Erin looked carefully at Mr. Gattlin. He was a short, fat, untidy little man with thin hair and extremely bushy eyebrows. His eyes were small and a trifle beady. There was very little about him which inspired confidence. But who else was there? His advertisement said he was a detective, and surely a detective was what she required. Besides that, Mr. Fielding had spoken well of him. Surely, a magistrate would not recommend an incompetent.

"Please start by telling me what brought you here?"

"I work for Lady Montague. She had a reception a few days ago. Mr. Henry Fielding was there, and Dr. Johnson was the guest speaker. Later when they were talking, I overheard their conversation. I confess I was eavesdropping," Erin admitted forthrightly. "Mr. Fielding was talking about the group of detectives he founded to root out criminals. He spoke briefly of you and your investigative ability."

Mr. Gattlin leaned back in his chair with obvious satisfaction. "Ah! The best advertisement is word of mouth." He ran his finger around his high collar. "I am quite well known," he said without the slightest modesty. "Is there criminal activity involved in your case?"

"Oh, no," Erin said. "In a way, it would be easier if there were. As I told you, I'm a widow. When my husband died, I was pregnant. I had nowhere to turn and no money. I went to the Gardner Home in Croydon. I had the baby and they took care of me. Mrs. Dudley, who ran the home, promised they would keep my child for a year before giving it over for adoption so that I could save enough money to keep him. But Mrs. Dudley died, and a Miss Agnus Atherton took over the home. She gave my child over for adoption. She won't tell me who adopted my baby."

"I can well imagine that is the usual course of action. Did you sign any papers?"

"I did, but only after Mrs. Dudley promised to keep my child for a year. I was to return and pay the costs of my room and board during the time I lived there, as well as the costs of their keeping my child."

"You know, of course, that they were quite within their rights to offer the child for adoption, promise or no promise. In order for Mrs. Dudley's promise to have meaning, it would have to be in writing or overheard by another."

"I fear only Miss Atherton knew about it." Erin felt dejected. Her quest was probably hopeless.

"I gather you want your baby back," Mr. Gattlin said, rubbing his chin with tobacco-stained fingers.

"Of course I want him back, but if I cannot have him, I want to know who has him and if he is all right. I know there is probably nothing I can do to get him back."

Again tears filled Erin's eyes. It was surely hard enough to lose her child, but not to know how he was and how he was being treated made matters all the worse. At least knowing would give her some peace of mind.

"I should like to help you," Mr. Gattlin said, sounding sympathetic for the first time. "But you must understand that looking into this matter would be costly. It is obvious to me that you are a girl of very modest means."

"Would you help me if I had the money?"

He rubbed his chin again and then raked through his beard with his stubby fingers. "I would," he said.

Erin nodded and stood up. All she could think of was the necessity to get another position, one which would provide her with more money than she had now.

"I shall be back, Mr. Gattlin," Erin said with determination.

"I trust you won't do anything illegal to get the money."

"I wouldn't dream of it. I want my child and I do not want to end up in prison."

"I shall look forward to seeing you again."

"You're moping," Pierre said, shaking his finger in her face.

"I'm only thinking," she answered. "I found a man who might be able to help me locate my son. But I have no money to pay him."

"Pierre would help, but Pierre has spent all of his money."

Erin did not have to ask on what he had spent his money. She knew he was investing in order to open his own coffeehouse, where the likes of Dr. Johnson and his friends could come. Pierre insisted he could do much better than the present establishments, which offered little variety. He muttered darkly that the English knew how to make neither decent coffee nor the little pastries and mouth-watering baguettes that went so well with his own dark brew. In Pierre's mind, the English culinary art was restricted to producing hard little biscuits and then covering them with gobs of clotted cream. "This is," he declared time and again, "a nation without culinary finesse, a land of roast beef and clotted cream."

"I shall have to find another position," Erin told him. "One which pays more than this one."

"You must be very careful. A young girl out on her own. I would try to stop you, but you're headstrong and willful. In any case, Pierre is leaving here too. He is ready to open his own coffeehouse. Of course, Pierre would hire you, but it is a place for gentlemen only, and if you were around the learned gentlemen could think of nothing but you and your red curls. Besides, if I hired a pretty girl, their wives would not allow them to come at all. Think how the arts would suffer!"

Erin smiled and doubted that she was that distracting.

"You must go to the grocer's this afternoon. I am quite out of certain items," he said, changing the subject.

Erin tried to hide her enthusiasm. Her heart skipped a beat at the thought of seeing Philip Lawson so soon again. "I'll go now, if it's all right."

"No time like the present," Pierre said.

By noon, large puffy clouds were moving across the sky and a brisk wind had come out of the south.

There was going to be a storm, Erin thought as she hurried along.

She stepped into the shop and looked around anxiously. As she had hoped, by coming at this hour, she avoided running into others. She was quite alone in the shop.

Philip came out of the back room. "Erin, good morning—or is it afternoon?"

"Eleven-thirty," she answered.

"As you know, I close the shop at noon and open at two, so there is often no one here after eleven."

She did not say that she was fully aware of that fact, nor that she had come at this hour hoping they would be alone.

"Has Pierre sent a list?"

Erin held out the list and he took it from her, but he kept his eyes on hers, and as she stared into them, she felt herself being drawn toward him. Was she imagining this? Did he feel what she felt when they were together?

Then, unexpectedly, instead of taking the list, he took her wrist and pulled her into his arms. "Erin—" he whispered, looking into her upturned face. He bent his head, and his lips brushed hers gently. His other arm encircled her waist and he drew her closer until she could feel his warm breath on her neck. The gentle motion of his lips on hers increased in intensity as he kissed her harder and held her even closer.

Her heart leapt. He most certainly did feel as she did! Erin felt incapable of moving. His body was against hers, his breathing heavier as he kissed her neck. He said nothing, but words were unnecessary. His body movements, his kisses, and her lack of objection spoke for both of them.

He withdrew and looked down into her eyes. "Erin, I'm sorry if I've been too bold."

She looked back into his gray eyes and wanted to say, *It's all right. I wanted you to kiss me.* But she did not say that.

She desperately wanted him to keep kissing her, to keep holding her. But a relationship between them now would not be fair. A pain filled her heart. She had to find her son and know his fate before she would be free to fall in love. But she could also not deny her feelings. What she was beginning to feel for Philip Lawson was something much stronger than the girlish infatuation she had felt for Jack Findley. It seemed to her as if Philip Lawson were, in reality, the man she had once thought Jack was, but again she cautioned herself to take care. She vowed to get to know him better, and most important, she vowed to find her son and put her anxieties to rest.

"We must wait," she said softly. "It's too soon for us."

He dropped his arm and stepped away from her. His face was flushed and she could tell he was as excited by her as she had been by him. But this could not be the right moment. She had to find her baby—she had to know.

"Yes," he said slowly. "We must wait, you are right." He did not say more, though he feared Erin might be frightened by the kind of responsibility a relationship with him presented. She was young, and even though she was a widow who had lost a child, she might not want to acquire an older man who had a small child to rear. Still, he wanted to know her mind better. She was kind and understanding, and when his lips touched hers, he felt something he had never felt with any woman before. He had been fond

of Adelle, and he had been completely faithful as
well. But there was neither passion nor lust in their
relationship. But he knew he wanted Erin. It was quite
a different feeling. He was aroused almost as soon as
he touched her. She was beautiful and warm. She was
truly desirable.

"I'll get these things for you," he said, turning
away.

Erin felt flustered and indecisive. She wanted and
she did not want. He was wonderful! "What were you
doing in the back?" she asked, trying to make small
talk, to go back to where they had been before his
kiss changed everything.

"Making a sign advertising for a shop assistant."

Erin's eyes widened. "What, if I may ask, are the
qualifications you seek?"

"An honest person, a hard worker, and of course
the person must be able to read, write, and do sums."

Erin stood straight and looked into his eyes. "I
should like you to consider me," she offered. "I need
a job that pays more than I get now. I can read, write,
and do sums. I will work very hard, Philip."

Philip looked down into her clear blue eyes. Of
course he would hire her! Then he could see her
every day all day, he thought happily. But naturally,
his personal feelings toward her might be a drawback.
Absurd, he told himself as he carried on his silent
argument with himself. Adelle had been his shop
assistant and they had been married. No, Erin would
be perfect, and when they knew each other better,
he felt certain that there could be something between
them. Moreover, she was pretty and friendly and she
knew a lot about food from Pierre. She would be a
great asset.

"Are you certain you want to do this?" he asked.

"Very certain."

"There's a small room in the back. You can live there if you like. It will save you spending money on room and board."

"That would be perfect."

He thought about it for a long moment. He would live upstairs as he always had. But no one would gossip if she lived downstairs. At least he hoped no one would talk.

"When can you start?"

"I must give Lady Montague a week's notice."

"That would be fine. You will miss Pierre, though."

"He's leaving too. He's opening his own coffeehouse."

"Then this is good for all of us! A coffeehouse? I must go there sometime," Philip said. Again, he was making small talk. All other words caught in his throat. How he wanted to tell her how delightful he found her. But now, he thought happily, they would be together all the time. Perhaps she would grow less resistant and he would learn to talk to her, really talk to her.

Philip stuffed the items on Erin's list into her basket. "Tell Pierre I'll see him soon."

Erin smiled. "I'll be glad to tell him."

The days slipped by quickly, so quickly that Philip felt as if time were truly flying. Erin was a hard worker, and even if he had not been infatuated with her, he would have recognized her talents. She was so charming that the women who shopped in his store adored her, while the few men who came in spent more money than they might have ordinarily. It was clear they just wanted to spend some time talking with Erin. But it wasn't just her rapport with the customers. She was very good with sums, and her handwriting was neat and clear. She helped him with every single detail of running his store, and for that he was grateful. Initially, he admitted that he had hired her to be near her, but it took little time before he found she was invaluable too.

Today, she was helping him stock the shelves. She stood on the ladder, putting various items of merchandise on the top shelf.

"Do you think it's a good idea that we begin to carry other items?" he asked her. He meant non-food items. It had occurred to him that a woman might well buy a toy for her child while buying groceries.

"It's a wonderful idea. I've always thought people had to visit too many shops to buy what was wanted. It's a unique idea, offering a variety of merchandise."

"Watch out!" he shouted, but it was too late. The rickety old ladder had buckled, and Erin came tumbling down right into his arms. He caught her and she looked both startled and grateful.

She was like a feather, he thought. He set her down on the floor, but he did not let go of her. "You must never get on that ladder when I'm not here to catch you," he said, staring into her blue eyes and feeling the inexplicable desire she aroused in him.

Erin drew in her breath, her legs feeling a little wobbly. She wasn't sure if it was the fall or being so close to Philip that made her feel so tiny and vulnerable.

Again he was looking into her eyes with that look of longing. He touched her cheek with his hand and then ran it over her neck. She shivered and was aware of breaking out in goosebumps all up and down her arms.

Then he bent, as if commanded by some secret voice, and kissed her. It was their second kiss, but it was even more passionate than their first. His lips moved on hers and she responded, unable not to, not wanting him to stop and yet still feeling guilty, still aware of her own unfinished business.

Again his lips sought her neck, and then his hand dropped and moved furtively over the swell of her breast and down to her waist. "Please," she whispered.

Again, he stepped back, his face red, his mouth dry. Never had he wanted a woman as he wanted Erin. He could think of nothing but undressing her, of holding her close to him, of running his hands over her soft white flesh and devouring her with the love he knew she deserved. God, she was beautiful! And so much a woman! There was even more—she was smart and funny, everything any man could hope for. This woman, he knew, would be not just a wife, but a true partner for a lifetime.

But he had to respect her wishes. "I'm sorry," he said. It was a lie. He wasn't sorry at all. He wanted to hold her forever. He wanted her to be his always. He wanted her as he had never wanted any woman.

Erin looked into his eyes. "I must have a little time," she said.

He nodded. "You may have all the time in the world."

Philip stood by the window and watched as Erin walked briskly down the street. They had been working together now for nearly a month, and while there were moments of great closeness between them, it seemed obvious to him that she was holding back.

Each time he dared to kiss her, she seemed to respond but then pulled away. He shook his head, mystified by the apparent contradiction between her actions and what he sensed she really wanted.

She disappeared around the corner. Was there another man in her life? It was not the first time he had asked himself that question. Perhaps she had some kind of obligation of which she had not told him. Perhaps she was afraid to tell him to leave her alone for fear he would fire her. No, he was sure that was not it. He was certain he sensed her attraction to him and that their feelings toward each other were mutual.

But still there was something—of that, there could be no doubt whatsoever. Perhaps it was as he had originally feared, simply a reluctance on her part to take on a man with a small child. Yet Erin seemed to be the type of woman who would make a good and loving mother—he shook his head as if to dispel his misgivings. He wanted to know what it was that made her so reluctant to become involved romantically with him, and clearly, she would not tell him. Not for the first time, he told himself to be patient.

Chapter Seven

Mr. Gattlin looked around the office of the Gardner Home and shook his head. He found, to his surprise, that the atmosphere of the place annoyed him. It proclaimed itself a charity, and yet he thought, being quite uncharitable himself, that the proprietors probably made a pretty penny out of their good works. After all, the girls who stayed here were kept busy and their children were undoubtedly sold for far more than it cost the home to keep their mothers.

He turned toward the door as Miss Atherton swept into the room. He wrinkled his nose in distaste. She was precisely the type of woman who should not be running a charity, while at the same time she was all too typical of those who did. She was tall and slim and had an expression of self-righteousness that immediately told him she would not be moved.

Still, he held a mental picture of Erin Findley in his mind. She had brought him money, and without telling her, he had accepted far less than his ordinary fee because he felt sorry for her and because there was something so likeable about her. In any case, he had children and had lost children. He did not like what this Miss Atherton stood for; he did not like the word "charity" applied to the selling of children. It was all too common, but it was a practice of which he did not approve.

"How do you do, Mr. Gattlin." Miss Atherton smiled warmly, but it was not a real smile. She thought him a client, and he decided to play out the role.

"I do quite well. I presume you are Miss Atherton?"

"I am indeed. Have you come about a child? We have none at the moment, but we have two girls who will deliver within weeks. I'm certain we can help you, whatever your needs."

"Whatever his needs." Good heaven, he could be any sort of person. No wonder Erin was so concerned and wanted to make sure her child was in fact in a good home.

"Well, my wife and I are interested in adopting a waif."

Miss Atherton circled him. "Unkempt as you are, sir, I note that your suit comes from a more than reputable tailor. I therefore suppose you can afford the cost."

He raised his brow. "Is the cost so high?"

"It depends on the child. Boys are more expensive than girls, fair-haired children fetch a better price than the dark-complexioned ones. And naturally, if you are in a great hurry, it could add to the expense."

"I thought this was a charity, one that attempted to place children in the best homes."

"We have our expenses," Miss Atherton said

haughtily. "If you are truly interested, I can be more specific."

"I am more concerned with who bought a child born here some months ago. The mother's name was Erin Findley."

Miss Atherton's expression hardened. "Did she send you here?" she demanded.

"I am investigating the whereabouts of her child."

"Until now I assumed you to be an intelligent man, if a bit untidy. I don't know who you are, or why you are acting for Mrs. Findley, but she signed the papers and the adoption of her child was quite legal. She lived here, she had the child here, and we cared for her and for the child. We had expenses and an obligation, it is as simple as that."

"She wants to know who took this child. She wants to be assured that he is in a good home."

"I will give her no information. None. I will give you none either. The child is in a good home."

"You were willing to sell me a child without knowing a thing about me, dear lady. Why should I take your word on this matter?"

Miss Atherton scowled. "Frankly, it is simply none of your business."

Gattlin stared back at her. She was a hateful woman, a woman of no scruples. "I imagine you got a very good price."

"We met our expenses."

"And then some, I imagine."

"I must ask you to leave."

He stood up. "I will make further inquiries."

"You will find out nothing about the child. I am the only one who knows to whom it went, and I will tell you nothing."

"No, dear lady. I shall make inquiries about you.

Perhaps you have heard the expression, 'there is more than one way to skin a cat?' ''

Miss Atherton paled slightly. "You cannot intimidate me.''

Mr. Gattlin smiled. He knew he already had. He might not find Erin's child, but he vowed that he would see this harridan put out of business. He picked up his hat and left without looking back. Erin would not find her child, but he would take steps to see that others did not lose theirs.

St. James's Park was full of summer flowers, green lawns, and ponds on which graceful swans circled. Erin stood uneasily by the fountain looking about. It was June fifteenth, and as she did on the fifteenth of every month, she had a special birthday thought for her son. He was eighteen months old today.

She watched with sadness as mothers walked with their children, and she found herself looking twice at the face of each child who appeared to be the same age as her own. She could not help asking herself if she would even know little John after so many months. He had never formally been christened, but she had decided to call him John the very first time she held him. She did not know the names of her own parents, but she had liked Jack's father, and it seemed only right that the baby be named after him.

She went back to contemplating what he might look like. When last she had seen him, his eyes had not changed color—if they were going to change color. By now, they might be brown, or gray, or even green. His hair too would be different. He still had soft, downy baby hair covering his little head the day she last saw him. Now he would have thicker hair,

and it most assuredly would be a different color. He
would be walking too.

Still, there was the birthmark. It was shaped like a
small duck and it was on his little rump. Erin knew
she would know her child by that mark, but naturally,
the children one passed on the street were dressed.
No, it was impossible for her to recognize her son
now unless she saw him unclothed. That was reality,
but in her heart she felt she would know him no
matter how he had changed. She thought perhaps
she would feel some instant affinity for him and that
he would feel the same thing for her. It was a belief
beyond all logic, this idea that she would have some
sort of divine insight and that he would be drawn to
her and know instantly that she was his mother. It
was as if she were waiting for a child to run into her
arms, to hug her, to call her mother.

But though all the children she saw aroused in her
an emotional response, no one child drew her close,
no one child seemed to be hers.

"Ah, Mrs. Findley, there you are. Very punctual, I
must say."

Erin looked up into the perfectly round face of
Mr. Gattlin. This afternoon he wore a rumpled red
waistcoat, matching britches, a white ruffled shirt,
and worn black shoes with somewhat tarnished buck-
les. He hardly looked as if he hobnobbed with the
likes of Lady Montague and Mr. Henry Fielding, but
she knew he did. He was simply one of those men to
whom shabbiness was a state of mind rather than a
financial necessity. Philip was quite the opposite. He
was not a man of great financial means, but he always
looked neat and he had a certain style. She supposed
he might easily pass for a gentleman rather than the
tradesman he was.

"I've brought you another payment," Erin said, forcing Philip from her thoughts. How often she retreated to daydreams of him, she realized. She recognized that Philip was coming to fill a void in her life, and she now thought seriously of telling him everything, all that she had not told him about herself and the son she had borne.

Erin fished into her bag and brought out a small purse. From it, she withdrew some coins.

"Ah, my dear Mrs. Findley, I cannot take any more of your money. I know how little you have, and though I have tried to earn it, unless Miss Atherton can be persuaded to talk, I feel there is no hope of finding your child."

Erin looked up at him. She felt drained. She knew all too well that she had allowed herself to be too optimistic, and though he had warned her earlier to be realistic, she had dared to hope.

"My dear, you look so crestfallen. You're a young woman. A beautiful woman. I'm sure you will marry again and have another child."

Aware that her eyes were filled with moisture, she looked up into Mr. Gattlin's eyes. "You're very kind, and I know you're trying to comfort me, but it cannot be the same. If I am fortunate enough to have other children, I will love them. But a mother cannot replace one child with another. To a mother, each child is special."

He hung his head and to her eyes resembled nothing so much as a basset hound. At first, she had found him gruff and impolite, but as she had grown to know him, she found him hard-working, honest, and quite kind.

"You are quite correct, Mrs. Findley. Forgive me for suggesting that your problem has so simple a solution. I once lost a child too—not the way you have, but to illness. I have other children, but they are not the same child. I do know better."

"I'm sorry. I didn't know that you too had lost a child."

"How could you? I am not a man who talks much of private matters."

"There is nothing I can do," Erin said dejectedly. "I shall just have to keep looking and praying."

"There is one thing. I am a detective, not a barrister. I have asked Henry Fielding to speak with you. Tell him what happened to you and to your child. He is an authority on the law, and he may have some suggestion. He may know if anything can be done legally."

Erin felt a bit overwhelmed. She had felt bold approaching Mr. Gattlin as she had, but he was at least in business. Mr. Fielding was a famous man. She was surprised that he would have time for her. "And he agreed to speak with me?" she asked incredulously.

"Henry Fielding is a man of honor. Heaven knows he is no snob. You may have heard that he married his wife's maid."

"I knew his first wife had died," Erin admitted. All she knew about Mr. Fielding, and indeed the rest of Lady Montague's friends, was gossip she heard from other servants. The truth of the matter was that since she had left Mrs. Montague's employ, she had heard little gossip.

"If he loved her, I think it is truly romantic."

"And I say it is no one's business. In any case, he is quite willing to speak with you. I took the liberty of making you an appointment a week from today at two o'clock in the afternoon. Here is the address at which he will meet you.''

He handed her a folded bit of paper, and Erin unfolded it and looked at it. She then carefully refolded it and put it in her little satchel. Perhaps, she thought hopefully, there was some quirk in the law that would compel Miss Atherton to answer questions.

"I want to thank you for everything," Erin said.

"I cannot expect this to help you, but I want you to know I went to Miss Atherton and I found her a most suspicious woman. I did not like her at all, and I began looking into her affairs. I have found her to be unscrupulous in the extreme, and indeed, I have discovered that she has committed several illegalities. I am having her charged formally."

Erin's mouth opened in surprise. But his words were far from comforting. If Miss Atherton was so bad, she might well have placed her child in jeopardy.

As if he guessed her thoughts, Mr. Gattlin put his arm around her shoulders. "Please do not worry. I'm certain your child is all right."

Erin nodded. "Thank you," she said. Then, before she once again began to cry, she turned and headed home.

Philip puttered around the store and looked up only when Erin came in.

"You're working on a Sunday?" she asked in surprise.

"Just a little tidying. Have you been out for a walk?" Even as he asked, he wondered if he were being too curious. But in truth, he was curious. He wondered where she disappeared to, and he could not help wondering if, indeed, she were seeing a man.

"Yes, just to Saint James's Park." She wanted to tell him everything, but she could not, though she knew she would soon do so. A part of her worried that he would be upset when he learned she had given up her child. But surely, when she explained that she had not intended to give him up, Philip would understand?

Philip watched her as she took off her summer cloak. Her dress was a plain design, a russet color with a white chemise underneath. But it did not matter how plain her clothing was. To his eyes, she was the most breathtaking woman in all of London. But why did she respond to him and then always put him off?

It was her day off, and she was most certainly entitled to a private life. He hadn't followed her, but he had wanted to. He wanted to know what mysterious secret kept her from him.

The truth was, the more he was around her, the more he wanted to be around her. He could hardly look at her now without wanting her. He daydreamed of loosening her lovely hair and letting it fall over her bare white shoulders. He thought constantly of what it would be like to taunt and tease her lovingly, to feel her responding, to hear her ask him breathlessly for fulfillment. It had not been that way with Adelle. He had loved Adelle as one might love a sister, but he had never felt this blinding passion for her. He had not dreamed of her writhing in his arms, hot with desire, filled with lustful wantonness. Not that he could be certain that Erin was the type of woman to respond in such a way—but most surely she was.

She seemed so warm, and when he had kissed her he had felt her desires awaken.

"Did you walk alone?" he prodded.

"I met a friend in the park," she replied.

It was as if a knife penetrated his heart. He was so afraid it might be a male friend. But he immediately chastised himself for even wanting to ask.

"It's lovely this time of year. I love the smell of the flowers."

Erin looked at him with admiration. This was not the first time he had revealed a soft side. A part of him cared about the sheer beauty of a summer's day, about the flowers, the graceful trees, the sound of little children playing. Something inside told her he had a poetic side. "Yes, it was very pretty. There were lots of children there playing, and several of the swans have given birth and have broods of cygnets."

"It's a lovely place. I hope one day the Crown will give over more land for use by commoners."

"When are you going to the country next?" Erin asked.

"Next Sunday. Erin, would you like to come?" The invitation popped out of his mouth so suddenly that it surprised even him. Then he added, just so she would know that this was no improper invitation, "My sister has room. You could sleep with one of the children."

She wanted to say yes because she wanted to spend the day with him, a day when they were not working, a day with no interruptions. But most of all she wanted to meet his small son, Adelle's child, a child the same age as her own. But she could not say yes to his invitation. She already had an appointment with Mr. Fielding. "I'm afraid I can't go next week," she said, frowning. "I could go another Sunday. In fact, I would like to go very much."

"I understand," he said quickly. But he didn't. Clearly, she had to see someone. Once again he felt an odd curiosity creep over him. If she had someone else, why did she just not tell him? He decided to be more forthright. "All right. I won't go next week, I'll go the following Sunday. Can you come with me then?"

Erin's face broke into a smile. "That would be perfect. I should enjoy it very much."

He grinned and felt relieved. "Good. It will do us both good to get away from the city and out into the country."

"I'm really excited about meeting your son," she said, smiling warmly at him.

Philip nodded. There were things he would have to tell her. Things he wanted to tell her. But they were things that could wait.

June had been a month of near perfect days, Philip thought. He tried to distract himself with the sights and smells of the day, with the outline of the buildings against the clear blue sky, and with the sight of the Thames as it flowed gently by the Houses of Parliament. As splendid as was the day, and try as he might, he could not make himself feel less guilty for following Erin, for seeing her meet a tall, handsome stranger. He fell into the depths of depression to discover that there was another man in her life, a man of obvious means who met her, talked and walked with her, and then returned to an ornate carriage and drove away in style.

It was true that the man Erin met had not kissed

her or held her. Perhaps it was not what he had assumed. He tried to tell himself it was all innocent, though he knew he was still doubtful. Again, he reprimanded himself for not asking her openly, and for following her about. "I've gotten what I deserved," he said to himself as he continued to walk along the Thames, trying to decide what to do. But what was there to do?

Next week they would go to the country together, and he told himself that nothing had really changed. But again and again, he asked himself what he should do. Finally, he decided he should speak with Pierre, who, after all, knew Erin better than almost anyone. Perhaps Pierre could set his mind at ease. Perhaps Pierre could solve the mystery that seemed to surround Erin.

Erin walked dejectedly home. Mr. Fielding had been extremely nice to her and had listened intently as she explained the circumstances of her son's birth, the promises made and the promises broken. He had asked her about what she had signed, if she could read, if she had understood the agreements the Gardner Home had required.

He had seemed surprised when she told him she could read and had understood. She patiently explained that she had trusted Mrs. Dudley and that the promise made was outside of the written agreement.

"It would have been better if you were illiterate," he said, shaking his head. "Then we might have initiated a case claiming you did not understand the consequences of your actions. Even that would be a difficult case, but there might have been a chance. The law," he explained patiently, "is made up of precedents—that is to say, on the weight of past decisions, on the thoughts and judgments of learned men. I would say that when a woman goes to a home to have a baby, and those who run the home take care of her, feed her, clothe her, and house her, and when there is a written agreement between them that makes it clear that they will take the child and offer it for adoption, the law cannot help you. I quite understand that the previous superintendent of the home made a special arrangement with you, but I think the law would still uphold the home's right to handle your case in the traditional way. But do not give up entirely. I shall look into it for you and I shall do a little research to see if I can find a case of this sort somewhere in the literature."

Erin had understood what he told her, but this time she decided she would not even allow herself the pleasure of hope. She turned onto Charles Street. She found herself looking forward to seeing Philip, and more than anything, she found herself looking forward to next Sunday in the country. Perhaps then she would tell him everything. If he still wanted her, she decided she would stop resisting his advances.

The coffeehouse was on a busy corner off Fleet Street. Inside, smoke drifted upward from the many small round tables, the smell of hot, dark coffee filled the room, and the noise of some dozen subdued conversations blended into a kind of hum. The denizens of the coffeehouse were like bees in their hive. They came here to talk, to exchange ideas, to get news from all parts of London and the world.

Pierre looked up at Philip Lawson and studied his facial expression. The British were so transparent!

Pierre could tell he was troubled, and he could tell that the trouble was a woman.

"You have come to seek Pierre's counsel?" he asked, indicating a small table away from the din of heady conversation.

Philip nodded. "I've come to speak with you about Erin."

"Ah, my little cabbage. How is she?"

"Working hard. She works very hard."

"As I told you she would. But that is not what you have come to see Pierre about."

"You're right," Philip confessed. "I find I have some questions about her."

Pierre frowned. "You British," he said scornfully. "And if you have questions about her, why don't you ask them of her?"

"I can't—I mean, I don't think it would be proper."

"Proper, proper, posh fosh! You're in love with her, is this the problem?"

Philip looked at Pierre and his mouth opened slightly. Yes, though he had not even thought of saying it, Pierre was right. He was in love with Erin. "I am," he said, so softly he could hardly hear himself.

"And how is this a difficulty? The difficulty as Pierre sees it is that you have not told her this."

"I have kissed her."

"Well, that's something. Sometimes I wonder why there are so many English. Your mating dance is so formal, so absurdly prolonged. And when you kissed her, what did she do?"

"I believe she liked it. But she always stops me."

Pierre raised both brows. "Ah, ha! You have kissed her more than once."

"Yes, more than once."

Pierre shook his head again. "No doubt she stops

you because she does not know if you are in love or just lustful.''

Philip's face reddened. "I am both," he confessed.

"Well, I'm glad to hear that. Then it is Erin you must tell.''

At that moment the door of the coffeehouse opened, and Philip looked up to see that the man who had entered was none other than the man Erin had met near the Thames.

Pierre too looked toward the door. He stood up and walked over, his hands extended. "Ah, welcome, Mr. Fielding.''

Philip stared at the two of them. Henry Fielding? The magistrate and writer? He watched dumbfounded as Pierre showed him to a table and then returned to talk with him.

"That man," Philip whispered. "Is that Henry Fielding?''

"Yes, indeed. A very good friend of Dr. Johnson.''

"I saw him with Erin. I thought—''

Pierre laughed. "You thought wrongly. Ah, you must love her. Pierre sees you are jealous.''

"I wondered if there was another man.''

"No. There is not. Pierre has always known that you and Erin were right for one another. You must talk with her. Ask her what you want to know.''

Philip nodded and stood up. Erin would be home by now, and he knew that Pierre was right. It was Erin he would have to ask. But he thought a better time would be when they were in the country together. After she met little Andrew, he would tell her how much he loved her. He would tell her about Adelle and share all his secrets with her.

He put on his cloak and left the confusion of the coffeehouse. His thoughts were filled with Erin as he left. Whatever her relationship with Mr. Fielding, he was sure it was not romantic. Yes, he vowed, he would declare his love for her, and he prayed she would feel the same. For the first time in his life he was in love. Truly in love.

Chapter Eight

The sun was warm as Philip guided the horse and cart down the rutted road. They had left London behind them, and now even its surrounding villages had disappeared and given way to rolling hills carpeted in lush, vibrantly green grass.

Erin sat beside him, and now and again he glanced over at her. She wore her plain blue dress with the white chemise. Her lush, red-gold curls fell down her back, and though they were tied with a ribbon, a few loose hairs had escaped and blew free in the morning breeze. She was to his eyes as breathtaking as the day, and he felt filled with anticipation and hope.

"It's a long ride out to Hendon. I don't go as much as I should." He imagined he still sounded all too formal. Pierre was right—the dance of love as performed by the British was agonizingly slow.

Erin let her eyes wander over the countryside. Cows and sheep grazed lazily behind white fences. Now and again, the air smelled of manure, a not entirely unpleasant aroma, though sometimes a trifle pungent.

"Is it your family farm?" Erin asked as they bumped along.

Philip shook his head. "My father was a tradesman too. No, the farm belongs to my sister's husband. They have five children, so Andrew has many playmates. You know, I didn't want to have him live separately from me, but I just couldn't run the store and look after him. I thought, at least while he is so young, that he would be better off with my sister, and so I pay her and her husband to keep Andrew. They need the money, and I know he's safe. Besides, he is at the age when he needs a woman's love."

"I wish I had that kind of choice," Erin said wistfully. "But I'm an orphan. I have no family, and Jack's father died a year after we were married. So really, there was no one. How could I work and take care of a baby?"

Philip turned toward her. "I don't understand. I thought you lost your baby."

Erin couldn't look at him. She was still concerned about what he would think of her. But she had to tell him. "I did lose him, but he is still alive."

"I don't understand," Philip said again.

"It's not easy for me to speak of it. I've worried about what you might think of me. Please try to understand—Jack left me penniless and in debt. I was pregnant, I had nowhere to turn. I had to agree to give my child over for adoption but—oh, I thought they would wait. I thought I would get him back. But they didn't wait, and they will tell me nothing."

"I still don't quite understand."

"They promised they would keep him. Then the

administration of the institution changed, and he was given over for adoption without my knowledge. They will not tell me to whom he was given.''

"Can't they be made to tell you?''

Erin felt relief flood over her. He did not think her a terrible mother; he was concerned. She shook her head. ''I hired a detective and even went to see Mr. Fielding. But the law is the law. I can do nothing, but I will never forget my child. I will always keep looking.''

Philp drew in his breath. He had thought there was another man, and in a way there was. The other man was her child. Poor Erin! He wanted so to hold her! He knew he could not compensate for or change the tragedy that had befallen her, but he wanted to do what he could. She would make a wonderful mother, and they would have children together. She would never forget her firstborn, but he vowed he would change her life and bring her happiness.

Philip guided the horse off the road and toward a shallow stream. ''We'll rest here for a while,'' he said, jumping down off the cart. He quickly unhitched the horse and led it to the stream; then he returned and lifted Erin down, but he did not let go of her. Instead, he kissed her. It was a long kiss, and he felt her returning his passion.

When he withdrew from her lips, he looked down into her face. This time she had not stopped him; she had not pulled away.

''Was that your secret, Erin? Was that why you always stopped me?''

Tears filled her eyes. ''Yes,'' she murmured. ''I wanted to find my baby, but I couldn't and I didn't think it fair to you . . . Oh, Philip, don't you see? I'm not emotionally whole. I'm so confused.''

He put his arms around her and drew her close once again, rocking her gently in his arms. "Erin, you've been through too much alone. I know about Jack. Everyone knew about Jack. Erin, I love you. I want to be with you. I want to help you find your child if that's what you want. Erin, I adore you."

Erin looked into his eyes. They were kind, and she felt safe when he held her. But she also felt much more. She felt on fire when he pressed her close. She felt passion when his lips moved on hers, and a deep desire to have him move within her. This was so different than it had been with Jack! She knew this man; she knew his moods because she had worked closely with him. She knew his tastes, and she knew he was good, kind, and reliable.

She almost smiled. At this moment, with his arms around her, reliability, as desirable a trait as it was, was not what she yearned for. She yearned to have him take her, to sweep her away, to hold her and make her cry out in his arms.

"Thank you for understanding about my child," she whispered. "I was so afraid of what you would think of me."

"Erin, I think you're the most wonderful woman in the world. I dream of you every night, I think of you every day. My darling, we all have secrets and we all have fears. I have things to tell you too," he said slowly. "But they can wait a little while. Erin, I want you to marry me. I want you to be my wife."

"Oh, Philip." She stood on her tiptoes and kissed him. "Of course I'll marry you."

Again his arms enfolded her. He kissed her lips, then her neck and ears. She moved in his arms, feeling the warmth of her own wantonness as his hands moved over her. He lightly touched her breast and then her hips and buttocks. She could feel the heat of his hands through the material of her dress. He kissed her again and again, and she trembled against him and felt almost faint in his arms. He could have her now if he wanted, but she trusted him. He was a proper man; he would wait and so would she.

"You are beautiful and filled with love, Erin," he whispered. "I have known love before, but I have never known this kind of passion. I have never known what I feel for you. Oh, Erin, I hunger for you."

Erin said nothing, though she tried to search her own emotions. Jack had awakened her passion, but he had not truly loved her, nor had she loved him. Theirs had been a youthful infatuation, but this was something very different; this was a whole love, a love of caring for each other, for sharing each other's troubles, a love of mutual respect, and it combined with a hot desire, a desire that they both felt. She looked into Philip's eyes and realized that she trusted him more than anyone she had ever known.

He touched the top of her bodice and undid a few of the laces. She did not stop him when he bent down and kissed the tops of her breasts; instead she felt herself weaken in his arms, fully awakened. She knew she did not want him to stop. She sensed he would be a good lover, a slow lover.

"There's a vicarage about two miles down the road, Erin. Why don't we stop and have him marry us now, this very day?"

"Whenever you wish," Erin whispered. She buried her face in his chest.

"I have been a fool to wait this long, I have been a fool not to tell you how I felt," Philip said.

He smiled at her. "Come on now, Erin. Let's find that vicar!"

He slipped his arm around her waist and, unable to resist one last kiss, he again bent and touched his lips to the top of her full breasts. It took all of his resolve to step away from her. "We'll be married and continue on to the farm. I want you to know my family. They will be your family too."

He lifted Erin back into the cart and then rehitched the horse and climbed in beside her.

The vicarage was a small cottage attached to a plain little church set in a garden filled with hundreds of blossoms.

"Had I picked a place to be married, I could not have chosen better," Erin said as Philip lifted her down. He kissed her once again and then, holding her hand, led her to the door. He knocked loudly and in a few moments, an elderly man opened the door. He had white hair and was small and round, with dark shoe-button eyes.

"We want to be married," Philip announced.

The vicar frowned. "I already have one wedding this week."

"Not this week. Now. This very day, this very moment."

The vicar raised his brows. "That's most unusual. Have you a witness?"

"No. Have you no wife who could serve as a witness?"

"Well, I suppose she could, though she doesn't hear well."

"It matters not. Come, my good man, I want to marry this good woman today, and if you can manage it, I'll make a good donation to your parish."

"Go and wait in the chapel and I shall find my wife."

Philip smiled and led Erin toward the little church.

"You're quite shameless," she laughed happily.

"I'm slow getting started, but I know what I want." He bent and kissed her again. "I do love you, Erin."

"And I you."

They waited for nearly half an hour, but then the door opened and the old vicar and his wife came in. His wife was as round as her husband, and she carried a large bouquet of wildflowers that she handed to Erin.

"Every bride should have a bouquet," she said, smiling a toothless smile. "I can just tell to look at the two of you that this is real love."

Erin blushed and looked to see that Philip too was blushing.

"Now the two of you stand right over here," the old clergyman instructed. "I've got my book and I'm ready to go."

"We're ready," Philip said.

The vicar opened his Book of Common Prayer and began to read the ceremony. Erin held Philip's hand and felt him warm and strong beside her. Whatever happened, she knew that at last she had a man who would always be at her side.

"I do," she answered when asked, and she heard him promise as well. Then Philip was kissing her and the vicar was smiling. "Ah, rare are moments like these," the old man mumbled.

Within the hour they were once again on the road and headed toward Philip's sister's home.

* * *

The farmhouse in which Philip's sister lived with her husband and children appeared large and rambling from the outside. As they stood in the entry hall, Erin looked about curiously. The house had a comfortable feel to it, though it was obvious its inhabitants were far from rich.

"This is my sister, Annabelle," Philip said, introducing a buxom woman with brown hair and lively eyes.

"Annabelle, this is Erin, and you should know right away that Erin and I were married this afternoon."

Annabelle smiled warmly. "My brother being spontaneous! What miracle have you wrought?" she asked, looking at Erin.

"Not so spontaneous. I waited far too long," Philip said.

"Your marriage is good news," Annabelle said, taking Erin's hand. "I'm so sorry you missed Andrew. You're a bit later than I expected, and he played hard all day, so he's been put to bed."

"I understand. We'll take a peek at him in a little while. Where's Bryce?" Philip asked.

Annabelle wiped her hands on her apron. "Still milking the cows. We have a larger herd than before, so it takes longer. But let's not stand in the hall all day—come on into the kitchen."

Philip followed his sister down the hall, and Erin followed Philip. In a moment, they entered a huge farm kitchen. It was obviously the center of the house.

Along one wall was a huge brick fireplace with walk-in ovens on both sides. In front of the fire was a long worktable. Further away, in the center of the room, was a large eating table with twelve chairs set around it. The rest of the walls held shelves of dishes and pots and pans. From the rafters, dried herbs hung, and there was even a braid of garlic and one of onions. The aroma of roasting meat filled the room.

"I knew you'd be hungry when you got here," Annabelle said, indicating the oven. "As soon as Bryce comes back, we'll sit down and eat."

"This is so wonderful," Erin said, looking about wide-eyed.

Annabelle laughed. "Wonderful?"

"I've never been in a house like this before."

"You mean you're a city girl?"

Erin shook her head. "No, I mean I've never been in a family home before. I was reared in an orphanage, and then when I was released, I came directly to London from Belfast. I got a position in the home of Lady Montague, and I moved into the servants' quarters. But Lady Montague lived in a mansion, not a real home. She had no family, so it was really not even like a home. This is—this is the way I always dreamed families lived."

Annabelle turned about and gave Erin a hug. "My house will always be your home, Erin."

"Where are the children?" Philip asked.

"Oh, you want children, do you? Well, I have an abundance of them as you well know, my fine brother. And now that you mention it, it's time they were fed and sent to bed. Then we can have a quiet evening, and you and Erin can escape together."

Annabelle turned about and walked to the back door of the kitchen. There she beat on a huge cow bell, and in a few moments it seemed that children had appeared from all over the house.

"This is part of my brood," Annabelle said proudly. The children all lined up in a row.

"Who's she?" one of the little boys queried.

"She is Erin Lawson, your new Aunt Erin."

"Erin, this is Phillipa, who is the eldest. She's eight. Mark here is seven, John is five, and Matthew is four."

A toothless four-year-old grinned up at her.

Philip laughed. "For a while we thought she might give birth to all twelve apostles."

Erin laughed. "And where is the fifth?"

"That would be Katie—she's only two and she's already been put to bed together with Andrew. They get so fussy if they're up after six."

Annabelle seated the children and began at once to dish up their supper from a steaming pot. "Bryce will be back soon," she said.

Hardly had Annabelle finished her sentence when a tall, lean man came through the back door. He had the ruddy complexion of a farmer, and Philip embraced him warmly and then introduced Erin with the same introduction he had given Annabelle.

"Then we must break out some wine and celebrate!" Bryce declared. He looked at Erin and smiled broadly. "You're a lucky man, Philip Lawson."

After dinner, Philip took Erin for a long walk around the farm. It was a clear, bright night, and the moon shone full over the rolling hills.

"One day I suspect London will sprawl all the way out here," Philip said as he slipped his arm around her slim shoulders.

"Then it would be a very large city indeed."

He laughed gently and turned her to look into her face. "I was a fool to wait so long to tell you how I felt."

"We've both had terrible tragedies befall us. It takes time to heal," Erin said.

He bent down and kissed her lips, and Erin pressed against him. The memory of his last kiss lingered, and this one seemed even deeper, even more passionate. She drew in her breath as she felt his hand caress her bare arm. His movements were slow and tantalizing as his lips moved against hers.

He put his hand on her throat and slid it slowly back under her hair. He moved his finger in a small circle round her ear, and again she felt goosebumps on her body and a chill go right down her spine. She had more than tasted his passion that day when he had bent and kissed the tops of her breasts. She knew that when he fully disrobed her and took her, it would be both deliberate and exciting. She was quite certain he knew where to touch her to arouse her, where to kiss and where to taunt her. Again she shivered and pressed against him.

Philip smiled to himself. She was warm to the touch, her skin flushed with excitement and her expression one of lustful hunger. He had always dreamed of a woman who would behave this way, a woman who wanted him as much as he wanted her. He had wondered how such a woman would be, how it felt to have a wanton woman twist in his arms and press against him. He felt himself completely ready for lovemaking and knew he would ache all night and want to possess her again and again. But what better place for their first tryst than here on the soft grass under the stars? What better time than now, when they were both filled with desire?

For a single flitting moment, he thought of Adelle. She had never really liked having him make love to her. It was something she did because she wanted a child, not something she did for the sheer joy of it. It had been the same with him. He looked down into Erin's face and Adelle disappeared from his thoughts.

"I love you, Erin," he said again. "I hunger for you. I want to devour you with kisses."

Erin reached up and touched his cheek. "And I love you, Philip. I love you more than I can say, though perhaps I can show you."

She put her arms around his neck and kissed him. "I love you," she murmured. "I love you and we're going to be a family."

He bent down and undid the laces of her bodice even as she opened his vest and then his shirt. Her hair smelled sweet, and the moonlight made her skin seem all the whiter. Her beautiful blue eyes looked up at him lovingly as he gently pushed the material of her chemise aside, revealing the swell of her breasts and the deep valley between them. He kissed them tenderly and felt himself warm and fill with anticipation as he held her close.

He pushed the material fully away and drew back and looked at her. "You're all I've ever dreamed of," he whispered as he lifted her skirts and slowly ran his hand over the inside of her thigh.

Erin felt him strong against her, his hands moving here and there. He touched her in magic places and drew from her lips moans of joy. Her hips undulated to the rhythm of his movements; his kisses covered her even in the most intimate of places. He was as slow and deliberate as she imagined, and her hunger for him grew with each of his taunting movements and each of his kisses. When he joined with her, she felt she might scream with joy, and the tension mounted within her as he moved slowly inside her. And then came the moment of total fulfillment! It was as if they had tumbled down the hill together as they held each other tightly and seemed to blend into one.

"You are my beloved," he whispered in her ear.

"I have everything any woman could ever want," she whispered in return.

For a long while they lay together in silence. Then Philip stood up and they both pulled on their rumpled clothing.

"Let's go and peek at Andrew," Philip suggested. "I want you to see my son."

Erin nodded and he took her hand, leading her back toward the house.

They walked together through the field and then wound their way back to the darkened house. They crept upstairs to the room Annabelle had declared the nursery and Philip opened the door. Erin followed him as they both tiptoed inside. Outside, the moon was full, and it flooded the room with light.

There in a little bed was a beautiful child, lying on his back with his knees folded beneath his stomach and his little head turned to one side. In another crib was a lovely little girl curled into a ball.

Erin crept up to the side of the crib and stared at the little boy who was Adelle's child. She could not think who he looked like, although she knew full well that in his present docile and unanimated state he probably appeared quite different than he would when awake and playing.

"He's adorable!" she said, gently touching his little fingers as he slept. Again, tears filled her eyes. Surely her own child looked this way when he slept. She felt a strong connection with this little boy, as if he were her own little John. She knew she wanted to hold him close. Erin closed her eyes and prayed that her own child was as warm and comfortable and loved as this one. "I love him already," Erin whispered. "I didn't think it possible to love another child as much as my own. But I can, I know I can."

Philip smiled and stroked her hair. "You'll make a wonderful mother, Erin. Not just to my son, but to all of our children."

Erin looked up at him with her huge blue eyes. "I want to be a good mother. God has given me another chance."

Philip laughed, "Just remember, they all look like angels when they sleep, but when they're awake they can be little devils."

"I know. Still, he is a little angel to me."

Philip took her arm. "Come to bed, my darling. I want to hold you once again."

Erin squeezed his hand.

He guided her down the hall and showed her into a small room. "It's not large, but at least we'll be alone."

Erin kissed him, and he pulled her down beside him in the darkness. Once again his arms were around her and once again she felt herself responding to him.

At last, Philip fell into a deep sleep. But Erin lay awake, tired yet clinging to the image of little Andrew.

What a strange feeling had come over her when she looked at Philip's sleeping son! She had felt a strong yet strange feeling of motherhood, but she could not really explain it. She could only think she had felt the instant bond because her son and Philip's son were more or less the same age. "That must be it," she thought, as she rolled over and curled close to her husband. "That must be it," she whispered to herself as sleep finally overtook her.

Chapter Nine

When Erin awoke, Philip was gone, and she sleepily recalled that he had told her he would go out to help his brother-in-law in the morning. She stood up and quickly put on her clothes, then hurried downstairs.

Annabelle was in the kitchen with the children. Little Andrew sat on a mat on the floor surrounded by wooden blocks, which he piled high and then knocked down with vigor. Erin stared at him. She felt as drawn to him in the light of morning as she had in the moonlight. She stepped closer to the infant.

"He can do that for hours," Phillipa said. She was at the table and held her younger sister, Katie, on her lap. She was feeding Katie gruel, which ran out of the sides of the child's mouth and down her chin. "She's not a very neat eater," Phillipa declared with the authority and superiority of an eight-year-old.

"That's because she's a girl," the youngest of the three apostles said. That was, in fact, what everyone called the three boys, and Erin thought it was amusing.

Erin laughed lightly and then turned to look once again at Andrew. She could hardly take her eyes off him for a second. The feeling that came over her when she saw him was indescribable, and the existence of other people did not lessen the effect. *It is because I love Philip so much and this is his child,* she told herself. That and the fact that Andrew was the same age as her own little John. Yes, there could be no other explanation for her feeling.

"Come to the table. I shan't even ask if you slept well," Annabelle said, grinning wickedly.

Erin smiled back and felt her face flush. She came to the table and sat down.

Annabelle set down a hot cup of tea in front of her. "In case he forgot to tell you, Philip's gone to help Bryce with the chores. They'll be back soon."

Erin sipped her tea, and though she tried to pay attention to the others, her eyes kept going back to Andrew, who smiled at her each time he caught her looking his way.

"You two seem to have hit it off right away," Annabelle commented.

"We worked together for many months before we realized how we felt," Erin said.

Annabelle laughed. "Not you and Philip, silly! You and Andrew. He hardly ever smiles that much, even though he's a good boy."

"I'm flattered," Erin replied.

"Oh, dear," Annabelle said with a sigh. "He's wet his diapers. I'll get you some breakfast as soon as I take him upstairs and change him."

Erin jumped up. "I'm a member of the family, and soon I will have to care for him all the time. You're treating me too much like a guest. I'll change him. I think I better get used to it."

"He's all yours," Annabelle answered.

Erin walked across the kitchen and lifted Andrew into her arms. He was heavy, a strong little boy at eighteen months. "Will you come with me?" she asked.

"Mama," he said, tugging at her hair.

Erin stopped short. She felt she might burst into tears.

"He calls all women mama," Annabelle said quickly. "But as I said, he smiles a lot at you."

"I think you're just trying to flatter me."

"You know where the nursery is. You'll find everything you need on the table. Here, better take a little warm water from the stove in case he needs washing."

Erin shifted Andrew to her hip and put one arm around him. It was how she had seen others carry children this age. She took the bowl of water. "Now we'll get you all cleaned up."

She climbed the stairs to the nursery room and lay the little boy down on the bed. He smiled up at her and giggled as he reached for her nose. "Don't you pull that," she said, winking.

Little Andrew giggled again and smiled. "Mama," he said again, this time rather more distinctly.

Erin stood for a long moment and stared at him. She turned when she heard Phillipa's voice. "He's a little devil sometimes. Mum sent me up to bring you a diaper. She said she forgot they weren't on the table because she hadn't folded them yet."

"Thank you," Erin answered. She took the clean diaper from Phillipa.

She bent over and undid the wet diaper, and when

Phillipa handed her a wet cloth, she turned the baby over to wipe him off.

Erin's hand stopped in mid-air. Her mouth opened, but she could not make a single sound. There on Andrew's round little rump was a birthmark—stretched a little, yes, but a duck nonetheless. The mark was identical to the one that was on her own son's bottom. Her mind raced. How could this be? This was Adelle's natural-born child! What terrible trick were her eyes playing on her? Was she going mad?

"What's this?" she stuttered.

"Just a little birthmark. We think it looks rather like a duck, don't you?"

It was real; she wasn't seeing things. "My heaven," Erin whispered. "My heaven, I don't believe this!"

"What is it?" Phillipa asked, obviously alarmed by Erin's reaction.

"Please, Phillipa, go and find Philip, wherever he is. Please go and get him! Tell him to come here at once! Please hurry."

She felt faint, but she commanded herself not to faint. With trembling hands she finished washing the baby, then put on the clean diaper. Unable to stop herself, she lifted Andrew into her arms and went to the rocking chair. "My baby," she whispered. She did not know how, she did not know why, but something very strange had happened. This was her child; she knew it. She felt it so strongly she could no longer deny it. And the birthmark was there, right where it had been the day he was born.

Philip fairly ran into the room. His face was pale and he stood for a minute staring at her. She sat in the rocker holding his son tightly and singing to him. It was a beautiful sight, but why had she called him?

Erin raised her eyes and looked at him. "How can this be Adelle's child?" she asked incredulously. "Philip, this is my child. He has the same birthmark as my child. I know this is my son."

Philip stared at her. Even though she had told him how she lost her child, it had never occurred to him that her son and his could be one and the same. He drew in his breath. It was some sort of miracle.

"He must be your son, then," he said, finally finding his voice. "Erin, I was going to tell you the whole story. I just had not got round to it."

"This is not the child Adelle gave birth to?" She could hear the disbelieving tone in her own voice.

Philip shook his head. "Erin, forgive me. I didn't know. I had no idea that this was your child. My son was born dead. Adelle carried him for nine long months. She was so sick, Erin. She was so terribly sick. I knew about this place, an institution in Croydon. We had once discussed adopting a baby."

"The Gardner Home," Erin said as tears began to run down her cheeks.

"When our son was born dead, I drove there in the middle of the night. They had a child, and I paid five times the normal fee for it. I signed all the papers right then and there. I brought Adelle the baby and she thought it was hers. She died never knowing it was not her own child. I did it to make her happy . . . Erin, I had no idea. You didn't tell me where you had your child. Dear heaven, if I had only known, I would have told you immediately."

Erin rocked the baby and closed her eyes. "It is I who told Adelle about the Gardner Home in Croydon. I heard about it from one of the maids. Oh,

Philip, this is my son. Dear heaven, there must be angels, or I would not have him back in my arms and I would not have a man as wonderful as you for his father."

"I'm so sorry you went through so much, my darling."

Erin looked up at him. "It gives me pleasure to think that Adelle died believing she had finally had a child."

Philip walked over to her and kissed her forehead.

Erin touched his face. "I'm so happy," she murmured. "This is truly a miracle."

"So is our love," he said, kissing her again.

PHILIP'S MOTHER

Lisa Higdon

For my mother, Sadie Carey, and my daughter, Natalie Higdon.
The two greatest blessings in my life.

Prologue

Santa Fe, New Mexico, 1866

The room was one of the loveliest Amanda Hamilton had ever seen. More beautiful even than her mother's bedroom at Rose Briar had been before the war.

Before the war.

The phrase served as an invisible chasm between what her life might have been and the life her father had tried to piece together in the face of defeat and poverty.

This room was what he managed to provide for his oldest daughter.

"You're marrying well," he assured her, "into a wealthy, prominent family . . . no differently than you would have if we were still in Mississippi."

Before the war.

After the war, there were very few wealthy or prominent families. Even the Hamiltons had been reduced to tending their own fields and performing household chores. Desperation had driven Papa to take them west in search of something—anything—better, but disappointment and hardship were just as plentiful in Texas and the New Mexico Territory. By the time they reached Santa Fe, Amanda overheard her parents agonizing over reaching the end of their rope and not knowing how the family would even eat, let alone push on to California.

Two days later, Miguel Ramirez came calling at Papa's invitation. Two weeks later, Amanda found herself looking around the opulent bedroom, not quite able to believe it was hers. Or that she would be sharing it with a husband she hardly knew.

"Go upstairs and get ready for bed," he had said and bent to kiss her hand. "I'll be up shortly."

Seated at an ornate dressing table, Amanda stared at her reflection, hardly recognizing herself. The silk nightgown and matching dressing gown were a pale shade of ivory, and the scalloped neckline was far more revealing than anything she'd ever worn. She tried to brush her hair, but her hands were shaking so hard that she couldn't manage it.

A soft knock came at the door and her head whipped around. "Yes? Come in."

The door opened, and Miguel Ramirez stepped inside the bedroom and closed the door behind him. He smiled approvingly. "Did you find everything you needed?"

"Yes, sir," she answered in a hoarse whisper.

"I'm your husband, Amanda." He smiled indulgently. "You don't call me sir."

She nodded. He had gently reproved her at dinner for addressing him as Mr. Ramirez, but she couldn't bring herself to call him by his first name. It felt too intimate.

She turned back to the mirror and watched as he crossed the room to stand behind her. He had removed his jacket, and his shirt was unbuttoned at the neck. His large hands settled on her shoulders, and she started.

"I did not mean to frighten you," he murmured against her ear, lowering his mouth to her neck.

She tried not to flinch as he kissed the side of her neck. "Y-you didn't."

"You are very beautiful, little one. You will become accustomed to my touch."

He was very kind and handsome, but he was nearly twice her age. She felt dwarfed by him, and the hungry look in his dark eyes frightened her.

He took hold of her hand and drew her to her feet, pulling her into his embrace. He kissed her, gently at first, and then his arms tightened around her, and his mouth grew demanding. He traced the narrow line of her shoulders with his thumbs, hooking them inside the opening of her dressing gown.

She tried not to flinch as the silk pooled at her feet, but she felt a blush crawl over her entire body. He noticed her embarrassment and seemed to be pleased by it. Without warning, he bent and caught her behind the knees, lifting her into his arms like a child, and carried her to the bed. He stood by the bed, unbuttoning his shirt, and studied her with a calculating look that made her shiver.

He put out the lamp on the bedside table, but the few remaining candles provided more light than Amanda would have liked. She closed her eyes, shaking with the knowledge that he was undressing right in front of her. She and her cousins had often whis-

pered about what husbands and wives did behind
bedroom doors, but none of them had known for
sure.

The feel of his hand on her shoulder startled her,
and her eyes flew open to find him leaning over her.
He smiled slightly and traced the scalloped neckline
of her nightgown with his fingers.

"You are afraid."

"N-no, sir." She winced, remembering he said not
to call him that. "I'm sorry."

"Don't be." He grazed his knuckles along her
cheek. He bent his head to the hollow of her throat
and kissed her softly. "Don't be afraid of me."

His mouth closed over hers, coaxing her lips to
open beneath his. She gasped at the feel of his hand
on her breast, and his tongue eased inside her mouth.
A peculiar warmth raced through her veins, and she
began to relax under his touch, but the fuzzy sense
of serenity dissolved at the feel of his hand drawing
her nightgown up over her legs.

"Raise yourself, pet," he murmured when the silk
bunched around her hips. "Let me see you."

The nightgown was up and over her head in a
matter of seconds, and he wasted no time destroying
every shred of modesty she possessed. He was touching her, looking at her all over, and she wanted to
die from the shame of being so exposed. She felt his
weight settling over her and froze as he kneed her
legs apart and moved between them.

"Relax, pet, relax." His words were soothing, but
she didn't miss the urgent tone in his voice. "This is
the way of things."

She felt the heat of his body straining at the
entrance of her own, and his first tentative thrust
succeeded only enough to assure her that this would

be neither easy or pleasant. She gasped and tried to twist out from under his weight. "Please, Mr. Ramirez! Please, don't hurt me like this."

His fingers tangled in her hair, holding her head down on the pillow. "Be still."

He shifted his weight and drove into her, barely clamping a hand over her mouth before she could cry out in pain. Tears spilled down her face and over his knuckles, but he took no notice, too absorbed in his own pleasure.

Through it all, she stared up at the ceiling, hating him and hating her parents. They had known. They had known what he would do to her, and they had offered neither warning nor apology. Indeed, they were gone within minutes of the priest declaring her this man's wife, leaving her for him to use as he liked.

She heard a deep groan and felt his body grow rigid just before he collapsed on top of her. He whispered something in Spanish and rolled onto his back. Amanda winced at the sticky, burning feeling between her legs, and she couldn't keep from turning her head when he moved to kiss her.

He gripped her chin and forced her to look up at him. His dark eyes glittered with anger, and she shrank beneath him. "Make no mistake, pet. Your life with me can be pleasant or it can be miserable. The choice is yours, but I will tolerate no disrespect."

She nodded meekly. "Yes, sir."

He brushed a kiss against her forehead and fell back against the feather mattress, drifting off to sleep. For the longest time, Amanda lay without moving, barely breathing, until she was certain he was asleep. She slipped from the bed, gathered her discarded nightgown, and hurried to the washstand.

Her hands were trembling as she washed away all

traces of him from her body, not surprised to find blood staining her thighs. Tears burned her eyes, but she fought to hold them back. The last thing she wanted was to awaken him. By now her family was long gone, but she couldn't ask them to take her with them anyway. Papa would have to give the money back to Mr. Ramirez, and they would all starve to death.

She slipped the nightgown over her head, but Amanda just couldn't bring herself to lie down beside him. Instead, she sank down on the window seat and stared out at the darkness, praying for escape. Desperate plans began to form in her mind.

She could run away, sell the expensive clothes he'd given her, and return home to Mississippi. Aunt Ginny would take her in, and her husband would never find her. If he did, Aunt Ginny would meet him on the porch with a shotgun.

The thought consoled her and saw her through the first months of her marriage. That fall, Amanda learned she was going to have a child and lost all hope of escape. Her husband's family was very powerful, and he would never let her take the child away from him. Leaving the baby behind was out of the question.

Amanda's son became the joy of her life, and she settled for the happiness she found with her child.

Chapter One

Santa Fe, 1879

Bone weary from the long journey, Amanda Ramirez was grateful to be home but sorry to end the brief absence from her troubles. She slipped off her gloves and reached to remove the hat she wore only for traveling, while her main trouble followed her inside and set his heavy traveling case in the foyer.

Her twelve-year-old son, Philip. He'd grown so much, but he was still very much a boy. Glancing back toward the open door, he hesitated before closing it behind him. She could almost feel sorry for him, except that she was the one he so desperately hoped to avoid.

"I'm sure Carmen will have dinner ready soon," she said by way of granting him a temporary reprieve. "Go on upstairs to your room and wash up."

"César said I should come down to the stables and

see the new foals." He tried to sound indifferent, but eagerness shone in his eyes. "I'll be back in plenty of time for dinner."

"Philip, we need to talk about other matters."

"Please, Ma, I won't be gone long."

"Ma? Where did you pick up that word?"

He shrugged. "I'm too old to call you Mama."

She didn't need to be reminded how quickly he was growing up or how their relationship had been changing. "Ma is too . . . common."

"Well, can I go? To the stable, I mean. I'm sure they can use some extra help with four new foals."

"If you plan to be a rancher, you'd better start learning your way around the stables now."

Amanda whirled around to see her brother-in-law strolling out of the parlor with an arrogant smile on his face.

"Uncle Victor!"

Philip was delighted, and Amanda tried to stifle her resentment as Victor caught the boy in a masculine embrace and ruffled his hair. "Look at you. Almost as tall as I am, but not nearly as handsome."

"Or as fat," Philip joked, elbowing his uncle's slight paunch. They laughed at that, and Philip wasted no time in returning to the subject of the horses. "You'll go to the stables with me, won't you?"

"Of course," Victor complied despite Amanda's earlier objections. He never missed an opportunity to supersede her parental authority, always claiming she didn't understand boys Philip's age. "Go on ahead, and I'll be there as soon as your mother and I have had a chance to talk."

She bristled at the remark. The last thing she wanted to do was argue with Victor, but she knew he wouldn't leave until he'd had his say. She watched

Philip bound out the door, still wearing his good suit, and head for the stables.

Amanda turned to find Victor waiting to pounce on whatever she had to say about the situation. "I didn't bring him home to be a stable hand."

"Why did you bring him home, Amanda?" He withdrew a thin cigar from his pocket and put it between his teeth. "To help you pack?"

Turning toward the parlor, she ignored the show he made of lighting his cigar. He knew she hated cigar smoke, but she wouldn't take the bait meant to shatter her defiance. "There's no need to pack anything. I'm not going anywhere."

"You weren't so bold when my brother was alive." He tossed the match into the fireplace and regarded her with contempt. "You'd taste the back of his hand if you so much as thought about disobeying him."

Her first instinct was to refute the spiteful remark and inform him that her husband had never raised a hand to her, but Victor knew that was only because Miguel never had to. Her husband's word had been law, and Amanda never dared disagree or question anything he did. Her brother-in-law, on the other hand, she felt had no right to run her life, and she'd had to learn quickly to stand up for herself and Philip.

"He was my husband," she countered. "And he never did anything that wasn't in our best interest."

"He did as he damn well pleased." A wicked grin slit Victor's face. "He said you jumped like a mouse if he so much as *looked* unhappy."

She hated the thought of Miguel discussing her with his brother.

"And he left control of his properties to me," Victor needlessly reminded her. "I'm sure he expected you to obey me as you would him."

"I doubt he expected you to gamble everything away," she needlessly reminded him, and the flash of anger in his eyes assured her that she had hit a sore spot.

"I gambled nothing," he snapped. "It was a business venture, something you wouldn't understand."

"I understand you lost every cent you invested, and now you think you can put me out of house and home to repay your debts." He was trembling with anger, but she wasn't about to back down. "Even I thought you were smarter than that."

Victor was a shrewd man, but too often he allowed greed to cloud his judgment. He'd been desperate to raise enough cash to invest in what was guaranteed to be a profitable venture, desperate enough to secretly mortgage his late brother's property. When the deal crumbled, he lost everything and still owed the money he'd borrowed. All that stood in his way was a tiny clause in his brother's will and Amanda's resolve not to suffer the consequences of his lack of foresight.

"You're being unreasonable, Amanda." Changing tactics, he admonished her as gently as he would a sulking child. "It's not as if you don't have options."

He *was* desperate if he thought he could make her see living in her father-in-law's home as an option. She merely returned his patronizing smile and mused aloud, "The land means so much to your father, perhaps we should discuss your dilemma with him. I'm sure he'll be very interested to know all about your little scheme."

Victor paled visibly, but she suspected it was due to fury more than fear. If there was anything Victor did fear, it was his father's disapproval. Miguel had been the favorite son, and their father still grieved for him after six years. Victor considered Amanda and Philip a constant reminder of his brother and resented the old man's fondness for his only grandson.

"You stay away from my father," he warned in a voice so ominous that Amanda flinched. "He's dying, and I won't have you disturbing him with your sniveling. I'm warning you, Amanda, don't push me."

Without waiting for a reply, he turned to leave but stopped before he reached the door. He glanced back at her and smiled ever so slightly. "I'll keep an eye on Philip for you. I know you wouldn't want anything to happen to him. The stable is a dangerous place; accidents happen all the time."

The threat went straight to her heart, and Amanda's despair increased. It was only a matter of time before old Señor Ramirez died and Victor would be free to take whatever action he chose.

Amanda had hoped a good night's sleep would put Philip in a better frame of mind, but he came to the breakfast table wearing the same sulking frown from the night before. His pride wasn't going to allow him to forgive her anytime soon, but she would rather deal with his anger than his impudence.

When he failed to return from the stables in time for dinner, she went in search of him only to find him eating in the bunkhouse, still wearing his good suit that was now crusted in dried mud and heaven only knew what else. Despite the raucous laughter and mingled voices, she clearly heard one of the ranch hands telling Philip all about a brothel in the nearest town that never charged for a first-timer.

She was appalled to realize that her sweet little

boy was old enough to be curious about such things. Without thinking, she confronted him on the spot and sent him to his room after a sound scolding.

Now was as good a time as any to tackle another unpleasant subject. "Philip, we need to talk about what happened at school."

He didn't look up from his plate. "I'm not going back."

"You were expelled. You couldn't go back if you wanted." She waited for a reply, but he only shrugged. "Could you please explain to me why you refused to cooperate with the headmaster? He did everything he could to help you, and you refused—"

Philip's sullenness bloomed into anger. "You're not even going to listen to my side, are you?"

"I wish you would explain your side," she countered. "Marshall Academy is one of the finest schools available."

"I hated it." He rose from the table. "I hated it, and I'm not going back. Uncle Victor said I don't have to do anything you say unless he approves."

"I am still your mother." She couldn't believe his belligerence. "Your uncle has no say in the matter."

"Don't I have a say? Or do you just not care?"

With that, he turned and bolted from the dining room, and she flinched at the sound of the front door slamming behind him.

Philip stalked out of the house and glanced toward the stables. He was anxious to see how the new colt had fared overnight, but he couldn't bear the thought of all the men laughing at him and calling him a mama's boy. He'd been so glad to be home, and the stable hands had welcomed him. He was fascinated by the workings of the stable, and the earthy subjects of conversation were intriguing. Following them into dinner had seemed only natural, until he saw his mother gaping into the bunkhouse.

"You come with me this minute, young man," she ordered, and he didn't miss the muffled laughter that followed him out of the bunkhouse. She fussed all the way back to the house and then sent him to his room after warning, "Don't ever let me catch you carrying on that sort of conversation again."

He tried to pretend he didn't care. She was already disappointed in him, and nothing he did would change that.

He trudged toward the corral hoping to get a few good scuffs on his new boots before anyone saw them, and waved when he caught sight of Rafael leading a dappled gray mare into the enclosure. Last night, the men had spoken of the wild horse Rafael had brought in with the intention of breaking. Uncle Victor had not liked it, and Rafael had told him to go straight to hell.

Rafael was only seventeen, but he seemed much older to Philip. He lived on his own with no parents to boss him, and he worked at the ranch only when he felt like it. Most of the men disliked him, but Philip secretly admired the way he refused to let anyone tell him what to do.

Eager to see how the mare would react to a rider, Philip settled himself on the top rung of the fence and watched.

The older boy dismissed him with a glance and returned his attention to the horse, urging her into a trot around the corral. At first she balked at the halter, but Rafael kept a firm hold on the lead without threatening her. Instead, he put a few extra feet between them and let her grow accustomed to the lead. A hundred questions ran through Philip's mind, but he knew to be quiet and not startle the wary mare as she grew accustomed to her master.

At last, he led her toward Philip and tethered her lead to the railing between them. Rafael picked up a currycomb and began brushing her as gently as he would a baby. He grinned up at Philip. "I heard they tossed you out of that fancy school. What did you do, spill warm milk on your uniform?"

Philip stiffened. "I hated that place, and I'm glad to be out of there."

"Your mama, she's not so happy."

Philip resented the way Rafael always took his mother's side, and Mama always defended Rafael, no matter what he did. "She doesn't understand. I belong here, not at some sissy school."

The older boy frowned over the horse's back. "So you thought if they threw you out, your mama would have no choice but to bring you home?"

Guilt forced him to look away, but Rafael only chuckled. Philip wondered if his mother also suspected that he had deliberately gotten himself expelled. Forcing a tone of defiance into his voice, he said, "She needs me to help with the ranch. I am old enough now, and it will be mine someday."

"Your uncle may have other ideas."

"What do you mean?"

"He seems to think your mother doesn't need this land. That she should sell it and move into the main house."

Philip gaped at him. "With him and grandfather?"

Rafael nodded.

"Who would he sell the land to?"

The older boy only shrugged. "Whoever he can, I suppose."

Philip couldn't imagine anyone living here but him and his mother. "Mother would never let him sell the land."

"I don't think he intends to ask her permission."

"You tell your boss I don't get mixed up in petty land squabbles."

Jack Noble drained the whiskey from his glass and started to rise from the table.

"Señor Ramirez will not appreciate being deceived by the likes of you."

"The telegram said he needed the likes of me to protect his land." Jack braced his palms on the table and glared at the fat little man. "Now you tell me I'm here to do nothing but run off squatters. If Ramirez can't handle something that tame, let him go to the sheriff."

"Since when do you care who you kill?" Juarez countered. "Or what is right or wrong?"

Jack only chuckled, rising to his feet, and slapped his hat atop his head. "Right and wrong doesn't figure into it. I'm just not interested in rat killing or wasting any more of my time."

Too late, Juarez realized Jack's intent and tried to snatch back the envelope containing the money due upon Jack's arrival in Santa Fe, but Jack was too fast. "Five hundred dollars when I arrived in Santa Fe, remember?"

"But you refused the job!"

"This is for my time." Jack folded the envelope and slipped it inside his vest pocket. "Ramirez could have saved us both a lot of trouble if he'd kept to the facts.''

Still smiling, Jack turned and made his way out of the saloon. He marched directly toward his horse, anxious to get out of the city. A town like Santa Fe offered too much temptation, and he had no intention of wasting one penny of this money.

Five hundred was only a fraction of what he had hoped to collect for his trouble, but it was better than nothing. He still had thirty days to clear another two thousand dollars, and then he might be able to buy back a portion of his soul.

Redemption, he was learning, didn't come cheap, and he'd waited too damned late to acquire a conscience Once Colson's widow had the land free and clear, Jack would be through with worrying about other people's problems, and he'd make damned sure the next man he delivered to the gallows was actually wanted by the law.

Chapter Two

Amanda honestly did not know what to do next, but she knew time was running out for her to have much chance to do anything. She knew a number of attorneys but none she could trust not to betray her confidence in deference to her powerful in-laws. Those not intimidated by the Ramirez name could easily be bribed.

Still, she had to find some way to fight Victor Ramirez. For six years, she had dug in her heels and withstood his every attempt to discourage her from remaining in Santa Fe. When Miguel died, she wanted nothing more than to leave, to escape, but her husband's death had rendered her penniless.

Everything was left in trust for Philip. The land, the house, everything. The only provision for Amanda was a generous monthly allowance and the privilege of living on the ranch—both of which she would lose if she remarried.

"Mother?"

Her head snapped up at the sound of Philip's voice. "Back so soon? I thought you were going riding."

"Is it true Uncle Victor is trying to force us to sell the ranch?"

Amanda felt the blood rush from her head. "Who told you such a thing?"

"Is it true?"

"Philip, you shouldn't meddle in grown-up affairs."

"Why would he do such a thing?"

Amanda considered her answer carefully. She had never spoken unfavorably about her in-laws to Philip, and she had never discussed the details of his father's estate. At last, she said, "If there was anything for you to be concerned about, I would tell you."

He looked stung. "You told Rafael, and he doesn't even live here."

Taken aback, Amanda had not considered Philip's friendship with the older boy. "I didn't tell him anything. There have been some problems, and he was aware of what was happening."

"Because he's here all the time, not away at school!" Philip shouted, his face flushed with anger. "You've always treated him better than you do me."

"How can you say that?" Amanda was on her feet now, stunned by the hurt in Philip's eyes. "Rafael would consider himself lucky to have the things you've had, an education not the least."

"The ranch is none of his business." Philip backed away from her. "You should have told me about the problems so I could help you."

"Philip, you're just a boy—" Amanda could have bitten her tongue. She had spoken hastily, forgetting Philip's tender pride, and the hurt on his face tore at her heart. "I mean, you're too young to worry about grown-up matters."

She reached to smooth her hand along his downy cheek, but he backed away from her. "This ranch is as much my business as anyone's. I'll show you."

"Philip, please—"

He turned and bolted out of the parlor, calling over his shoulder, "I'll show you, just wait! I'll show everyone!"

Philip was determined not to cry. He was no baby! Still, his chest ached and his eyes burned as he urged the horse into a fast trot, hurrying away from the barn toward the vast expanse of plain. The roan mare delighted in the unexpected freedom and wasted no time stretching out into a full gallop.

The wind made his eyes sting all the more and dried the dampness on his cheeks, but he didn't slow the horse. He let her run and run, wishing he could keep riding and never look back.

At last, the mare stopped of her own accord and tossed her head before she began nibbling at the grass. Philip slid out of the saddle and kicked the ground with the toe of his boot. Nothing was working out as he had planned!

All he wanted was to come home and live on the ranch with his mother. Not only did she not want him there, now the ranch might not even be theirs anymore. She would waste no time finding a new school for him, and he would be sent away without a home to return to.

He neared the fence separating their property from the road, surprised to find the wire cut and dangling along the ground. Though no one was in sight, his insides shrank at the thought of confronting rustlers alone with no weapon. His mother didn't allow him to have a gun, and he had been foolish to ride so far alone. He glanced around once more, assuring himself that no outlaws loomed behind him, and edged closer to the damaged fence.

A shallow ditch lay between the fence and the road, and he saw where several horses had trampled the grass and left hoofprints in the hard-packed dirt of the road. He swallowed hard, wondering how closely he had come to riding up on them in the very act, and turned to claim his horse and hurry back home.

He'd taken only two steps before realizing that he was running like a child. A man would find a way to mend the fence and come back later with tools to do the job properly. Squaring his shoulders, Philip dashed back to the fence and tried to decide the best way to repair the damage.

He needed a hammer to secure the wire in place and decided to find a heavy rock to use instead. He scrambled along the ditch, searching for a good-sized rock, and froze at a groaning sound. The guttural cry faded, and Philip forced himself to turn and see for himself who was calling out for help. He edged cautiously down the slope until he caught sight of a figure at the bottom of the ditch.

The man lay sprawled in the dense brush, facedown as if he'd tried to crawl toward the road. Philip's first instinct was to bolt and run, but stubborn pride forced him to inch closer to the stranger.

Even from a distance, it was easy to see the man was badly injured and posed no threat to anyone. Blood had run down from his temple, matting his dark hair and smearing his face. Gingerly, Philip closed the distance between himself and the stranger and knelt beside the man's prone body.

"Mister, can you hear me?" He had once seen his uncle feel the throat of an injured man to tell if he was alive or not, but Philip couldn't bring himself to touch what might be a dead man. He cleared his throat and spoke a little louder. "What happened to you?"

A faint groan that sounded more like a curse was enough of an answer to assure Philip that he was indeed alive, but he could only guess how badly the man was hurt. He wore no gunbelt, but Philip recognized the man's clothes and boots as those of someone who made his living outdoors. No doubt he had been robbed of his gun and horse and left for dead.

Philip caught sight of a hat lying nearby and snatched it up before the wind could toss it farther down the road. He looked inside, hoping to find a name etched on the band, and found several folded pieces of paper wedged inside the crown. He unfolded and read the first of several wanted posters depicting men who bore no resemblance to the injured stranger.

The posters described bank robbers, murderers, cattle thieves, each more notorious than the last, and Philip was astounded by the large sums of money offered for their capture. He glanced back at the stranger with a shock of realization. The man had to be a bounty hunter or a gunfighter! Left for dead by ruthless outlaws until Philip came along.

A desperate plan began to form in Philip's mind. If he helped the gunfighter, the man would be honor-bound to repay the favor, and such a man could persuade Uncle Victor to forget any plans of selling the ranch. His mother, however, would surely disapprove and send the man away before their problems could be resolved.

The only solution was to keep the man out of sight until he was well enough to take care of Uncle Victor. Then his mother would see that she couldn't get along without Philip and wouldn't dream of sending him back to school.

Jack awoke to a haze of pain so intense that he nearly cried out, but he managed to school his thoughts enough to realize that the slightest sound would lead the enemy to where he was hidden. Slowly, he opened his eyes, wondering just where in the hell he was.

The last thing he remembered was riding east of Santa Fe, and now he found himself in the shadowy confines of some sort of hayloft, hurting like hell. He inhaled the sweet smell of freshly cut hay and the warm scent of animals, but a sharp pain cut across his ribs before his lungs could draw any more air. He groaned and cursed, staring up at the dust motes floating overhead.

"Are you awake?"

The voice brought Jack to full alert and he tried to sit up, only to have the heel of a boot grind into his chest.

"Not so fast, mister."

He blinked slowly and opened his eyes to find the face of a boy looming over him. He was tempted to give the kid's knee one good twist and set him on his ass, but Jack needed a few answers first. Glaring up, he demanded, "Who the hell are you?"

"You'd better answer my questions first." An arrogant smile accompanied the reply. "What were you doing on my property?"

"Your property?"

"I found you passed out in a ditch." He paused in feigned thoughtfulness. "I decided to hear your story before sending for the authorities."

"Sounds like you've already figured things out."

"You're a gunfighter, aren't you?" Easing his foot off Jack's chest, the kid knelt beside him. "I knew it. I just knew it. What's your name?"

"Jack Noble, and I guess that's what some folks call it." Hesitantly, Jack raised his hand to his face and gingerly fingered his nose and left eye. "Right now, I can't call myself any kind of a fighter."

"Who did this to you?"

Jack had a pretty good idea, but everything was fuzzy. He remembered the money he'd had in his pocket when he left the cantina, but after that—He felt the pocket of his vest, found it empty, and growled, "Shit!"

"What is it?"

Ignoring the boy, Jack sat up and felt the pockets of his jeans. Empty. Both of them. His gunbelt was also missing, and he knew there was no point in asking about his horse.

"I'll make a deal with you, mister." The boy rose to his feet and smiled down at Jack in a way that left no doubt the kid needed a few trips to the woodshed. "You can stay here until you're feeling better, and I won't tell anyone. When you feel better, you can repay me."

"Repay you?"

"I can use a man like you," he remarked jauntily. "You know, to work around the place."

"Don't get any ideas about me punching cows or

cleaning out stalls." Jack levered his weight on one elbow and got to his feet. "I can fend for myself enough to be on my way."

His legs felt heavy and useless, and his head began to swim with the first step he attempted. Jack weaved backward, trying to gain his balance, and would have fallen if Philip hadn't caught him by the arm. Swearing with every breath, Jack had no choice but to return to the bed of clean straw.

"Where the hell am I, anyway?"

"I brought you to our barn."

"There wasn't any room at the inn?" Jack sneered, closing his eyes against the pain throbbing full force in his head.

"Plenty of room in the jail."

Jack glared up at him. The kid was the least of his problems right now. He had a score to settle with Ramirez, and time was running out before the bank would foreclose on Colson's land.

"All right, kid," he finally said. "You give me a few days to rest up and I'll be at your service."

"You swear?"

"On my honor," Jack assured him.

That night at dinner, Philip could hardly sit still. His mother's curious gaze settled on him more than once, but the conversation remained neutral. She looked tired, and his guilt mounted over the trouble he'd caused at school and the hateful things he'd said to her earlier.

All the more reason to hang onto Jack Noble. Every time Philip thought about the deadly gunslinger con- valescing in their barn, he felt better. The man was ill-tempered and surly, and no doubt the perfect solution to the dilemma regarding their property.

Philip noticed that his mother had hardly touched the food on her plate, and he knew she was worried about their home.

"Mama?" he ventured. "I'm sorry for what I said today. I didn't mean to hurt your feelings."

She smiled slightly. "I know that, sweetheart."

He was dying to tell her that their troubles would soon be over, and she had nothing to worry about. Instead, he returned her smile and hurried to finish dinner. Philip didn't think he could wait until Jack Noble was feeling better.

"Damn, kid, all you had for supper was cornbread?"

"That was all I could sneak out here without my mother seeing."

Jack only shook his head, setting the leftovers aside. For two days he'd lived on sleep and table scraps, but he could finally breathe without pain and had regained a good deal of strength. A steak dinner and a few shots of bourbon would have him right as rain, but for now he'd settle for what he could get.

"I appreciate the clothes." He smoothed his hand along the buttons of the chambray shirt. "Are you sure they won't be missed?"

Philip shook his head. "They were left behind by a man who only worked here for a few days."

"A cowhand?" Jack asked, remembering the half-hearted promise he'd made to help out around the place when he recovered. He'd just been stalling for time and he didn't want the kid getting any ideas. "I told you, I've got no tolerance for cows."

"That's not what I want," Philip countered, arrogant as always. "I need a gunfighter. A good one. You haven't lost your nerve, have you?"

"What the hell does that mean?"

"I mean, whoever beat you up got the better of you."

"Not if they meant for me to die."

"I kept you from dying."

"When was the last time your pa took his belt to you?"

"My father died when I was just a boy." Philip's expression grew serious. "There's only me and my mother."

Another widow. Jack swore under his breath, and he had a pretty good idea what the situation was. A penniless widow with a son to raise trying to save her farm from foreclosure. No wonder there was nothing but cornbread for supper.

Amanda hesitated before opening the barn door. Philip had been acting very odd since their argument the other morning, and twice she had seen him sneaking out to the barn. She didn't want to spy on him, but she didn't want to wish she had later.

Just as she stepped inside, she saw Philip climbing down from the hayloft. "What are you doing up there?"

He started and lost his footing on the bottom rung, stumbling to the ground. "Ma! What are you doing out here?"

"I asked you first."

"I'm not doing anything."

"You were just sitting up in the hayloft? Doing nothing?"

"Nothing," he insisted. "Just . . . thinking."

"Philip, I can't cope with any more of your mischief." Amanda felt her throat closing up. "If you're smoking cigarettes, you'll set the barn on fire and yourself with it."

"I told you, I'm not doing anything."

He stormed out and she let him go, forcing herself to admit she had overreacted and never should have accused him of wrongdoing. Everything was closing in on her. Philip was all she had, and she feared losing him more than a house or land.

Amanda reached out and wrapped her fingers around one of the rungs leading up to the loft. She hesitated, not wanting to spy on Philip, but she couldn't bear the thought of anything happening to him.

She sagged against the ladder, letting her head rest against her wrist, and swallowed hard against tears. She had fought so hard for so long, and the thought of losing everything now was tearing her apart. A sob escaped her throat and the dam burst, leaving Amanda helpless to stop the tears she'd held back for so long.

From his vantage point in the loft, Jack had watched the exchange between Philip and the woman he called Ma. She looked nothing like the weary, workworn woman Jack pictured as Philip's mother. She was a lady, young and beautiful. Too young to have a son Philip's age.

When she turned toward the ladder, Jack braced himself for the confrontation. Would she believe he meant her no harm? But instead of climbing the ladder, she'd slumped against it and begun crying her heart out. Maudlin females had always been high on his list of dislikes, but something told him this was a woman who rarely succumbed to tears, even when she had a right to do so.

Her narrow shoulders were shaking but her sobs were silent, and it occurred to him that she was also a woman who'd learned not to let anyone hear her crying.

Suddenly, the barn door burst open and the woman whirled around as if she expected the devil himself to barge in on her. The man who did walk in wasted no time railing at her.

"How dare you order anyone off this property?"

"You mean your lackeys?" Defiance straightened her backbone and snapped her chin high. "They had no business here, and I told them so."

"Lackeys!" His face grew mottled. "My attorney brought important documents for you to sign and you sent him away. He is furious. What do I tell him?"

"That you wasted his time, because I'm not signing anything."

"You are pushing me too far, Amanda. I'm warning you."

"I will not sign away what my husband intended to be mine." She swept past him, moving toward the door. "Nor what he left for his son."

The man reached out and took hold of her arm, and Jack saw the fear on her face before she could school her emotions. He cursed himself for a fool but moved to the back of the loft and slipped through the trap door used to pitch hay down to the livestock, hoping the rope ladder would hold his weight. The dull ache in his side sharpened, and he barely swallowed back a curse as his boots landed silently on the hay-strewn floor.

Lingering in the shadows, Jack waited to see what she would do next.

"Let go of me." Her voice was calm and level. "I will not—"

He hauled her away from the barn door, twisting her arm, and shook her. "My patience with you is gone! You will be sorry—"

"Unhand the lady, *compadre.*" Jack seized the handle of a forgotten pitchfork propped against the wall and brandished the gleaming tines at his opponent. "Now!"

The woman gasped and scrambled backward when she was released. Her assailant, however, froze and paled so quickly that Jack suspected the man nearly swallowed his tongue. To the contrary, he found his voice and demanded, "Who the hell are you?"

"Does that really matter right now?" Jack held the pitchfork level with the man's soft belly, applying the slightest amount of pressure. He grinned slightly. "Just like giggin' a frog."

Backing away, the man said a few choice words to the lady and bolted for the door. Silence filled the barn, and Jack turned to find the woman gaping at him. "Now, if you tell me that was your husband, I'm gonna feel like a fool."

She blinked and shook her head, stammering, "N-no. No, he's not my husband."

"You're probably even happier about that than I am."

"Indeed, I am." She smiled slightly. "Thank you for stepping in when you did."

Jack propped the pitchfork against the wall and studied her while she made her own appraisal of him. Her eyes flicked from his unshaven jaw to his faded clothes, and he knew he looked every bit the common tramp. He cleared his throat and began the explanation she didn't want to demand. "I hope you'll pardon me for helping myself to your barn. I didn't mean any harm. Just wanted a place to bed down for the night."

"My goodness, I'm fortunate you were here!" she exclaimed, closing the distance between them. "I can't thank you enough . . . Mister . . .?"

"Noble," he said, "Jack Noble."

"You're more than welcome, Mr. Noble."

He nodded, breathing the delicate scent that rose from her hair and no doubt lingered on her skin, and he knew it was no dousing of perfume. Nothing that sweet could come from a bottle. "You're mighty kind, ma'am."

She nodded and held out her hand. "I'm Amanda Ramirez."

Ramirez! Jack froze, refusing to believe that even his luck could be this bad. Her expression grew puzzled, and he forced himself to shake her hand. "Pleased to meet you, ma'am."

He was anything but pleased at the prospect of being holed up in a barn belonging to the son-of-a-bitch who had tried to have him killed. Philip had said his mother was a widow, and Jack could only guess what their relationship was to Victor Ramirez. He noted her fair complexion, light hair, and blue eyes. Obviously, she was no blood kin to the family, and her son's dark features had come from his father.

He needed to put some distance between them before he started thinking of her in any way other than the mother of a smart-mouth kid. Now that she knew of his presence, he would have to hightail it out of there tonight.

"I'll just bed down in the loft and be gone by

sunup." Taking a step backward, he said, "Thank you again, ma'am."

He almost made it to the ladder before she caught up with him. "You're hurt! Why didn't you say something?"

Turning around, he realized that he was favoring his right leg and bracing his aching left side with the opposite hand. He shrugged and tried to ignore the tender concern in her green eyes. "I just fell off an ornery horse, that's all."

"A horse with knuckles?"

He fingered the still puffy bruise under one eye. "Just my luck."

She smiled. "You don't owe me any explanations, but I must insist that you come into the house and let me put some salve on that eye."

The house was the last place he needed to go. For all he knew, Ramirez was right inside, waiting to finish the job his thugs had started. "Ma'am, that's not necessary. I couldn't intrude on your family."

"You wouldn't be intruding," she insisted. "Only my son and I live here, and you're more than welcome."

He hesitated, and she studied him carefully. "When was the last time you had a home-cooked meal?"

"A good while," he admitted.

Her smile was sweet but determined. "I won't take no for an answer."

Chapter Three

It had been so long since Amanda had entertained company that she could barely contain her delight over Mr. Noble's presence. At first, she had been so stunned by his sudden intervention that she could do little more than nod and thank him.

He stood just inside the kitchen while she put a pot of coffee on to boil. She dried her hands on a dishtowel and motioned for him to be seated at the plank table. "Please, sit down. I can doctor that eye while the coffee perks."

He glanced around and sat down as if he were wary of her. She brought the salve and a basin of warm water to the table. "Mr. Noble, I have a twelve-year-old son, and I've tended my share of cuts and scrapes. I won't blind you."

The grin that softened his face made her shiver, and she suspected that a very handsome man was lurking beneath the bruises and whiskers. Raising a damp cloth to his forehead, Amanda tried to concentrate on the task at hand, but her fingers were none too steady as she dabbed salve on the nasty cut over his cheekbone. The heel of her hand brushed against his mouth, and she felt him flinch at her touch.

Her fingertips grazed the growth of whiskers on his face, and she couldn't help but wonder what he would look like clean-shaven. Much younger, she suspected, and she wondered what hardships had hardened his features into the impassive mask of indifference. Only his eyes held a warmth that drew her attention, and she realized he was studying her with the same blatant interest.

"There, that's much better." She turned toward the stove, thankful for the diversion of filling two coffee cups. She cleared her throat and tried to sound unruffled when she asked, "How long have you been in Santa Fe?"

"I'm just passing through," he spoke quietly. "Didn't figure on staying this long."

She brought the coffee to the table. "Are you headed home?"

He shook his head, taking neither cream nor sugar, and sipped the strong black coffee. "Just passing through."

With a nod, Amanda let the subject drop and set about warming supper for Mr. Noble. Rarely did she have use of the kitchen all to herself, and she was never more grateful that the cook didn't live in the house.

She joined him at the table while he ate, curious to know more about him, but she sipped her own coffee and refrained from asking any personal questions. Instead, she told him once again how much she appreciated his help. "It was very chivalrous of you to put yourself at risk for my sake."

"It wasn't much of a risk," he countered, and a sly smile lent a wicked gleam to his eyes. "Even the devil carries a pitchfork."

She could laugh about it now, but she hated to think what might have happened if Mr. Noble hadn't been there. Victor had been badgering her for weeks about selling the land, but tonight was the first time he'd threatened her directly.

Her smile faded and she said, "I suppose I'd better keep that in mind."

"You'll have to do better than that." His expression sobered. "If he comes back, he'll mean business."

They heard the front door open and close, then footsteps on the polished floors.

"Philip?" Amanda called, noticing the way Mr. Noble tensed, and she explained. "My son, Philip."

"Yes, ma'am?" the boy answered.

"Come in the kitchen for a moment."

Philip walked into the kitchen and froze in place, gaping at Jack Noble in disbelief. Amanda was embarrassed by his wide-eyed astonishment.

"Philip, this is Mr. Noble," she said by way of prompting him to remember his manners.

Only then did the boy turn his aghast expression toward her. "What's he doing here?"

"Philip!" Amanda was taken aback. "Mr. Noble is our guest."

"Our guest!" He turned to Jack. "What big stories have you been telling my mother?"

"That is enough out of you, young man." Amanda rose from the table, horrified by Philip's rudeness. "Go on upstairs to your room if you can't keep a civil tongue in your mouth."

"You don't know anything about him. He could be—"

"Go upstairs. Now!"

Once more, Philip glared at Jack Noble and stalked out of the kitchen, leaving Amanda to explain his insolence. "Mr. Noble, I apologize—"

"Don't apologize." He held up his hand when she tried to continue. "It's his place to look out for you."

She nodded. "He's going through a very difficult time right now."

"I think you both are." Before she could say anything else, he rose from the table. "I'd best get on out to the barn. I've taken up enough of your time."

"Mr. Noble, I won't hear of you sleeping out in that barn." Amanda didn't give him a chance to argue. "I have a perfectly nice guest room that hasn't been used in years, and you're more than welcome. In fact, I insist."

He glanced in the direction Philip had stalked off earlier, but nodded in acceptance. "You're mighty kind, ma'am. I'll be on my way first thing in the morning."

"Mister, please, you got to believe me. I'm no cattle rustler."

"My job is just to bring you in. I'm not a judge."

"I got a wife and kids. What will they do without me?"

Jack's eyes flew open. The voice was so clear, he wouldn't have been surprised to find Colson's ghost standing over the bed.

It had been a long time since Jack allowed himself to sleep so soundly, but he was so exhausted, the soft bed had felt like heaven. His eyes drifted open before daylight, and the room was still dim. Gradually, he became aware of an insistent knocking at the door, and he knew exactly who was out in that hallway.

Wearing nothing but his long johns, Jack crossed the room and opened the door. Without a word, Philip stormed inside and closed the door.

"What did you say to my mother?"

"About what?"

"You know what I mean!" Philip glared at him. "Did you tell her about our agreement?"

"What makes you think we talked about you at all?"

The boy was taken aback by that. "How did you get yourself invited into the house?"

"Your mama had a little trouble in the barn after you stormed out." Jack went to the washstand against the wall and studied his battered face in the mirror. "I never have been able to resist helping a pretty lady."

Jack turned around to find Philip watching him with an uneasy expression. The boy swallowed and asked, "What kind of trouble?"

"A man stormed in on her and started carrying on like something crazy."

"Who was he?"

"I don't ask questions, kid," Jack reminded him. "I would have just kept out of sight, but I draw the line at standing by while a woman gets smacked around."

Philip's eyes widened, and the pretense of maturity disappeared. "He hit her?"

Jack shook his head. "He didn't get a chance."

"She didn't say who he was? What he wanted?"

"All I heard was something about lawyers and papers that she wouldn't sign."

Philip paled and opened his mouth to say something, but closed it quickly, as if thinking better of telling secrets to a stranger. That suited Jack fine. He wanted to know as little as possible about Amanda Ramirez's troubles. He did need to know just how Victor Ramirez figured into things.

He poured fresh water into the basin and bent to splash his face, pausing long enough to ask, "So, why didn't you tell me your name is Ramirez?"

Jack toweled his face dry and watched Philip in the mirror, struggling to find an answer. By way of prodding the boy, Jack suggested, "Did you think I'd kidnap you if I knew you had a rich daddy?"

"He's my uncle," Philip clarified. "My father died when I was a boy, and Uncle Victor has taken care of the ranch ever since."

Victor Ramirez. Damn. Jack swore under his breath, though he'd already suspected as much. Whatever troubles *Uncle* Victor was having with the squatters was spilling over to his family. The man harassing Amanda in the barn the night before was probably trying to get back at Ramirez by threatening her.

Jack fingered his stubbled chin and grinned slightly. "You mind if I borrow your razor?"

Philip blushed and frowned at Jack's teasing. "I'll get one for you."

Jack watched the boy leave and suspected the problem Philip wanted his help with was the squatters who threatened their land. He tried not to think about the boy and his mother getting caught in the middle of a range war or what Philip's mother would do the next time she faced the enemy. Jack would be long gone by then.

Philip returned shortly with a razor and a shaving mug. Jack began lathering his jaw and Philip paused before he closed the door. "What did you mean when you called my mother a pretty lady?"

Jack looked up to see Philip's reflection as well as his own. "Don't you think she's pretty?"

"Well, I never . . . I mean, yeah. I suppose she is." The boy frowned. "I just never thought anyone else did."

Jack scraped the razor across his cheek. "She seems awful young to have a boy your age."

Philip nodded. "She was very young when she married my father."

Jack's curiosity was piqued, but he focused on the mirror and the task at hand. It would serve him right to cut his own damned throat for asking questions when he was better off without such answers.

Amanda scrutinized the table once more and straightened the vase of flowers in the center. She hoped breakfast would make up for the humble supper she'd offered Mr. Noble last night.

"Is very pretty, Señora?" Lupe asked hesitantly. "Do you like?"

"Of course, dear," Amanda assured her. "You did a wonderful job."

The young girl smiled proudly, but the door leading from the kitchen opened before she could say anything else. Carmen, the cook, snapped at Lupe in Spanish and ordered her back to the kitchen.

Amanda returned her attention to the flower vase while Carmen placed serving dishes on the sideboard. She had been none too happy when Amanda instructed her to prepare a formal breakfast in the dining room. She was even more unhappy that she knew nothing of their guest. As ususal, Amanda ignored the woman's vehement complaints, pre-

Take 4 FREE Books!

Zebra created its convenient Home Subscription Service so you'll be sure to get the hottest new romances delivered each month right to your doorstep — usually before they are available in book stores. Just to show you how convenient Zebra Home Subscription Service is, we would like to send you 4 Zebra Historical Romances as a FREE gift. You receive a gift worth up to $24.96 — absolutely FREE. There's no extra charge for shipping and handling. There's no obligation to buy anything - ever!

Save Even More with Free Home Delivery!

Accept your FREE gift and each month we'll deliver 4 brand new titles as soon as they are published. They'll be yours to examine FREE for 10 days. Then if you decide to keep the books, you'll pay the preferred subscriber's price of just $4.20 per title. That's $16.80 for all 4 books for a savings of up to 32% off the publisher's price! What's more...$16.80 is your total price...there is no additional charge for the convenience of home delivery. Remember, you are under no obligation to buy any of these books at any time! If you are not delighted with them, simply return them and owe nothing. But if you enjoy Zebra Historical Romances as much as we think you will, pay the special preferred subscriber rate of only $16.80 each month and save over $8.00 off the bookstore price!

We have 4 FREE BOOKS for you as your introduction to
KENSINGTON CHOICE!

**To get your FREE BOOKS,
worth up to $24.96, mail the card below.
or call TOLL-FREE 1-888-345-BOOK**

Take 4 Zebra Historical Romances FREE!

MAIL TO: ZEBRA HOME SUBSCRIPTION SERVICE, INC.
120 BRIGHTON ROAD, P.O. BOX 5214,
CLIFTON, NEW JERSEY 07015-5214

YES! Please send me my 4 FREE ZEBRA HISTORICAL ROMANCES (without obligation to purchase other books). Unless you hear from me after I receive my 4 FREE BOOKS, you may send me 4 new novels - as soon as they are published - to preview each month FREE for 10 days. If I am not satisfied, I may return them and owe nothing. Otherwise, I will pay the money-saving preferred subscriber's price of just $4.20 each... a total of $16.80. That's a savings of over $3.00 each month and there is no additional charge for shipping and handling. I may return any shipment within 10 days and owe nothing, and I may cancel any time I wish. In any case the 4 FREE books will be mine to keep.

Name _____

Address _____ Apt No _____

City _____ State _____ Zip _____

Telephone ( ) _____

Signature _____
(If under 18, parent or guardian must sign)

Terms, offer, and price subject to change. Orders subject to acceptance.

KC0599

AFFIX
STAMP
HERE

KENSINGTON CHOICE
Zebra Home Subscription Service, Inc.
120 Brighton Road
P.O.Box 5214
Clifton, NJ 07015-5214

Ill..l..ll...ll.l.l.l.l.l...l..l.l.l.ll.l..lll...l

tending not to understand the steady stream of irate Spanish.

Early on, Amanda had gradually learned Spanish but she kept her knowledge to herself. The family and the servants spoke freely around her, thinking she didn't understand a word they said, and she let them think she only knew what they wanted her to know.

Hearing Philip's voice and footsteps on the stairs, Amanda was pleased to see her son leading Mr. Noble toward the dining room. Philip was a good boy, and she was very proud that he was making amends for his poor manners the night before.

"Good morning," she said as they entered the dining room. She was somewhat startled by the change in Jack Noble's appearance. The swelling under his eye had lessened considerably, and he had shaved, revealing the face she'd imagined almost boyishly handsome. There was nothing boyish in the intense set of his jaw or the harsh lines that spoke of age and experience. Amanda realized that she was staring and forced her attention to what Philip was saying.

"Ma, I told—" Philip paused, somewhat chagrined, and started over. "Mother, I told Jack I would try to find his horse today."

"That would be very good of you," she said as Philip held her chair out for her. As they were seated, Carmen brought out the last of the dishes and began serving the meal. "I hope you're feeling better this morning, Mr. Noble."

"Yes, ma'am." He reached for his coffee and smiled slightly. "A good night's rest was the best medicine."

The meal was pleasant, though Philip did most of the talking. Amanda tried to concentrate on the boy's stories about the new foal, but she couldn't keep her eyes from drifting back to their guest again and again. He was such a puzzle. His table manners were impeccable, and his language was neither coarse nor vulgar. Yet he'd been sleeping in barns, and didn't even have a horse or a gun.

At last, Philip asked to be excused. "I'll find your horse, Jack. Don't you worry."

"Find Rafael," Amanda told him. "Have him go along. I don't want you riding alone."

"Ma, I can manage—"

"Your ma's right, boy," Jack cut in before Philip could argue further. "You never know who you might find out there."

Philip's cheeks reddened slightly, but he left the dining room without argument. Amanda smiled slightly. "Thank you, Mr. Noble. Philip wants to grow up so quickly, but I'm not ready to let go."

He made no reply, and an awkward silence fell between them. Carmen emerged from the kitchen to collect the empty plates and refill their coffee cups.

"Mr. Noble, you're welcome to remain here until you're fully recovered." Amanda spoke the words in a rush and winced at the anxious sound of her own voice. She took a breath and continued as casually as possible. "What I mean is, it would be in the best interest of your health."

"I really need to be moving on, ma'am." He sipped his coffee and spoke over the rim of the cup. "Besides, it wouldn't do for a lady like yourself to take in a tramp like me."

It was on the tip of her tongue to ask him if he was running from the law, but offending him was the last thing she wanted to do. He fingered the rim of his coffee cup, and his expression was that of a man wrestling with a moral dilemma.

"Mr. Noble, I don't trust easily, but when I do I'm usually right." She paused, not wanting to stoop to begging. "You're the first person I've trusted in a long time."

"You've got no reason to."

"I've lived my whole life with people I couldn't trust," she informed him. "I know the difference."

He didn't answer.

"Mr. Noble, would you at least consider working for me?" She didn't want to sound desperate. "You need a few days rest, and I can pay you for your time."

"Lady, are you sure your troubles are worth asking a stranger to help you?"

"Mr. Noble, there *is* no one else for me to ask."

Chapter Four

Jack slipped out onto the porch and lit a cigarette, carefully considering his situation. He was out more than the five hundred dollars. His horse, his guns, all his gear, everything was gone, and the last thing he needed to do was spend what money he did have on himself.

He weighed his options and found them lacking. If he did leave, as he should, he would be on foot and unarmed, and he would have no hope of confronting Ramirez. He didn't want revenge. Ramirez was a coward, and revenge on a coward yielded little satisfaction. He had learned a long time ago that money was what mattered to men like that, and Ramirez would pay for what he had done in cold, hard cash.

Not so much for what he'd done to Jack, but for the lives that were now in jeopardy if the money didn't reach the bank in time to save the Colson farm.

He thought of Amanda Ramirez and wondered

what loyalty she held for the family of her late husband. She must be close to them; otherwise she would have returned to her own family as most widows did. The boy was at least twelve, maybe older, and he wondered how long she'd been alone, how she'd lost her husband.

He glanced down toward the barn and then the stable, where several men were grooming horses in the spacious lot outside. Mrs. Ramirez had been left well provided for—land, a fine home—and she seemed to want for nothing. Still, he felt guilty at the prospect of taking her money even though there was no reason to. She needed his help and wouldn't have offered money she didn't have.

He turned at the sound of riders approaching to see Philip and another boy nearing the house, leading Jack's horse behind their own mounts.

"I told you I'd find your horse!" Philip called out as they reached the house. "Here she is."

"Is this your mare, mister?" The older boy all but glared at Jack. "I found her two days ago. She'd wandered off the road and got herself tangled up in some briars. She's a fine horse. You should take better care of her."

"I'll remember that next time I get ambushed."

Jack stepped down off the porch and examined the series of cuts and scratches crisscrossing the horse's flanks. She seemed to be well on the mend but was no more ready to ride any great distance than he was. Jack swore under his breath.

Philip grinned at his irritation. "Looks like you won't be going anywhere anytime soon."

* * *

"Why did we have to come here?"

Philip's voice was barely a whisper, but Amanda could hear the fearful reluctance in his tone. She caught his hand in hers, squeezing it reassuringly, and tried to sound soothing when she said, "Your grandfather is very ill, and he wanted to see you."

"Is he dying?"

Amanda didn't want to lie, but she didn't want Philip to be frightened. "He's been sick for a long time, and he's very weak. He has some time left, but he won't be with us much longer."

Philip nodded and squared his shoulders, but he didn't let go of Amanda's hand as they neared Señor Ramirez's bedroom at the far end of the hall. She knocked softly, and Victor opened the door almost immediately. Amanda didn't miss the flicker of loathing that flashed in his eyes before he forced an indulgent smile for his nephew.

"Your grandfather has been waiting for you." He ushered them inside, catching Amanda by the arm before she followed Philip toward the bed. Lowering his voice, he warned her, "He wants to see the boy, not you."

She didn't flinch. "I'll wait right here."

Reluctantly, Victor released her arm, but she knew he would have preferred to drag her out into the hall. Glancing over his shoulder, Victor saw that Philip had his grandfather's undivided attention, and he turned back to Amanda, demanding, "What game are you trying to play with me?"

"I haven't the slightest idea what you're talking about."

His face flushed with anger, and he sneered, "I'm talking about your guardian. The man who tried to run me off. Who is he?"

"That is none of your business." She smiled slightly. "And he *did* run you off."

"Not for long." His eyes narrowed, but he made no move toward her. "I'm just biding my time. Soon it will not matter if you have an army to protect you."

"Mother?"

Philip's hesitant voice drew her attention. "Yes, dear, what is it?"

"Grandfather wants to speak to you."

Amanda was surprised but she ignored the warning look Victor gave her. Approaching the bed, she was stunned by her father-in-law's appearance. He was only a shell of the man he'd once been, pale and feeble, but his dark eyes were still sharp with keen awareness.

Coughing slightly, the older man held out his hand to her and spoke in a raspy voice. "You have raised a fine son, Amanda. You should be proud."

"I am proud of him," she assured him.

He nodded and closed his eyes, drained from the effort of speaking, and drifted off to sleep. Amanda drew Philip away from the bedside and, without a word to Victor, led him out of the bedroom and down the stairs.

Once outside, Philip ran on ahead to bring the buggy around from the stable. Victor lounged in the doorway, studying Amanda with a smug expression. "You should have left here years ago."

Amanda caught sight of Philip nearing the house. "Then you should have helped me, because that was what I wanted most in the world."

Jack groaned aloud as he hoisted himself into the borrowed saddle, cursing every bruise on his body for refusing to heal as quickly as he would have liked. He'd have liked to believe his injuries were worse than he thought, but the truth was, he was getting plain lazy. It hadn't taken him long to get accustomed to sleeping in a feather bed, having his meals served on fine china, and most of all having a pretty woman fuss over him.

For the past three days, Amanda Ramirez had plied him with food and comfort, doing everything she could think of to lure him to stay on a few days longer.

She just never got around to telling him exactly what it was she had to fear. He already had enough on his conscience without getting tangled up in her problems. She had the means to hire a dozen guns to protect her and her property. Time for Jack was running out.

He turned his mount and kneed the big mare into a full gallop. Soon they were clear of the stable, and the house was far behind him. He reached the road and turned in the direction he'd been traveling less than a week before. He tried not to think about Amanda being disappointed when she discovered he was gone.

The crack of rifle fire broke the silence, and Jack's insides went cold at the sound of a woman's screams. The horse shied slightly as he wheeled his mount around in the direction of the frightened cries.

He topped the hill and saw a buggy weaving down the road. Immediately he recognized Amanda as the frantic driver, struggling to gain control of the frightened team. Another shot rang out, and Jack drew his pistol and urged his horse into a full run. He reached the buggy just as one of the horses reared in fright, nearly toppling the buggy.

"Jack!" Amanda cried, her grip on the reins never loosening. "Help me!"

He vaulted from his horse, caught the bridle of the rearing horse just as the animal dropped to his feet, and steadied the other. Returning his attention to Amanda, Jack saw Philip slumped against his mother, his face pale and his eyes closed.

"Jack, please help me," she begged. "He's been shot!"

"Hold the horses," he ordered, releasing the harness and climbing into the buggy. "What the hell is going on?"

"I don't know." She shook her head. "I didn't see anyone."

Jack inspected the gaping wound in Philip's arm, relieved to find that it wasn't serious. "It's just a flesh wound, but we need to get him back to the house right away."

"You take him on your horse," Amanda insisted. "It will be quicker, and I can manage the buggy myself."

He started to argue, but the grim determination in her eyes assured him he was dealing with no cowardly female. He nodded and scooped Philip from the buggy. "Don't let me get too far ahead of you."

"You just get Philip home safe," she told him. "I can take care of myself."

Amanda rushed into Philip's bedroom just as Jack tore away the shredded sleeve of the boy's jacket. The wound was still bleeding, and Amanda gagged at the sight of Philip's torn flesh. She swallowed hard against the bile rising in her throat and managed to say, "I thought you said it was just a flesh wound."

Jack glanced up for only a moment before turning his attention back to Philip. "The bullet passed clean through the flesh, and the bone isn't broken. He'll be fine."

Amanda neared the bed, her legs shaky. "Shouldn't I send for the doctor?"

"How long will that take? An hour? Two, maybe?" Jack shook his head. "You want him to lie here bleeding all that time?"

"Of course not!" she snapped, resenting his arrogance. "What should we do?"

"Fetch me a kettle of hot water, bandages, a needle, and some stout thread." When she was almost to the door, he called, "And a bottle of whiskey."

Amanda wasted no time in gathering the items Jack needed, along with a bottle of bourbon from the liquor cabinet. Being Sunday, the servants were not in the house, and Amanda prayed she was not making a mistake by not sending for the doctor.

Philip was starting to wake up by the time she returned to the bedroom, still groggy, and he called out to her. "Mama, what happened?"

"Shh . . . don't worry, sweetheart," she soothed him, kneeling beside the bed. "Everything is going to be all right."

Jack had already filled the basin from the washstand with hot water, and Amanda soaked a cloth in cool water from the pitcher. She bathed Philip's sweat-beaded forehead and urged him to lie still as Jack began to clean the wound. Philip flinched as the strong-smelling solution seared his torn flesh, and he squeezed Amanda's fingers tightly in his.

Once again Jack assured her that the wound was not serious, but she couldn't look as he began to sew the gaping wound closed. Philip's grip on her hand tightened to the point of being painful, but she endured it in silence until Jack was finished. He smeared a foul-smelling salve on the stitches and swathed Philip's arm in the clean white bandages.

Grinning slightly, Jack tousled Philip's hair. "I think you'll make it."

Philip smiled weakly, and Amanda whispered, "I want you to take something for the pain, sweetheart. Just a little something, so you can rest, all right?"

The boy nodded and she mixed a few drops of laudanum in water and urged him to drink it. Philip's head fell back against the pillows, and anguish knifed through Amanda's heart. Now that the crisis had passed, she felt no relief. Instead, the hysteria she'd staved off until now threatened to reduce her to tears.

"Here." Jack's voice drew her attention. He was standing over her, holding a glass partially filled with whiskey.

"For Philip?"

He smiled slightly. "For you."

Her fingers were trembling, but she took the glass and raised it to her lips. The whiskey tasted smooth and slightly smokey but turned to fire in her stomach. She managed another swallow and handed the glass back to him.

She hugged herself and began rocking back and forth, fighting against tears, but her shoulders began shaking.

"Come on," Jack whispered, gently taking her by the arm, and drew her to her feet. "He needs to rest."

"N-no, I can't leave him," she protested. "What if—"

"He'll sleep for the next couple of hours, and then he'll need you—calm and rested." When she started to protest further, he silenced her objection with an undeniable truth. "Seeing you so upset will only frighten him."

He led her out into the kitchen and eased the door closed behind them, his hand lingering on Amanda's arm. "Do you have any idea who would do this?"

There was no point in suggesting it had been an accident, even if there hadn't been a second shot, but she couldn't bring herself to dump the whole mess out into the open. If Jack Noble had an ounce of sense, he'd bolt and run before getting mixed up with a woman so badly outnumbered. She only shook her head, and doubt flashed in his eyes.

"Amanda." He spoke her name softly when she turned away from him. "Amanda, tell me what's going on."

Her breath grew ragged and she buried her face in her palms, trying not to think how close Philip had come to dying, how close she had come to losing him. She stiffened at the feel of Jack's hands on her shoulders, but her protests were halfhearted when he turned her round and drew her into his embrace.

His palm eased down her spine in a gesture so tender and comforting that she was helpless to resist, and Amanda wept in his arms.

At last she quieted and, weak from vented emotion, let her head rest against his shoulder. Suddenly, she realized the picture she made—a sobbing, hysterical female—and she bristled, desperate to regain her composure. Jack gathered her closer when she would have pulled away, and she glanced up to search his face for dismay or chagrin.

Instead, she found understanding and longing.

His thumb traced the line of her face, wiping away the tears, and she shivered at the feel of his breath on her damp cheek. He lowered his mouth to hers, and the feel of his lips moving over hers caused her to shudder. She leaned forward, clutching at his shoulders to keep from slumping against him.

His hand still lingered against her face, and he held her firmly as he deepened the kiss. The last of Amanda's reserve dissolved and she returned the kiss, giddy from the medley of whiskey and desire. When his mouth left hers, she felt bereft of his touch, his taste.

Gently, he set her apart from him and an awkward silence fell between them. At last he backed away, combing his fingers through his dark hair. "I'd better see to the horses, ma'am."

She watched him leave, more stunned by his abrupt retreat than by the unexpected passion that had flared between them.

Jack stormed into the barn and kicked a wooden bucket with such force that it splintered against the wall. His horse glared at him in disapproval, but Jack ignored her. He had enough disapproval for himself.

What the hell was he doing? Just that afternoon, he was all set to run out on her, without so much as a thank-you or good-bye. Next thing he knew he was playing knight in shining armor and kissing her as if he'd known her all his life. The dazed, hungry look in her eyes had startled him back to his senses before he did something stupid, but he was still breathless from the effort of pushing her away.

It was too late in life for him to start developing a sense of honor. Once he put the matter of Colson's farm behind him, things would go back to normal. A man like him lived by the gun, and he would be dead in six months if he started playing nursemaid to every widow and orphan he met up with.

Even the widows he helped create.

He swore out loud at the thought and turned to unsaddle the horse as if he could turn his back on the guilt that festered on his newly developed conscience. Over the years, he'd faced down dozens of men in gunfights and hauled twice as many into the law for a hefty bounty, never once considering what consequences their doom would bring to others.

Everything had been so simple before Colson.

Jack tossed the saddle on the railing and led the mare into a stall before removing her bridle, silently reminding himself that he'd done everything by the book. The warrant had been legit, signed by a judge, and Jack had no reason to doubt that Colson was a wanted man. The man's pleas of innocence had fallen on deaf ears.

"Save it for the judge," he'd told Colson as he'd told countless other fugitives. "My job is just to bring you in to face the charges."

"Do you really think Pratt will let me live to go to trial?"

Those words haunted Jack still. Why hadn't he stopped to wonder how Colson knew who had placed the reward on his head? Because he'd been so hell-bent on collecting the fat reward, he hadn't given a damn. Not until he learned Colson had been dragged from the jail and lynched.

His thoughts turned back to Amanda Ramirez, and he realized he knew even less about her situation than he had Colson's. He didn't doubt for a minute that the trouble had to do with her brother-in-law's feud with land grabbers, and his new-found scruples were plagued by the knowledge that his refusal to work for Ramirez might very well have left Amanda and Philip vulnerable.

He was positive she knew who had taken a shot at her, so why would she lie to him about it? Her reluctance troubled him.

He hadn't exactly been honest with her, either. He didn't want to tell her, "Your brother-in-law tried to hire me to kill innocent people and then tried to have me killed when I turned him down." No doubt, she would be horrified to learn she had taken a hired killer into her home, trusted him with her son, and let him kiss her until they were both nearly at the point of losing control.

He swore again and headed out of the barn to take Mrs. Ramirez's team of horses and her fancy rig down to the stables.

"Señora Ramirez! What are you doing up so early?"

Amanda turned from the stove to find Carmen standing in the open doorway, gaping at her. Too tired to be tactful, Amanda told her, "Philip was hit by a stray bullet yesterday. He ran a fever for most of the night, but the worst has passed."

Disbelief registered on Carmen's face first, followed by shock. "A bullet? *Dios mio!* He could have been killed!"

"Thankfully, the injury wasn't serious." Amanda turned back to the kettle of beef broth she was making for Philip, stirring the clear liquid. "He's going to be fine."

A moment passed, and Amanda started at the touch of Carmen's hand on her shoulder. "You should rest, señora. I will see that young Philip takes some nourishment."

That was the first kindness Carmen had shown Amanda since she'd come to work in the household. Graciously, Amanda smiled and nodded. "I would appreciate that, Carmen, very much."

Exhausted, Amanda slumped into a chair at the long plank table and propped her forehead on her upturned palm. She'd spent the night sitting at Philip's side as he slept fitfully. Once his fever broke, he had slept soundly, but Amanda did not relax her vigil.

Jack Noble, she decided, was probably twenty miles from there by now, and she couldn't blame him. What man wouldn't run from a lonely widow turned spinster, fawning over him like an old maid at a Sadie Hawkins dance.

The kitchen door suddenly burst open and Rafael marched in, his face mottled with anger. "No one sent for me."

It was a statement, not a question, but Amanda sensed he was waiting for an answer. "I haven't sent for anyone. There wasn't time."

The young man's expression softened with concern. "Is he going to live?"

Amanda rose to her feet and hugged him. "Oh, Rafael, he's going to be fine."

Awkwardly, he returned her embrace, insisting, "You should have sent for me."

"Well, you're here now. Why don't you go upstairs and check on him for me?"

Jack lingered just inside the doorway until Rafael was out of earshot. "Who is that cocky kid? I told what happened to Philip and he nearly took my head off."

"He's Philip's brother," she whispered, sinking back into her chair.

"His brother?"

"His half-brother." Amanda felt her face burning. She had never discussed the matter with anyone. "He was born before my husband and I were married. His mother was not a—she was—"

"I think I understand."

Amanda would never forget the first time she found Rafael peering up at her with those huge brown eyes. She had been little more than a child herself, and they had formed a bond of loneliness and rejection. Miguel never acknowledged the boy, and his hasty marriage to Amanda had been an effort to spare his family embarrassment.

"Does Philip know?"

Jack's question startled her. "No, I felt I should wait until he's older to tell him . . . to tell them both."

"Who told you?"

She grinned. "I overheard the housekeeper discussing it with the cook. They didn't think I understood Spanish."

Jack sat down at the table, and Carmen brought him a cup of coffee, her disapproval of him tempered slightly. He asked, "How's Philip this morning?"

"Much better." She wanted to ask why he hadn't come back to the house the night before, but she knew the answer. "I should apologize for my behavior yesterday. I suppose my emotions were running rampant."

"Are you?"

"Am I what?"

"Going to apologize?" He brushed his fingers over the top of her hand, and she shuddered from even that slight touch. "Are you sorry?"

Amanda knew her face must be flaming, but she had to admit, "No. No, I'm not."

She paused. "I just don't want you to think—I

mean, I know men think widows are always looking to snare another husband—"

"I'm the last man you'd want for a husband."

"That's not true." She floundered. "I mean, that's not what I was trying to say. I just don't want you to leave because you think I'm scheming to trap you."

He rose from the table and smiled slightly. "Ma'am, I was the one who kissed you. Perhaps we both ought to be worried about traps."

Chapter Five

Jack had never known himself to be so good at making excuses, but every day he managed to come up with another reason he needed to stay on with Amanda. First there was Philip. He didn't feel right taking off and leaving Amanda to care for him alone. A lady like her knew nothing about gunshot wounds.

Then there was the trouble she remained reluctant to talk about. She wouldn't let Philip out of the house, even with Rafael, and every time Jack entered the house she looked relieved to see him. He couldn't, he told himself, leave until he knew she and Philip would be safe.

The real reason was the sickening dread he felt every time he contemplated leaving. When he left, it would be for good. He wasn't the kind of man to ask a woman to wait for him to return. He had nothing to offer, and the life he would be returning to would be an offense to a decent woman.

He'd sworn not to kiss her again, but he only learned that his need for her went beyond any physical desire. Jack couldn't imagine a day without hearing her laughter, seeing her eyes glow with affection for her son, or catching the faint scent of her perfume when she crossed the room.

There was no escape, and he was beginning to believe he would always be haunted by a sense of loss where she was concerned. Even as he readied his horse to leave, the thought of never seeing her again tore at his guts.

The barn door opened and Amanda stepped inside, quickly assessing the curried horse and his neatly packed gear waiting nearby.

"She certainly seems to have recovered from her ordeal."

Jack nodded. "Yeah, the old girl's going to be all right."

"I'm glad," she said. "Glad you're both doing well now."

The breeze picked up and played with a loose strand of her hair. Jack couldn't resist fingering it away from her face. "Thanks to you."

He felt her shudder beneath his touch. "I wish things were different, Amanda."

She nodded, not saying anything, but he didn't miss the way her lip trembled. Jack cupped the back of her head with his palm and coaxed her to look up at him. "For the first time in my life, I wish I could be something I'm not."

He brushed his lips against her forehead, and she slipped into his arms. "Oh, Jack, don't wish for things that can't be. It's such a waste."

When she looked up, her eyes shimmered with unshed tears, and he was helpless to do anything but kiss her, knowing it might be the last chance he ever had. Her lips parted beneath his, and he savored the sweetness of her mouth and the feel of her hands clinging to his shoulders.

"Señora Ramirez!"

The shout startled them both, and Jack straightened immediately, easing Amanda away from him. She hurried out of the barn just as a rider slid off his horse and scrambled toward her. "Señora! Señor Ramirez sent me to tell you his father has died. The funeral will be tomorrow at one o'clock."

Jack stepped out of the barn just in time to hear the news and to see the terror in Amanda's eyes. She only nodded to the messenger and turned toward the house, her steps none too steady. Jack followed her inside the kitchen and found her seated at the table, her hands folded against her lips.

She looked up at the sound of his boots on the kitchen floor. Her face was pale but held no grief, only fear, and he knew that whatever trouble was facing her now was worse than any before. He also knew he couldn't leave. Not now.

Amanda kept her head bowed throughout the drawn-out prayer, but her eyes were trained on Victor. He had barely spoken to her prior to the funeral service, but he'd made a big enough show of concern over Philip's condition, incredulous that the boy had not seen a doctor.

"I'm just fine." Philip reveled in discussing the incident, now that he was recovering, and wore the sling on his arm like a medal. "Mama just worries too much."

Amanda noticed that Victor didn't demand to

know why no one had sent for him or let him know about Philip being injured. It was all she could do not to confront him and let him know she knew what he had tried to do, but she couldn't prove it. Not yet.

The priest concluded the prayer and those gathered for the final service in the family cemetery began to recede, offering a word of sympathy or encouragement to Victor. Amanda waited until everyone was gone to lay a single rose on her husband's grave and cross herself as she had learned to do in the Catholic church. Philip came to stand beside her.

"I don't remember very much about when he died," Philip told her. "Mostly what I remember is the time he taught me to ride a pony."

She, too, could remember the fat little pony and the way Philip's legs could barely reach the stirrups. She'd been so afraid he would fall that Miguel sent her to the house and wouldn't let her watch. "As time passes, we only remember the good things," she explained.

"That's good advice," Victor commented as he joined them. "Have you been making good memories with your guest?"

Amanda glanced at Philip. "Why don't you have our buggy brought around from the stables?"

Once he was out of earshot, Amanda countered Victor's accusation. "I will do whatever is necessary to protect my home and my son. The land is not yours to do with as you please."

"It's not yours, either, Amanda. You keep forgetting that."

"I forget nothing. The land was left in trust for Philip. His father wanted it passed on to him, but no one was given the right to put me out of my home."

"I'm warning you, Amanda. If you value your life,

get off that property." He glanced down at his brother's grave. "It would be a shame to have to dig another grave so soon."

Her insides were quaking, but she managed not to falter at the malevolence in his eyes. Backing away from him, she said in a cool voice, "Be careful you don't dig your own grave, Victor."

Amanda paced the length of the parlor, her nerves on edge. When she and Philip returned home from the funeral, Jack Noble was nowhere to be found. His horse was also gone, and no one had seen him all day.

Now what will you do?

Nearing the fireplace, she stared at the glowing embers. There was a great deal more at stake than losing her home. She and Philip were all that stood between Victor and enormous wealth. Philip stood to inherit a portion of his grandfather's estate as well as his father's.

Outside, she heard a horse approaching, and her heart leapt at the thought of Jack returning. Peering out the front window, Amanda recognized Jack leading his horse into the barn and breathed a prayer of thanks. He hadn't left. Not yet.

He had long since recovered from his injuries and would have already left if not for caring about Philip. Now that Philip was getting better, there was no reason for him to stay. Unless she asked him.

She had managed to remain calm and collected in the face of Victor's threats, but inside she was truly frightened. Even if she could find an attorney willing to challenge Victor in court, the chances of a widow successfully contesting her husband's will were slim.

In the meantime, she had to protect herself and Philip or all the lawyers in the world wouldn't be able to help her. Amanda plucked a shawl from a hook near the door and hurried out into the darkness toward the barn. She rushed inside, and the wind slammed the heavy door closed behind her.

Jack whirled around, his gun already drawn. She hadn't even seen him reach for the holster.

"Damn, woman, you could get killed busting in on a man like that." He holstered the pistol and eyed her warily. "What's wrong?"

Amanda swallowed. "I was afraid you had left."

"I went into town to take care of some business."

"You don't owe me any explanation—I mean, it's none of my business." She was babbling and felt her courage weaken. "I just thought you had left."

"Not without saying good-bye." He closed the distance between them and caught her trembling hands in his. "I take it you didn't have a very pleasant day."

She shook her head. "My father-in-law was a good man, but I barely knew him."

His fingers began kneading the inside of her palm, and she understood her alarm at the thought of his leaving. For the first time in years, she felt safe. Unable to resist the comfort Jack was offering, Amanda pressed her forehead against his shoulder and reveled in the feel of his arms closing around her.

Closing her eyes, she drew a ragged breath and said, "I need you to stay, Jack. Please don't leave me. Not now, please."

The hand stroking her shoulder stilled in the center of her back. "Can you tell me why?"

She drew back and decided the time had come for her to be honest with him. "My husband's brother is trying to take away my home ... sell off the land and put us out."

His eyes narrowed. "How can he sell your land?"

"It's not mine," she explained. "When my husband died, he left everything in trust for Philip and appointed Victor as trustee."

"Why would he do that?"

"To prevent the land from leaving the family in the event I remarried."

"But his brother can sell it if he wants to?"

"Until Philip is twenty-one, Victor has complete authority over the property. He was merely biding his time until his father died." She drew a deep breath. "He wants the money to cover a bad investment, and nothing will be left for Philip."

"What's stopping him?"

"He can't sell unless Philip and I leave, and I have refused to do so."

He came up behind her and let his hands settle gently around her waist. "Does that explain why someone would take a shot at you?"

She nodded, longing to throw herself into his arms. "Everything would be a lot less complicated for Victor if Philip and I weren't here."

Jack turned her around and drew her against him, holding her close. She buried her face against his shoulder. "I shouldn't burden you with my problems, but I don't know what else to do."

He raised her face to his. "Amanda, I'll stay as long as you need me."

His mouth settled over hers, and she realized that she had needed him all her life. She believed he would stay, but knew it wouldn't be forever. He deepened the kiss, and she wound her arms around his neck, clinging to him.

When he ended the kiss, his expression was grim. "You'd better get back inside the house. I've never been much of a gentleman."

Amanda knew he was right, but she also knew that if she left now, she would regret it the rest of her life. She raised her palm to his cheek and brushed her lips against his, whispering, "Are you accusing me of trying to take advantage of you?"

He stared down at her with a mix of surprise and desire, but his arms tightened around her. "I'd say we're about even on that."

The next kiss was unlike any they had shared. With none of the haste or apprehension she'd felt before, Amanda savored the slow, willful rise of her own desire and reveled in the hunger she felt in his touch. His lips grazed the line of her jaw, seeking the soft hollow of her throat.

He put enough distance between them to search her eyes for reassurance, and she took his hand and drew him to her for a kiss that spoke volumes of her need for him.

Like teenagers, they scrambled up the ladder leading to the hayloft, and Amanda grinned at the sight of blankets strewn in one corner. "So this is where you've been trying to hide from me."

"Did you think I was sleeping with my horse?" He gathered her close and lowered them both to the makeshift bed. "I couldn't sleep in that house knowing you were in the next room . . . in bed alone."

His fingers found the row of tiny buttons and, starting at her throat, undid each one until only the thin material of her chemise veiled her from his sight. Impatient, he bent his head and kissed the swell of each breast where the garment was laced together. Amanda started at the feel of his mouth on her flesh, the pleasure so intense, and arched against him seeking more.

Jack was only too willing to accommodate. His tongue circled the shadow of her nipple as he slowly unlaced her chemise and she shuddered when his mouth closed over her naked breast, her entire body throbbing at his touch. He kissed a path to her other breast and eased the dress from her shoulders, and she squirmed to rid herself of the garment when he hesitated.

She laughed at the startled expression on his face and reached for the buttons of his shirt. He drew her back into his embrace, and she shivered at the feel of her naked flesh burning against his. Jack let his hand move over her ribcage and down the flat of her stomach, kissing her with a tenderness that made her want to weep. His hand found the ties of her undergarments and skimmed the dress down and off.

Amanda kept her eyes focused on his face, trying to guess his thoughts as his gaze traveled the length of her bare body, and she suddenly felt shy and uncertain. She was no seductress, only a woman who'd been alone for too long, and she braced herself for his disappointment.

When his eyes met hers, her misgivings vanished. His desire was undeniable. He shed his own clothes and gathered her against him, touching every inch of her body with his. He bent to kiss her, whispering, "You're beautiful, Amanda. Don't ever doubt it."

He splayed his palm across her belly, tracing her navel with one finger, and she shuddered as his hand slid between her legs. His touch was gentle, awakening her body to pleasures she'd never dreamed of, and she forgot her shyness and moved her hips in search of what only he could bring her.

Jack whispered something, but she was lost in a haze of aching desire and all reason was lost as his mouth returned to her breast. Amanda clenched her fingers in his hair and arched against his touch, desperately clinging to him as her body shattered in completion. He held her close while she lay limp in his arms, too stunned to do more than whisper his name.

Jack smoothed dampened tendrils of hair behind her ear and brushed a kiss against her throat. Easing her thighs farther apart, he settled his weight between them and entered her as gently as if she were a virgin. Amanda gasped as her body opened to the slow, steady pressure, and she dug her nails into his shoulders.

He gave her time to adjust to his penetration, kissing her until her desire once again matched his own. Only when she arched beneath him and twined her legs around his did he begin to move within her. Amanda was mesmerized by the raw need on his face and the tension she felt in his body, so enthralled she didn't think to object when he slid his hands to her bottom and drew her into the urgent rhythm of his desire.

Amanda let him guide her movements to match his, and her loins tightened around his as he brought her to ecstasy once again. She heard his own muffled groan of pleasure and held him close as he spilled himself inside her.

It was nearly daylight before Amanda slipped out of the barn to sneak back into the house. Jack watched her hurry across the yard, hugging a shawl tightly around her shoulders, and cursed himself for a fool.

He'd been fully prepared to explain his situation to her, apologize for not being honest with her, and leave.

If only that were the problem. The real problem was going to be explaining the correlation between his presence and Ramirez's search for a gunfighter. The "squatters" to be eliminated were Amanda and Philip.

Amanda was in more danger than she realized and explaining the situation would only incriminate himself, wrongly so. He'd refused the job outright and planned to leave Santa Fe that day. He couldn't expect her to believe he just happened to end up on her property, injured or not, and she would be a fool to let him remain.

He couldn't leave now, not with Ramirez intent on being rid of her. But he couldn't stay unless she knew the truth.

He stepped inside the kitchen and found Amanda humming to herself. She had changed clothes and coiled her braided hair at the nape of her neck. She turned and smiled at him. "Good morning."

He nodded, reaching to stroke the delicate skin at the base of her throat, and her expression sobered. Reluctantly, he said, "I need to tell you something."

"Later," she insisted, pressing her fingers against his lips. "Please, let's wait until later. I haven't felt this happy in years, and I don't want anything to spoil it."

He shouldn't put it off any longer, but he nodded. He took her hand and brushed a kiss against her knuckles. "Later."

She smiled and slipped her arms around his waist. "Thank you."

His arms had barely closed around her when he

caught sight of Philip standing in the doorway, glaring at them. Jack drew back and Amanda whirled around just as Philip demanded, "What's going on here?"

"Philip!" Amanda gasped, her face flooding with color. "There's nothing—you shouldn't—"

"I'm not stupid," he snapped. "I know what it means when a woman lets a man grope all over her."

"Philip!" Amanda was mortified, her expression stricken.

If anyone was to blame, Jack thought, it was him, but Philip had no call to lash out at Amanda that way. He leveled his gaze with the boy's and warned him, "Don't ever talk to your mother like that."

The boy drew back, bristling with anger. "Why do you care? You're just using her!"

"No, Philip," Jack countered. "I wouldn't hurt your mother. You know that."

Philip ignored him and turned back to his mother. "You can t believe anything he says. He's nothing but a hired killer, a gunfighter, and I'll bet he's wanted by the law. He's just after your money, Mother."

"Young man, you go right back up those stairs and don't come down until you're ready to apologize to me and to Mr. Noble."

"Apologize! For telling you what you're too daft to see for yourself?"

Amanda's palm smacked loudly against Philip's face, and he staggered back a few steps. His eyes filled with accusation as he cupped the cheek bearing the outline of Amanda's hand just before he turned and ran out of the kitchen toward the front door.

"Philip!" Amanda cried, hurrying after him. "Philip, wait, I'm sorry!"

The front door slammed shut just as she reached the foyer, and Jack waited to see if she would go out after Philip. When she reached the door, she hesitated and then slumped forward, pressing her forehead against the solid wood.

His first instinct was to reach out to her, but his instincts with her had been wrong from the beginning. So he waited until she sensed his presence and turned around.

"Jack, I'm so sorry," she began. "Philip had no right to say those things about you."

"Yes, he did."

She shook her head. "Last night was my choice, Jack. I won't let you blame yourself."

"I mean, Philip is right. I am a gunfighter, sometimes a bounty hunter, but still a hired killer."

She blinked, disbelieving. "What do you mean?"

"That's why I came to Santa Fe in the first place." He decided to be as truthful as he could. "A man hired me to resolve a feud, but he exaggerated the situation, and I turned down the job. He didn't take kindly to being refused and had me beaten up and left for dead. Philip found me and hid me in your barn. Otherwise I probably would be dead."

Her jaw went slack, and he could only guess what she was thinking. She opened her mouth and closed it quickly. Jack supposed that whatever she was going to ask him was better left unanswered.

"I'm sorry, Amanda. I should have told you before—before now."

"Being a bounty hunter isn't the same thing as a hired killer." She sounded as though she was trying to convince herself rather than him. "And you didn't take just *any* job."

"This time I didn't."

"Let's sit down." She took his arm and led him

into the parlor, but he remained standing when she settled on the sofa. She looked up at him. "Tell me."

"I had a reputation for being ruthless, and I was proud of it." He paused. "I was so good that there were times I would be hired to track a man down rather than competing for a bounty, and I didn't ask questions."

The troubled look on her face was more than he could bear. He turned toward the window and looked out. "Six months ago, a rancher in Texas sent me to track down a man wanted for a killing. It only took a week to find him and haul him in. The whole time, he kept telling me he was innocent, that Pratt had set him up, but I'd heard it all before. Only this time it was the truth."

"What happened?" Amanda asked softly after several minutes of silence.

"I hauled him into the sheriff, collected my money, and left. That night a mob stormed the jail and lynched the poor bastard." He shook his head. "He never had a chance."

"Did they ever find the real killer?"

The question startled him. She was still trying to believe the best about him. "There was no killer, no murder. The charges were false. The whole thing was a setup to get rid of Colson—that was his name, Jacob Colson. Pratt wanted him eliminated because he stood in the way of a sweet deal with the railroad."

"But you didn't know that." He turned to find her standing just behind him. "You were only doing what you thought was right."

"Right?" he sneered. "I didn't care about right or wrong, just the money. If I hadn't been so hell-bent on collecting a fat reward, I would have seen that Colson was no killer. Hell, the man wasn't even trying to hide. He just kept begging me to think about his wife and kids."

Amanda's eyes widened slightly. "My God, what happened to them?"

"Nothing yet. I sent his wife the reward money I'd collected . . . anonymously." He held up his hand to silence any praise she was about to pay the deed. "All that did was buy her a little time. If she doesn't pay off a bank note by the end of the month, she'll be thrown off her land with four children to raise—alone."

"So you came to Santa Fe to earn the money," she concluded, as if there was no problem. "I said I would pay you for helping me."

"Amanda, I'm not taking your money." He was stunned. "That's not why I told you about Colson."

"I know that," she whispered. "But I want to help you, Jack. The way you've helped me."

Jack shook his head and turned from the room, needing to put some distance between them. He couldn't convince her what kind of man he was unless he was willing to tell her what had brought him to Santa Fe. She would hate him, of course, and he wasn't ready to face that.

Amanda started at the sound of riders approaching the house. Philip had been gone nearly three hours, and she was growing more worried. He had not taken a horse, so she knew he couldn't go far.

She stepped out onto the porch, recognizing Victor's horse right away. He was flanked by at least six men, and the grim determination on his face assured her that he meant to put an end to her resistance.

"Good afternoon, Amanda." He leaned forward

in the saddle, smiling down at her. "You're looking well."

"What do you want?"

His smile faded. "Defiant to the end. I admire your courage, but it takes wisdom to know when you're defeated."

"And you're here to tell me I've been defeated?"

"The sale will be completed tomorrow. You have until then to get out."

"You can't put me out of this house."

"No, but I can give you the choice of leaving or having it burned down around your head."

"I told you once to leave the lady alone." Jack stepped out onto the porch, brandishing a shotgun. "Don't make me tell you again."

Several men reached for their guns, but Victor held up his hand. "So, we meet again. I don't know who you are, but there is nothing you can do to change matters."

A man at the back of the assembly moved his horse forward and stared down at Jack, his face a mask of disbelief. "Señor Ramirez, this man is Jack Noble."

Jack and Victor both look shocked, but Victor recovered first. "Mr. Noble, I should have introduced myself the first time we met. It would have saved us both a great deal of trouble."

Amanda looked to Jack for an explanation, but Victor continued, "Although it seems you've enjoyed your little stay with my sister-in-law."

"What does he mean, Jack?"

"Amanda, you didn't know?" Victor shook his head in mock sympathy. "Mr. Noble came to Santa Fe at my request. I thought he might be able to . . . persuade you to leave. I certainly never expected him to move right in with you, but obviously you are willing to do anything that pleases him now."

Jack swore vehemently. "God damn you, Ramirez, you know I refused to take that job."

"Of course, you refused," Victor agreed, flashing a knowing smile Amanda's way. "Then you just happened to show up and seduce the very woman I wanted you to eliminate."

He turned to leave, calling over his shoulder, "Remember, Mr. Noble, I want her gone by tomorrow."

The stricken look on Amanda's face silenced any denial Jack might have made. She backed away from him, reaching behind her for the door. "Why didn't you tell me?"

"I told you I refused the job I was offered."

"You failed to mention that I was the job."

"I didn't know that until last night. I'd never met Ramirez, but I sure as hell didn't think he'd hired me to do away with a woman and a child."

He tried to close the distance between them, but she opened the door and stepped inside. "Please, Jack, just go away."

"Amanda, listen to me—"

"I should have listened when you told me you were a hired killer."

Chapter Six

It was late afternoon when Philip returned to the house, his emotions still in upheaval. The house was eerily quiet, and he'd expected his mother to meet him at the door.

She wasn't in the parlor or the kitchen, and he nearly panicked to think she might have gone somewhere with Jack. Instead, he found her in her bedroom lying down.

"Mother? Are you sick or something?"

She sat up on the bed, startled by his presence. She shook her head. "No, I'm just tired."

Her eyes were red and puffy and her voice was scratchy. Guilt plagued him for the hateful things he'd said to her. "Can I do anything for you?"

Again, she only shook her head.

"Where is Jack?"

She stiffened, but her bottom lip trembled slightly. "Mr. Noble left this afternoon."

Philip nodded, but part of him was sad to see Jack go. He liked the man, but he couldn't let a gunfighter take advantage of his mother. "I'm sorry for what I said this morning. I know you wouldn't do anything wrong."

She nodded. "Thank you."

Philip made his way downstairs and out to the stable. The only matter remaining to be settled was convincing Uncle Victor not to sell their ranch. Now that Jack was gone, Philip would have to handle the matter himself.

He saddled his horse and rode the short distance to the house that had belonged to his grandfather. Now it belonged to his uncle, and Victor had no reason to bother with their property.

Philip slid from the saddle and tied the horse near the front of the house. Gathering his courage, he marched toward the front door and knocked firmly.

Victor opened the door. "Philip, what are you doing here? Did your mother send you?"

"No, I came to talk to you. Man to man."

"Is that so? What about?"

"My property." When Victor made no reply, Philip explained, "I want to settle the matter of my inheritance."

His uncle nodded. "Come right in."

Philip followed him into the library.

Victor placed a bottle of liquor on the table along with two glasses. "What do you want to know about the property?"

Philip hesitated when Victor slid a glass full of whiskey toward him. His uncle raised his own glass and said, "First, let us drink a toast to our first man-to-man talk."

Philip took a tentative sip and grimaced at the

strong, bitter taste. The way he'd seen men tossing back liquor as if it were water, he'd always expected it to taste rich and sweet. Victor was watching him, and he gulped a mouthful and gasped for breath when the fiery liquid pooled in his throat, nearly choking him to death.

His uncle thumped him soundly on the back, and Philip barely managed to swallow the whiskey. He could feel the heat scorching a path toward his stomach, and his insides scrambled to escape the invasion.

"It takes some getting used to," Victor assured him, refilling his glass. "Have another."

Philip shook his head, and Victor laughed. "Come now. We have much to celebrate."

Philip took his next drink much more slowly while Victor detailed the problems facing them as landowners. He began to feel woozy and his stomach found its way into his throat. Sweat popped out on his forehead. "I think I should go home now."

"Home? You just arrived."

"I don't feel well." He tried to rise from the chair, but Victor clasped his shoulder and shoved him down. "Please, I'm going to be sick."

"Did your mother send you here?" Victor demanded, forcing Philip to look up at him. "Did she?"

"No, she doesn't know I'm here." Philip didn't miss the rage on his uncle's face, and, too late, he scrambled to escape the man's fury. "Let me go!"

Victor twisted his fingers in Philip's collar and hoisted the boy to his feet. "She should have listened to me when she had a chance. Maybe she'll listen now that she stands to lose more than her home."

* * *

Amanda knocked on Philip's bedroom door a second time and waited for an answer, only to be met by silence. Turning the knob, she peered inside and found the room empty. Her alarm began to mount. He was nowhere to be found in the house, upstairs or down, and she desperately wished she had gone out looking for him rather than crying over Jack Noble.

She went out to the bunkhouse and listened outside the door, hoping to hear Philip's voice, but she recognized only the tired voices of hard-working men anxious to rest. She debated whether or not to question them about Philip's whereabouts.

"Señora?"

She turned to find Rafael approaching.

"Is something wrong?"

"Have you seen Philip?"

He shook his head. "Not since this morning."

They hurried to the barn and found Philip's gelding missing, and Amanda's worry quickly gave way to panic.

"Where would he go?" Rafael asked.

"He's been so upset since he came home from school." She shook her head. "And I've only made things worse. I had no chance fighting Victor. I should have taken Philip and left a long time ago."

"Staying took more courage than leaving," he reminded her. "It always has."

She nodded. "We have to find him."

Dusk was settling in Santa Fe by the time Amanda found Jack at a back table in a smoke-filled saloon. A bottle of whiskey sat on the table in front of him, and an empty glass rested in his hand. He glanced up, and his eyes widened slightly before a cynical smile settled on his features.

He leaned back in his chair. "Mrs. Ramirez, what a surprise."

"Jack, I need your help."

He shook his head. "No, not my help, you don't."

"Please, Jack. Philip is missing."

His shoulders tensed and a flicker of alarm flashed briefly in his eyes. "What do you mean missing?"

"I can't find him anywhere."

"He's just off sulking somewhere." As if dismissing the matter, he reached for the whiskey and poured himself another drink. "Won't you join me?"

"Jack, I have to find him." Amanda couldn't believe his indifference. "He's been full of foolish notions about the ranch since he returned from school. He keeps saying he wants to prove he can take care of things."

"Then let him." Jack raised the glass to his lips. "Let him take care of things."

"He's just a boy!"

"And I'm nothing but a cold-blooded killer," he reminded her. "Why would you want my help?"

She straightened. "You're right. I should never have wasted my time coming to you."

She whirled around and marched out of the saloon. Jack watched her leave, shouldering her way through the rowdy crowd of drovers and saloon girls, and resisted the urge to go after her. Amanda had come here wanting to believe the best about him, wanting to prove to herself that he wasn't a man capable of the things he'd done, but he had refused to let her do that. Regret didn't change the facts, and the fact remained that he was everything Ramirez had accused him of being.

He'd already destroyed innocent lives, and he didn't intend to see Amanda and Philip hurt, but he wouldn't let her make a hero out of him. He tossed a coin on the table and left the half-empty bottle behind.

Finding Philip was no problem. Jack merely followed the blatant trail that led from Amanda's stable to the home of Victor Ramirez. There was no sign of Philip's horse anywhere around, but Jack suspected that Philip had not been able to return home.

The instincts that had kept him alive all those years cried out for him to confront Ramirez and put a bullet through his skull. The irony was that, had he done that in the beginning, Amanda's future would not be in peril nor would Philip be in danger.

Jack decided first to find Philip's horse before charging into the house without proof that the boy was indeed there. Slipping quietly into the barn, he recognized none of the horses stabled inside, and he knew Ramirez was shrewd enough to do away with any evidence of Philip's presence.

A muffled sob reached his ears, and Jack made his way to the empty stall in the back. He peered over the railing and caught sight of Philip, bound and gagged, huddled against the back wall. When he opened the door to the stall, the rusty hinges groaned in protest, and Philip struggled to sit up, his eyes wide with fright.

"Quiet," Jack ordered in a tight whisper. He knelt to cut the ties binding the boy's wrists and noticed the ugly bruise marring one side of his face. "Your mother's worried sick about you."

Philip nodded, and his lip began to tremble. The

tears that spilled down his cheeks reminded Jack that Philip was only a child. "Let's get you home, boy."

Clinging to Jack's arm, Philip struggled to his feet but didn't hesitate to leave the barn as quickly as possible. Once outside, Jack motioned for Philip to be quiet as they stole past the corral and several out-buildings. The boy stumbled twice, and Jack paused to let him rest.

Philip was breathing hard, and Jack feared he was hurt worse than he looked. Finally the boy gasped, "I can't leave my horse."

"Mine can carry the both of us," Jack assured him.

"We can't leave him," Philip insisted. "My uncle is going to shoot him. He said so."

Jack knew it was crazy, but he asked, "Where is he?"

Gesturing over his shoulder, Philip whispered, "The corral."

Jack swore to himself. "You wait here."

A dozen or so horses mingled in the corral and Jack was barely able to pick out Philip's in the dark. He grabbed a rope draped over one of the railings and led the gelding toward the gate. As he closed the gate behind him, Jack caught sight of Philip walking toward the corral.

"I told you to stay put."

"The boy never listens." Victor Ramirez came into view, a pistol trained on Philip's head. "He is just like his mother."

Jack barely stopped himself from drawing his own pistol, a reflex as natural as breathing, for he knew the slightest move on his part would only get Philip killed. Instead, he spread his empty palms wide.

"Come on, Ramirez, he's just a boy. This is between you and me."

"Actually, it has nothing to do with you," Victor replied. "I had hoped bringing you to Santa Fe would provide a means to an end, and it still may."

"How is that?"

Ramirez shrugged, as if the answer were obvious. "What choice do I have but to kill the man who killed my nephew while trying to steal the boy's horse?"

Philip's face filled with terror, and Jack willed the boy not to provoke Ramirez further by panicking. "That's pretty clever, but what about Amanda? She's the one who sent me here to get Philip."

Unshaken, Victor only smiled. "I will deliver the sad news to her myself, and she will not be able to prove otherwise."

Before Jack could respond, the sound of riders shattered the silence and drew Victor's attention— only for a moment, but Jack knew better than to waste so much as a heartbeat. He lunged forward, shoving Philip to the ground and drawing his pistol just as Ramirez realized his intent.

A man shouted, "Ramirez! Drop the gun!"

But Jack saw the desperation in Ramirez's face and fired without hesitation. Victor dropped to the ground, swearing and groping for his weapon, and Jack fired again as Victor reclaimed the weapon. The bullet slammed into his chest, tossing him backward onto the ground, motionless.

"Philip!" Amanda rushed forward and knelt beside her son. "Philip! Are you hurt?"

Philip was shaken, badly so, and reached for his mother like a frightened child. "He was going to kill me. He was. If Jack hadn't saved me, I'd be dead."

* * *

Amanda was shaking even as she held Philip tightly, rocking him back and forth. "Thank God. Thank God you're all right."

"I'm sorry, Mother," he whispered. "I'm sorry."

He looked up at her and she brushed her fingers against his swollen cheek. "Why on earth did you come here?"

"I wanted to take care of you."

"Take care of me?"

He nodded. "I thought I could make Uncle Victor leave you alone, so you would need me and not send me away to school again."

With her fingers, she combed his dark hair away from his face. "Philip, you don't have to prove anything to me."

"But you were so young when I was born." He looked away. "I know you've always been sorry you had to stay here because of me. I wanted to make it up to you."

"Philip, having you is the best thing that ever happened to me. My only regret is that I would have been a better mother to you if I'd been older."

Huddling in her embrace, Philip whispered, "You couldn't. No one could be a better mother."

"Oh, Philip," she whispered against his forehead.

Amanda glanced up and saw Jack talking with the marshal, explaining the bloody scene to the lawman, who could only shake his head in disbelief. At last he turned and ordered two men lingering nearby to collect Victor's body. Jack made his way to stand over her and Philip.

He helped Amanda to her feet and then Philip. Already, she could sense his retreat, but she wasn't going to let him go so easily this time. "You saved my son's life."

He nodded. "You don't deserve any more grief in your life."

Amanda drew a deep breath. "I'm sorry for the things I said. I should never have believed anything Victor told me."

"He told you the truth," Jack insisted, clasping her hands in his. "I'm everything he said I was, and worse. I just want you to know I never meant you or Philip any harm."

"I know that," she whispered.

"I wish things could be different." He pressed his forehead against the top of her head. "But I am what I am, and I can't change the past."

"I want to pay off Mrs. Colson's land for you."

He backed away. "That's my debt, Amanda."

"No, it's mine." He started to protest, but she wouldn't hear it. "If it weren't for Mrs. Colson, I would never have known you. I can never repay her for that."

"I won't take your money."

She smiled. "You don't have to. I'm sure the bankers around here are going to be mighty nice to me. They'll help me find her."

Philip brushed past her, following after Jack. "Noble, you promised me something. Now you're backing out."

Jack eyed Philip warily. "What are you talking about?"

"You promised me. You promised me that you would never hurt my mother."

Jack pulled Philip aside. "That's why I'm leaving, to keep from hurting her."

"That doesn't make sense."

"She'll be better off in the long run," he tried to explain.

"In the long run, I'll be a grown man with a family of my own." Philip wouldn't be dissuaded. "She'll need someone to take care of, and you need taking care of more than anyone in the world."

Jack glanced back at Amanda, and she immediately recognized the hopeless need in his eyes, the same need she felt in her own heart. She wasn't about to wait for him to decide what to do. She closed the distance between them and took the choice away from him. "Do you love me, Jack?"

Jack couldn't look away, but neither could he answer her. Loving Amanda was easy, but telling her so and leaving would be impossible.

"Jack, answer me," she demanded. "Do you love me?"

He hauled her into his arms and kissed her until she was breathless. "Does that answer you question?"

"No," she managed. "Do you love me?"

"Yes, Amanda, I love you," he declared, sealing his fate and hers. "Do you want me to prove it?"

"Every day," she told him. "Every day for the rest of our lives."

A MOTHER FOR LUKE

Maggie James

Chapter One

Philadelphia, 1852

With a jolt of terror, Bonnie realized she was not alone in the darkness.

The bedroom door had opened, as quietly and softly as the whisper of an angel. But the intruder could only be her stepfather, and, as far as she was concerned, he was akin to the devil himself.

Sitting up in bed, she yanked the sheet up to her chin and angrily cried, "Nate, I know it's you, and I want you to get out of here right now."

There was no response, but she could hear his heavy breathing from across the room.

"I know you've been drinking, but that's no excuse, and this time, I'm going to tell my mother."

In the two months that he and Addie, her mother, had been married, Nate had let Bonnie know that his regard for her was anything but fatherly. Whenever he could catch her alone, he would try to kiss her and put his hands on her. She had pushed him away and threatened to tell, but he had laughed and said she didn't dare. And, so far, she hadn't, because she didn't want to hurt her mother.

But enough was enough. Nate was obviously not going to give up, and even though her mother would be devastated, she had to know what a fiend she had married.

Bonnie sadly thought how thrilled Addie had been when Nate asked her to marry him. The hard times were over, she had exulted, because Nate was a man of means. He owned a profitable hardware store in a busy section of Philadelphia, with comfortable living quarters above.

Never again, Addie had declared, would she and Bonnie have to live in a tar-paper shack down by the river and take in other people's laundry to keep from starving. There would be someone to take care of them forever.

The floor creaked.

He was getting closer.

Angrier, louder, Bonnie repeated, "Get out of here, Nate. You've no right to come in here."

"I got every right," he said, voice slurred. "It's my goddamn house, remember? And if you want to keep living here, you'd better be nice to me."

Bonnie had been leery of being alone in the house with Nate after her mother went to stay the night with a sick neighbor. With no bolt on her bedroom door, she had tried to shove the furniture in front of it, but everything was too heavy. She had then vowed to stay awake all night and was now thankful she had. Otherwise, she would not have heard him come in.

She had also thought to extinguish the bedside lantern so if he did sneak in, he would have to fumble around in the darkness.

In addition, she had positioned a water pitcher on the bedside table within easy reach. Though not much of a weapon, she would have a fighting chance if she could smash it over his head when he got close enough.

"I'll hurt you if I have to, Nate," she warned.

"You're the one who's gonna get hurt. I'm gonna take what I want—one way or the other."

"My mother will—"

"Your mother won't do a damn thing, 'cause she won't believe you. I've told her how you've been teasing me when she's not looking. She said she'd have a talk with you, that you don't know how to act around a man. You've never been around one . . . never been courted . . ."

No, Bonnie thought, she had not been courted. She had done nothing but work since her father died the year she was fifteen. With no time for beaus to call, she had been passed by. Now, nearing nineteen, she was considered a spinster.

She gripped the pitcher tighter. "I don't tease you, Nate, and you know it. I try my best to stay away from you."

". . . always swishing around." He hiccupped. "Making me crazy with want . . . trying to take me away from your momma, 'cause you wish it was you I'd married instead, so you'd have a man to take care of you. I know your kind."

"Nate, it doesn't have to be this way. Turn around and leave, please."

He snickered. "Oh, but it does. Now stop arguing,

damn you. You're wasting time. She might not stay gone all night, and I plan to love you real good."

"Stay away from me, Nate. I'm warning you for the last time." Dear Lord, she prayed the pitcher would knock him out. If it didn't, he would be so mad there was no telling what he might do.

"Ungrateful little bitch. After all I done for you—"

"I've worked for my keep. So has my mother. All you do is loaf all day and drink with your lazy friends."

"I'll teach you to sass me," he growled.

He bumped into the chair she had purposely left in the middle of the floor and yelped, "Gonna get you for that, too, you little bitch."

Bonnie drew back against the bed's iron posts. She gripped the handle of the pitcher with both hands. He knew the layout of the room, knew where she was, and the only reason he had not yet reached her was because he was stumbling drunk.

"I took you in and gave you a roof over your head, put food in your belly, and then you dare to stick your nose up like you're too good for me."

She got to her knees. Once she hit him and he fell to the floor, she intended to run down the steps and out of the house, screaming all the way. She didn't care how embarrassing it would be when all the neighbors found out her stepfather had tried to rape her, because she and her mother would be moving. A tar-paper shack down by the river suddenly seemed like heaven, and never again would she begrudge living there.

"Gotcha. . . ."

He had managed to silently cover the last few feet to take her by surprise, grabbing her from behind.

Propelled forward, she dropped the pitcher, spilling water on the bed.

Holding her facedown with his body, he reached underneath her to fondle her breasts. "Now you're gonna give me what I want, or I'll break that pretty little neck of yours." His lips were hot and wet against her ear.

Her face was mashed into the mattress. Struggling to breathe, it was all she could do to choke out the promise, "I'll kill you for this . . . I swear I will . . ."

Instantly, he wrapped one hand around her throat and squeezed. "The only one who's gonna die is you if you keep fighting, damn you. Now settle down till I get inside you, and then you can wiggle all you want." He managed to yank her nightgown up to her waist, then tried to spread her thighs.

He kept pressure on her neck, and Bonnie felt as though the bones were being crushed. A great roaring began in her head, and she fought to stay conscious, to try and fight him off to the very end.

Suddenly, he cried, "Hell, the bed's all wet." Then he abruptly let go of her neck, grabbed her by her shoulders, and jerked her up. "We can't stay here."

Bonnie opened her mouth to scream, but at the first sound, Nate smacked the side of her head—hard. "Shut up. You bring the neighbors running, and I'll wring your neck."

The blow dazed her, and the room seemed to spin.

"Stop fighting me, damn you. How many times have I got to tell you?"

Through a fog of pain, Bonnie felt herself being roughly hoisted over his shoulder.

"We'll go to my room," he grumbled as he stalked out. "I'm not laying in a wet bed. You're gonna clean it up, too. I don't want your momma asking questions, 'cause I aim to keep her. She's a hard worker and a good cook. Maybe later, when she sees how it is between you and me, she'll be smart enough to accept it. She knows she's got it good here. And other folks won't know about it, 'cause if you ever tell, I'll make you wish you hadn't.

"All of us can have a good life," he droned on. "And you'd be smart to realize that."

Above the roaring in her head, Bonnie struggled to gather her wits about her. She had to be ready to seize any chance to get away from him.

Ahead, she could see light. He had left a lantern burning in the room at the end of the hall where he slept with her mother. The door was ajar, and he kicked it open, then crossed to the bed and threw her down.

"Now we're gonna have some fun," he said in triumph, peeling his suspenders off his shoulders.

Eyes darting around the room, she searched for anything she could use to defend herself. The table beside the bed held only the lamp. To grab that and hit him with it might set them both on fire.

He was stepping out of his trousers. "I think we'll go ahead and get the first time over with, and then I'll show you what I want you to do for me. Your momma won't be back for hours. Maybe not till daylight. I locked her out, anyway. If she comes back early, she's gonna have to clang the bell outside, and that will give me time to get you out of here."

Bonnie knew how a trapped animal had to feel— helpless, desperate, and, yes, maybe even wishing to hurry and have it over with rather than dread the inevitable. But she was not the sort to give up and would fight to the end.

He came at her, naked, grabbing her by her ankles to yank her legs apart and fall between them.

"I'll bet you're no virgin. And I'll bet you took in something besides laundry in the dump you lived in by the river. I've heard about the whores down there, how they'll do it for whatever they're offered, and—"

Bonnie raised her foot, aiming for his crotch, but even in his drunken state, he saw the movement coming and caught her ankle and twisted. Her cry of pain was drowned by his bellowing, "You want me to break it? I will, little bitch. I'll break every bone in your body if I have to."

He was a huge man with a thick neck, muscular arms, and a barrel chest. Bonnie was no match for his strength, and all her twisting and struggling was in vain as he lowered himself between her legs and began to probe with his swollen penis.

She twisted her face from side to side as he began to rain wet, hot kisses over her face.

"Don't like to kiss, huh?" he laughed. "Well, there's a lot of things you won't like, but I promise you'll learn to. You're gonna do everything I tell you to, and you're not gonna argue about it, either. Now be still"—he grunted—"got to get it in . . ."

His hardness jammed against her.

Mustering every ounce of strength she possessed, Bonnie managed to bring her knee up and then jerk violently to the side, knocking him off her—but only for a second. Quickly he was upon her again, pressing so hard she could not move. He tried to maneuver himself inside her, and she was squashed and once again unable to breathe.

She felt his first, sharp probe and knew he was going to have his way with her.

And she prayed to die then and there.

"What . . . what's going on here?"

It was her mother, and Nate instantly rolled to the side.

Bonnie scrambled to sit up, dizzy but grateful he had not succeeded in penetrating her.

It was, she knew, a terrible way for her mother to find out about him, but thank God she had come when she did.

She held out her arms to her and began to cry.

But Addie made no move to go to her. Her face was frozen in horror, her skin the color of ashes.

Bonnie scrambled from the bed, but Nate grabbed her and pushed her back down.

"Stay away from her, you little hussy," he yelled. Reaching for his trousers, he fired words from his mouth like bullets from a revolver.

To Addie, he said, "Thank God you came when you did to save me from your whore of a daughter. I had too much to drink, 'cause I was lonely, missing you, and I went to bed to sleep it off, and the next thing I knew, she was crawling in bed with me, begging me to take her. I didn't know what I was doing."

Once he had his trousers on, he jerked Addie into his arms. Her expression had not changed, shocked eyes still fixed on Bonnie.

"So many times I wanted to tell you how she was acting," he rushed to continue, "but I knew it would break your heart. Now you have to know, 'cause she's gone too far. She'd been after me since the two of you moved in—said I should've married her instead of you. I told her she was crazy and to leave me alone, but she wouldn't, and tonight, after you left, she

sneaked in here and did things to make me crazy.
But you've got to believe me and forgive me, Addie,
because I love you so much."

Bonnie shook her head wildly from side to side,
stunned that he could lie so easily, so well.

She tried to push by him to get to her mother, but
he shoved her away so hard that she fell back on the
bed.

"Get away from her," he snarled. "You're not fit
to touch her."

Bonnie bounded off the bed. Ignoring Nate, she
tried again to make her mother listen. "He's lying.
He sneaked into my room tonight. If you don't believe
me, go look at the bed. It's wet from the pitcher he
knocked out of my hand when he grabbed me from
behind—the pitcher I was ready to hit him over the
head with. I'd been expecting him to try something,
don't you see? Ever since you married him, he's tried
to touch me, kiss me, when you weren't around."

Nate lifted an arm as though to strike her. "You'd
better get out of here, whore of Babylon, before I
unleash the wrath of God on you myself. You're a
witch. You cast a spell on me—your own stepfather—
to have your way with me. I'm taking you to the
preacher in the morning and have him pray the
demons out of you."

He turned to Addie, cupping her face in his hands
as he said, "That's what we'll do. She's been taken
by demons, and we'll have them driven out of her.
But you've got to say you believe me, Addie, that you
know it's you I love and want. Get her out of here,
and I'll prove how much."

He crushed her against him once more, but Addie
maneuvered to stare over his shoulder at Bonnie.

"Leave us," she said quietly, coldly. "We'll talk in the morning."

Bonnie stood her ground. "No. We have to talk now, because I can't have you thinking such terrible things about me, Mother. Come with me to my room. Let me show you the water, the pitcher, and—"

"And I think we've heard enough of the demons inside you for one night."

Nate slapped her before she knew what was happening, and she reeled beneath the blow and stumbled backward.

Cooly, Addie stepped between them. "Nate, that's enough. I'm too upset to talk about this anymore tonight."

Nate reached out to push back a strand of hair that had fallen on Addie's forehead. "Of course, darling. It's been a shock, I know. How come you're back early? Of course, I thank God all over the place that you are, otherwise . . ." His voice trailed off as he gave a helpless shrug.

Bonnie saw so many emotions mirrored in her mother's eyes—sadness, anger, resentment. But perhaps most vivid was the hopelessness that was also evident in her voice as she murmured, "Miss Lila took a turn for the better and told me to come home."

"He said he locked you out," Bonnie told her. "He wanted you to have to ring the bell so he'd have time to get me out of here. How did you get in?"

"I didn't want to wake anyone, so I crawled in a back window." Addie motioned her to the door. "Go now. I'm very tired. I can't talk about this now."

"Mother, please . . ."

Again, Bonnie reached out for her, but Nate grabbed her and shoved her into the hall. "Leave her be. Can't you see you've broken her heart?"

Bonnie fought against him, begging her mother to listen. "It's not like he said. I swear it—"

Nate pushed her so hard that she fell. Then he towered over her, shaking his fist. "I'd rather the preacher pray the demons outta you, girl, but I'm losing patience, and I might just beat them out of you instead. Your spell on me is broken, and I know you for the vixen you are. Now get to your room and don't come out till you're told or I'll rip the skin right off your witch's hide."

With an evil smirk on his face that only Bonnie could see, he slammed the door.

At the first light of dawn, her mother came to her.

Bonnie had been sitting all night in a chair by the window, dozing off and on from weariness but never soundly sleeping.

Seeing her mother, she leaped to her feet. "Thank God you came so we could talk without him around. You have to leave him. He's a monster—"

"Silence," Addie said, holding up a hand. "I'll not have you speak disrespectfully of your stepfather."

Bonnie gasped. "Surely, you don't believe him. I could never do what he claims, and you know it. He came here, like I said, to my bed, and—"

"If he did it was because you tempted him."

"Tempted him?" Bonnie echoed, astonished. "How can you say such a thing?"

Addie was standing like a wooden statue, her gaze vacuous. "Perhaps you didn't realize you were doing it, but it doesn't matter now. You're leaving. I'd like you to pack your belongings now and go before he wakes up."

Bonnie thought she had to be dreaming, caught

in the throes of some horrible nightmare. "I'll do no such thing. I won't leave you with that—that lecher."

Addie's eyes narrowed. "I've already told you, Bonnie, that I won't tolerate your talking like that about Nate. He's a good man. A good provider. At my age, I'm lucky he wanted to marry me, and I won't have you ruin it for me. I won't go back to the river and live in squalor, scrubbing other folks' laundry till my fingers bleed."

Slowly, painfully, it was dawning on Bonnie that her mother was so desperate to have a man take care of her that she was willing to turn from her only daughter. "You really mean it, don't you?" she asked in quiet horror. "You're willing to lose me in order to keep him."

For the briefest of seconds, Bonnie thought she saw her mother's expression pulled by regret, but then the cold mask of resolve took over once more. "If I can find a husband, so can you."

She turned to go, and Bonnie burst into tears and threw herself against her. As though she were once again a child seeking comfort from its mother, she sobbed, "Please, don't do this. You have to stand by me. I'm your daughter, and—"

Addie pushed her away but did so gently. "I'm sorry, but this is how it has to be."

Bonnie saw the tears trickling down her mother's face.

"I'm sorry," Addie said. "I truly am. But I do what I must . . . and so should you."

And then she ran from the room and down the hallway, running, Bonnie knew, towards the hell she had made of her life.

* * *

Bonnie was out on the street within a half hour. She did not have much to pack. Nate had bought her some nice dresses to wear working in the store, but she was not about to take them. All she carried with her was the other dress she possessed, cheap muslin like the one she was wearing, and a hopsacking nightgown.

Philadelphia was only starting to awaken, and there were few people out and about. With no other family, she had no idea where to go or what to do. She had no money, and already her stomach was growling from hunger.

Never had she known such despair.

Though the day was clear, there might as well have been a heavy, blinding fog, because Bonnie saw nothing but bleakness before her.

She bumped into someone and apologized, then glanced about to see where she was.

The poster, tacked to the side of a building, seemed to leap out at her.

It was a solicitation for single women to travel to Texas to marry and settle there. Travel expenses would be paid.

With each word she read, Bonnie felt excitement creeping to think of making a new life somewhere else . . . not that she had any intention of marrying a stranger. All she wanted was to get out of Philadelphia. She could worry later about how she would survive.

As for swindling the company, well, she would pay them back once she had a job. Then she wouldn't feel so guilty about what she was about to do.

Just then a man walked up and unlocked the door of the building next to her.

"Excuse me," she said and pointed to the address listed at the bottom of the poster. "Could you tell me where this would be?"

He smiled and tipped his hat. "Why, it's right here, little lady, and I'm the man you need to see."

Chapter Two

The journey west was long and arduous, the covered wagons trundling over roads thick with choking dust. The sun beat down mercilessly, and there was seldom even the merest whisper of a breeze.

But Bonnie did not complain as did so many of the hundred or so women on the wagon train with her, all heading for Texas to take a husband. Instead, she forced herself to look upon her present misery as nothing more than a brief inconvenience that she would soon forget in the joy of the new life awaiting her.

She was aware, however, that it might be a fool's dream. After all, when the wagon train reached their destination of Houston, Texas, she planned to sneak away. She would be no worse off than she'd been in Philadelphia, and she would find a way to survive, somehow. She was willing to do almost any kind of work but hoped to find a job singing. She had been told she had a fair voice, and she could play a guitar if she had one.

There were five other women in the wagon with her. Four of them whined constantly and fought among themselves. Bonnie distanced herself from them as best she could. So did Alice Brandine, who was talkative and outgoing and eager for company.

Alice knew a lot about Texas because her sister, Lorena, had been living there for two years. She had also gone west to take a husband and had written Alice that she was quite happy and urged her to join her.

"Texas is really growing," Alice told Bonnie, elaborating, "You see, all newcomers are given free land—over three hundred acres—and they can do what they want to with it. Lorena said in her last letter that she'd heard the population has trebled in the past ten years and the number of farmers alone has doubled."

Bonnie listened politely but was not really interested. After all, she only planned to stay in Texas until she could save enough money to move on to California. She had heard about the bustling city of San Francisco, with lots of music halls where she could surely find a job. She had heard that tickets to Lola Montez's concert there had sold at auction for up to sixty-five dollars, but even women of small talent could make a living on the stage.

Then one day, out of the blue, Alice bluntly asked, "What made you decide to come all the way to Texas to find a husband? Usually women do it because they're either too old or too homely to get one back home. Me, I'm fat, and I know it. But you're different. You're not so old, and you're pretty to boot. You could easily get a man on your own."

Bonnie had never thought much about whether

or not she was pretty. Not in the past few years, anyway. She'd never had time, because she'd had to work so hard. But she supposed, without too much conceit, that she was more comely than the other women on the wagon train. She had a nice, slender shape, not too tall, but neither could she be called short. She wasn't crazy about her hair—the color of strawberries—but her mother had told her men liked women with bright red hair. They also liked blue eyes, though she thought hers a bit too large, too bright.

Alice prodded, "So, why are you doing it?"

"I was bored." It was all she could think of to say and wondered how she could lie so glibly. Dodging the lecherous advances of her stepfather could hardly be considered a tedious pastime, but she was determined to put the bad memories behind her.

Alice hooted. "Well, you won't be bored out here. Especially if the man you're marrying has land on the plains. Lorena says there are Indians there, and they raid and steal the animals, burn houses, kill the men, and take the women and children to make slaves of them."

Bonnie shuddered to imagine such horror.

"I'll be living in town," Alice said, relieved. "The company agent told me my man is a blacksmith. His name is Seth Hollowell, and he's pretty old, but what the heck"—she shrugged—"I'm no spring chicken. I'll be nineteen my next birthday. What about you? What's your man do?"

"His name is Tom Parsons. I don't know anything else about him."

"They pay a lot for us, you know."

Bonnie didn't know, but Alice was only too eager to explain.

"Not only do they pay for our passage, but they

give what's called a premium to the company for signing us up."

Bonnie wondered if Tom Parsons would get his money back and hoped he did. After all, it wasn't his fault that she was going to run away and not keep the bargain she had made.

The day they rolled into Houston, Bonnie watched, awed, as crowds of men converged on the wagons before they even came to a stop. They called out their names loudly, so their brides could find them.

Bonnie cringed, waiting to hear the name of Tom Parsons. She did not want to face him, intending to disappear into the throngs as soon as she got off the wagon.

Alice was at the reins, and when she heard Seth Hollowell's name, she broke into tears of joy as she answered, "I'm here, Mr. Hollowell. It's me—Alice."

A tall man with shoulders like an ox, his face etched with the wrinkles of his years, pushed his way through to the wagon.

Bonnie hoped his disappointment would not show on his face when he realized that the woman who was to be his wife was almost bigger than he was. But all around, couples were getting acquainted, and from the sounds of it, they were all delighted with their intended spouses. The marriages were for convenience, after all, and they had no expectation of meeting the great love of their lives, anyway.

Seth Hollowell's face crinkled even more when he grinned at the sight of Alice. He reached right up and, trying not to buckle beneath her weight, lifted her down off the wagon and gave her a big hug and kiss.

"Welcome to Texas, little lady," he said when he finally let her go "You and me are gonna have a good life, I promise."

Bonnie slipped to the back of the wagon and dropped to the ground, heading into the crowd.

"Miss, wait up."

A hand clamped on her arm, and, with a jolt, Bonnie found herself staring up at a man wearing a tag identifying himself as Barton Willis, an agent for the company in charge.

"Who are you looking for?" he asked.

"No ... no one," she stammered, trying to pull away from him, but he held her tightly.

His eyes narrowed. "You just got out of that wagon. That means you came in on it. You aren't trying to renege on your contract, are you? Because if you are, you'll either pay back what it cost to bring you out here, or you'll go to jail."

Bonnie tried to think fast, tried not to let her nervousness show. "Uh, no. It's not like that at all."

He continued to hold her. "Then what's the name of your husband-to-be?"

She groaned under her breath. It was no use, and she should have known escape would not be easy. For the time being, she had to pretend to cooperate, but surely it would take time for weddings to be arranged.

"How many times have I got to ask you, Miss? What's the man's name?"

"Tom Parsons," she replied, then saw a strange look come over his face. "Is something wrong?"

"Yes, I'm afraid there is. Come with me." He began steering her away from the wagon.

Alice saw them and came running, leading Seth by the hand like a puppy. "Wait, Bonnie. I don't want us to lose touch with each other. Did you find out about your man—where you'll be living?"

Dully, Bonnie said, "No, but I'm about to."

Seth was all over himself with excitement and urged Alice to hurry. "The preacher is waiting. We're one of the first in line to get married."

Barton gave Bonnie's arm a tug. "Come along."

She tried to shake free of him and was annoyed that she couldn't. "At least tell my friend where she can find me before you drag me off."

Alice looked from Bonnie to the agent and frowned. "I don't understand. Everybody else has met her man. Where's hers? You're with the company. Just tell me where you're taking her."

He gave an airy sniff. "It's none of your concern, ma'am. Just go your way now."

Alice took a step closer, bumping him with her stomach and pushing him back a step. "I think you're gonna tell me now."

Barton paled, swallowed, then said, "Oh, very well. I wanted to tell her in private, because it's embarrassing, but you give me no choice." He turned to Bonnie. "Tom Parsons already has a wife."

Bonnie was washed with relief, because it meant she was free, but Alice exploded, "What a dirty, rotten thing for him to do—send for a wife when he had one. He oughta be horsewhipped."

Barton corrected, "No, no. It's not like that. He wasn't married when he ordered a wife. He took one while he was waiting, someone he met and fell in love with. It happens sometimes, even though women are scarce out here."

"So what do you intend to do about her being stranded now?" Alice demanded.

"There is a man in my office who didn't sign up

in time for this wagon load, and he's eager for a wife. He said he'd take her since she's left over. It really doesn't make any difference. She came out here to find a husband, and she'll have one."

Bonnie stiffened. Even though she'd never had any intention of marrying anybody, she did not like being considered part of a *wagon load*. Neither was she pleased at the thought of being a *leftover*.

"I need time to think about all this," she said quietly. Actually, she wanted time to figure out how to disappear.

Bernard brusquely informed her, "You have two choices—either marry the husband we are providing for you or go back where you came from. While it isn't company policy to pay return passage for someone who changes her mind, in this instance we will, due to the circumstances. It's up to you."

Seth motioned to Alice. "Honey, the preacher is waiting, and if we miss our turn, there's so many waiting in line behind us he might not get to us for days. We've got to go."

Alice argued, "But I want to know what's going to happen to my friend."

"Go ahead," Bonnie urged, then asked Seth, "Where's your blacksmith shop? When I know what I'm going to do, I'll come and see you."

"Down the street, two blocks on the left. My name's over the door."

Reluctantly, Alice allowed him to lead her away, but she called back to Bonnie, "Remember, you promised to find me. You're my only friend out here. . . ."

After they melted into the crowd, Barton seized Bonnie's arm once again. "Come on. You're getting married."

She pulled against him. "No, I'm not. I want to go home. Just give me the money for my passage." She knew she could live on that until she found work.

He shook his head. "It doesn't work that way. If you don't want to marry the man we're providing, then be ready to leave in the morning for the return trip. That's all we'll do for you."

"Then I'll stay here." Even if she wanted to go back—which she didn't—she had no intention of going on another wagon train.

With a sigh of disgust, he let her go. "Very well. You're on your own. The company is no longer responsible for you."

He walked away, leaving her standing in the middle of the street.

The crowd had broken up. Onlookers went back to whatever they had been doing. Happy couples rushed to get in line for their wedding ceremony.

She was all alone.

By the time darkness fell, Bonnie was exhausted.

With her tiny satchel in hand, she had gone door to door along the businesses on the main street. She asked for any kind of work—washing dishes, cooking, scrubbing floors.

Everyone had turned her away—except for the yellow-haired lady at the Wild Horse Saloon.

Hearing piano music, Bonnie peered over the wooden swinging doors. There weren't many people inside, but it was early. The nighttime revelers were not out yet.

She eased inside and walked over to the man playing the piano.

He looked her up and down. "You looking for somebody?"

She mustered her nerve to say, "I thought maybe you could use a singer. You play really well, by the way."

"Thanks, but I don't do the hiring. You'll have to see Goldie over there." He nodded in the direction of the bar.

Goldie was wearing a purple satin gown, her huge breasts threatening to spill from the deeply plunging bodice. Her eyelids were colored a shimmering green, her cheeks smeared with orange rouge, and her lips painted a bright red.

But it was her hair Bonnie found most fascinating. It was the brightest yellow she had ever seen. Drawn back from her face, long, curled ringlets trailed down her back.

"Excuse me . . ." Bonnie tapped her on her arm to get her attention. She was facing the bar and sipping on a foaming glass of beer.

She turned. "Yeah, what do you want?"

"Are you the owner?"

She sneered. "I run the place. The bank owns it. The name's Goldie. Who the hell are you?"

"Bonnie . . . Bonnie Craven. From Philadelphia."

Goldie exchanged an amused glance with the bartender, who was watching as he polished glasses with a white cloth. "Well, Bonnie Craven from Philadelphia, what can I do for you?"

"I'm looking for a job."

"*Here?*" Goldie's incredibly long eyelashes dusted her cheeks as she blinked in surprise. "You want to be one of my girls? You ever done this kind of work before?"

"I've never sung professionally, but back home I

did sing in church a few times, and everyone said I had a nice voice, and—"

Goldie cut her off. "We can talk about that later. I've got something else in mind for now. I need another girl to work the bar. Do you want the job?"

"I certainly do, but you already have someone to make drinks, don't you?" She nodded to the bartender.

"Yeah, but you wouldn't be making drinks. You'd be selling them."

Bonnie shook her head. "I don't understand."

"Don't worry about it. I'll tell you everything you need to know. With a face and figure like yours, the men will flock around you like bees to honey. Wait here while I go in the back and see if I can find you a gown that will fit."

She walked away, and for an instant, Bonnie was tempted to leave but decided to see it through. After all, she was desperate.

A man pushed through the swinging doors and walked up to the bar. He was tall and well-built, his shirt strained across his broad chest. Rolled-up sleeves revealed deeply tanned and muscular arms. His thick, dark hair brushed his collar, and when he glanced at her she noted a sadness in his brooding gray eyes.

She decided he was handsome in a rugged kind of way, then chided herself for paying him any mind at all. She was so hungry, she was dizzy and she needed to concentrate on finding work instead of staring at men, for heaven's sake.

"Sam, give me a whiskey," he said, slapping some coins on the bar. "Make it a double."

"That bad, huh?" Sam asked with a grin. "What's wrong? You aren't having second thoughts about all them longhorns you bought, are you? I told you to stick with cotton."

"Cotton means having slaves or hiring workers. I don't believe in one and can't afford the other."

Sam set his drink down. "You can't exactly raise cattle by yourself, either."

"Well, I'm doing all right for now."

Sam swept the coins from the bar and into his hand. "Then how come you're drinking double?"

"Could be I'm in a hurry to get back to my boy."

Bonnie wondered why he suddenly sounded so angry, but then Goldie returned, and she forgot all about the stranger.

She held up a green velvet gown, trimmed in feathers. "I think this might do just fine. It'll be pretty with your red hair. Go try it on."

For some reason she could not understand, Bonnie felt her gaze pulled to the stranger. He was staring at her with—what? Amusement? Disgust? She could not tell and there was no time to study his expression because he tossed down his drink and abruptly walked out.

Goldie prodded, "Well, are you gonna put this on or not? You'll have plenty of time later to gawk at men, though I can't say as I blame you for taking a fancy to that one right off. He's a cut above the ones you'll be cozying up to, but he don't come in much, and when he does, he don't want any part of my girls. A real woman-hater, he is."

Sam cut in. "Aw, go easy on him, Goldie. He's got reason to be sour after what his wife did. And Lord knows, he can't get nobody to keep that bratty kid of his."

"I don't care about that, Sam." Goldie pushed the gown at Bonnie. "Hurry up now. We'll need time to fix your face and hair before things get busy. I'll have one of the other gals show you the ropes, but all you've got to do is get men to buy you drinks to keep them drinking. Sam will water yours down, so you won't get tipsy. As for the ones who want to take you to bed, you send them to me, and I'll collect the money and tell you which room upstairs to take 'em to, and—''

Bonnie shoved the gown into her arms. "I'm not interested."

"What? Hey, come back here."

Bonnie was almost to the door.

"You think you're too good to be one of my girls?" Goldie shouted after her. "Well, you can just starve, 'cause you're not gonna find any other kind of work around here."

Bonnie paused just long enough to tell her, "That's exactly what I'd rather do—starve."

And she pushed through the doors and out into the gathering dusk of the hot Texas night.

Chapter Three

"Good Lord, honey, what are you doing here?"

Bonnie slowly opened her eyes to see Alice towering over her.

Alice called to Seth, "Get out here. It's Bonnie. I found her behind the water barrel." She leaned to place her hand on Bonnie's forehead. "Are you sick? Are you hurt anywhere?"

"No, just stiff and sore all over from sleeping on the ground." She managed to stand, her knees wobbling.

"Well, why on earth did you sleep *here*? What happened after I left you yesterday?"

Bonnie gave her head a dismal shake. "I couldn't go through with it, Alice. I couldn't marry a stranger. Some women can do it—like you—and it works out fine, but I can't."

"But that's why you came out here."

"No, it wasn't. The fact is, I had some bad problems at home, and with nowhere else to go, I figured the west was as good a place as any to make a new life. But I never intended to get married."

Alice moaned, "Oh, dear me. Then what were you going to do?"

"Get a job. Only I found out there's none to be had—unless I want to go to work in a saloon enticing men to buy drinks . . . and more . . . which I don't."

Alice put a comforting arm around her shoulders and began guiding her toward the back entrance to the blacksmith shop. "Of course, you don't, and everything will be all right. Seth will know what to do. He's a fine man, and we're going to be real happy. I can already tell. So you see? These kinds of marriages can work out. Maybe you'd better think about it some more."

"No. I'll find work." Bonnie knew she didn't sound convincing, even to herself.

Seth appeared, bare chest gleaming with sweat from the smithing fire. "Goodness, little lady, what are you doing here?"

"Things got rowdy on the streets last night, and I knew I had to find a spot where I wouldn't be seen. I figured you two would show up sometime this morning."

"Well, we live upstairs," Alice said. "You should've hollered or knocked and let us know you were down here."

Bonnie laughed. "On your wedding night? I'd have to be pretty desperate to do that."

"Fix her up with some breakfast," Seth told Alice as he went back to his shop. "I'll be up when I get the fire going good."

"Thank goodness I went to fetch water for coffee," Alice remarked as she led the way up the steps. "Otherwise, the marshal or one of his deputies might've found you and hauled you to jail for vagrancy. Now let's get some food in you and then we'll have ourselves a talk."

Alice got busy in the tiny kitchen making coffee and scrambling eggs.

Bonnie saw that there were only two rooms, both in need of a woman's touch.

Happily, Alice said, "Seth says he'll take me to visit my sister as soon as he gets caught up on all his work. I can't wait. It's been so long since I've seen her."

"That's wonderful. He seems like a very nice man."

"He is, believe me. I wish you had a husband just like him."

Bonnie didn't say anything, the delicious smell of frying bacon making her feel faint with hunger.

When Alice at last set a heaping plate in front of her, Bonnie's hands were shaking with anticipation. But hard as it was, she politely waited for Seth to sit down and say grace.

Alice told him Bonnie had decided she did not want to get married, after all.

"Then what's she going to do?" he asked as though Bonnie weren't even there.

"Stay in Texas."

He looked at Bonnie then. "And do what?"

Bonnie shrugged as though it were nothing, even though she was terribly worried. "Try to find work. I haven't had any luck so far."

"Why don't you just go back home?"

Alice answered for her. "She doesn't want to, Seth. She had some problems at home, and that's why she left."

He spoke around a mouthful of eggs. "Seems to me, you've got two choices, little lady—let the company find you a husband to take care of you or hightail it back east. There's just not much work for women in these parts, and a woman alone won't survive."

"*I* will," Bonnie declared fiercely, almost angrily.

He sighed and shook his head. "Well, I wish you all the best. And I'd like to help, but you can see we don't have much room here."

"Even if you did, I wouldn't impose," Bonnie was quick to say. "And after I've eaten, I'll be on my way."

Alice reached across the table to squeeze Seth's arm. "You can help her with some money, can't you?"

Bonnie protested, "No, I couldn't do that."

"I ain't got none to give you, anyway," he said with candor. "I spent everything I had to get Alice out here."

"Well, we can feed her—"

"No," Bonnie said with a firm shake of her head. "I'll find a way to look after myself. I'm not your responsibility. You've given me a nice meal, and I'm grateful. I don't expect more than that."

Seth shook his fork at her. "Now you listen to me. I might not be able to help you with money, but as long as me and Alice got food on the table, you won't starve, and"—he stopped waving the fork, eyes going wide—"hey, I think I know where you can find work."

Bonnie and Alice stared at him.

"Zach Pressley needs somebody to look after his boy while he's working his farm. The boy's a handful since his momma left, I hear, and Zach worries about him getting hurt. He left him with Preacher Henry's wife for a spell, but she got tired of him. Zach was in here just the other day saying he didn't know what he was going to do, that nobody could handle the boy, and it was keeping him from tending the cattle he's trying to raise."

Alice nudged Bonnie excitedly. "That sounds perfect for you." She asked Seth, "Where does he live? Is it far out of town?"

"Oh, maybe an hour's ride. Zach settled here right before the government reduced the land grants in '44. He got the twelve hundred and eighty acres families were being given back then, which is around two square miles."

"Can you take her to see him?"

"No, but she can borrow my mule and wagon, and I'll point her in the right direction."

"I'll go with her."

Seth looked at her with warm, shining eyes. "I'd rather you didn't. I want you with me, honey."

Bonnie squirmed uncomfortably in her chair, feeling like an intruder on a very private moment.

Alice, beaming at Seth, asked Bonnie how she felt about going alone, then remembered she'd not said she was even interested. "Maybe you don't want that kind of work."

Actually, she didn't, but if it meant food in her belly, a roof over her head, and the chance to save some money to move on, she was willing.

"You'll be living alone with a man in his house," Alice pointed out, frowning.

"He built himself a cabin," Seth interjected. "I rode out there once to show him how to shod his horses himself, back when he was just a greenhorn, and—"

"Greenhorn? What's that?" Bonnie asked.

"That's what you call somebody new, somebody that don't know beans about what he's doing. It's different now, though. Seth knows everything he needs to. He's smart and hardworking. You can tell by the cabin he built. He made the shingles himself, and instead of weighting them down with stones and poles like most do, he nailed every one of them in place. It's got three rooms, too. It was Seth's intent to have a big family. So you'd have a room of your own."

Alice grinned. "It sounds like the perfect solution for you, Bonnie."

"Oh, it would be," Seth agreed. "Zach's a fine man. Very polite. He come out here from New York, determined to make a new life. Only his wife couldn't take it."

"She died?" Alice asked, eyes going wide with sympathy.

"Nope. She left him."

Sympathy turned to anger. "And the boy, too?"

"Yep. The way I heard it, Zach told her if she was hell-bent on leaving, he wouldn't try to stop her, but he'd be damned if she was taking his boy. So she took off back east with another man, and so far as I know, Zach never heard from her again."

"How long ago was that?" Alice asked.

Seth thought a minute. "I don't know exactly. Over a year, anyway, I'd say."

Alice gasped. "That long? Well, why hasn't he signed up to get himself a new wife? Seems to me he'd be first in line, with a youngun to raise."

"I asked him the same thing, and he said he never wanted to get married again. He's real sour on women."

Bonnie wondered if the man they were talking about was the same one she'd seen in the saloon the day before but didn't ask. After all, she would find out soon enough.

She asked Seth if he had time to hitch up the mule and wagon. "I'd like to ride out there right away and see if I can get your friend to hire me."

"Oh, I'm sure he will," Seth grinned. "After all, he's desperate—and so are you."

Bonnie had learned to handle a team of horses by taking her turn at the reins on the way west. She had thought a single mule would be simple by comparison.

How wrong she was.

Blackjack, the lumbering mule, set his own pace and could not be hurried. As a result, the ride that Seth had predicted would take an hour, more or less, had turned out to be more.

She was wearing the same muslin dress she'd had on the day before, because there had not been an opportunity to launder her other one. Every stitch was soaked. Her hair hung limp about her perspiration-slick face. She knew she looked a sight but supposed it didn't matter. After all, if Zach Pressley was as anxious to hire someone to tend his unruly son as Seth said he was, it would make no difference what she looked like.

Now and then, she would pass a cabin but saw no sign of life other than a few chickens pecking at the ground. Everyone was probably out working their crops.

It was lonely, and for the most part desolate, but Bonnie found herself reveling in the beauty of such tranquility.

She also thought about Zach Pressley, wondering what kind of man he was. She hoped he'd be kind and tolerant.

She also hoped she could bluff him into hiring her by making him think she could cope with his son. Being an only child, she had never been around many

children and had no idea what she should do. But
she supposed she would learn quickly. Besides, how
hard could it be? The boy might be six years old, but
he was, after all, still just a child.

Seth had given her a canteen of water, and it was
empty by the time she reached the sign he said she
should watch for. NEW HOPE, the carved letters proclaimed, perched on a post stuck in the ground. An
arrow pointed to a trail leading behind a thick grove
of hardwoods.

The mule did not want to turn in, but after jerking
and tugging the reins, accompanied by a few words
she seldom used, he was finally persuaded.

Bonnie tried not to think about what to do if no
one was home. If Mr. Pressley had taken his boy and
gone out somewhere on his lands, she'd never find
them. Two square miles, Seth said he had, certainly
too large for her to go out looking for him. So if he
weren't around, she would wait as long as possible
and then return to town and try again tomorrow.

Finally, rounding another stand of trees and cross-
ing a rough-hewn bridge over a stream, she reached
the cabin.

Like the other places she'd passed, chickens
clucked about, and there were a few sheep grazing
and some ducks waddling around at the water's edge.

"Hello," she called. "Is anybody home? I'm looking for Mr. Pressley."

Standing up in the wagon, she shaded her eyes
with her hand against the sun and looked all around
but could not see anyone.

With a disappointed groan, she got down from the
wagon and went to sit in the shade of the front porch.

Suddenly a movement at the window to her left

caught her eye, and she whipped about. "Who's there?"

Hearing quick, shuffling footsteps inside, she went to the door and knocked. "I know you're in there, and I've come a long way. Please answer me. I have to talk to Mr. Pressley."

Suddenly the door flew open, and she found herself staring down into the angry, belligerent eyes of a little boy.

"He ain't here. Now git."

He started to close the door, but she stuck out her foot. "Wait a minute. You've no cause to be rude. Besides, I'm thirsty and my canteen is empty."

"Get some water from the well and then git."

He shoved at the door with all his might, but Bonnie kept her foot wedged tightly in the crack.

"You'd better leave," he warned. "I got a gun in here."

Bonnie met his angry glare with one of her own. "If that were so, as unfriendly as you are, you'd have already shot me. Now where's your pa?"

"None of your business. Now git," he repeated.

"I'm not leaving till I see him."

"He's never coming back."

"Nonsense." She gave the door a mighty push, and the boy stumbled backward. "Why are you being so mean to me? I'm not going to hurt you."

"You got no right to be here. We don't need you. My pa and me don't need nobody."

"Don't be silly. Everybody needs somebody."

She glanced around the room. It was sparsely furnished but neat. There was a table with benches on two sides. Carved rockers sat in front of a stone fireplace. She assumed the closed doors on either side went to bedrooms.

The boy backed away from her, fists doubled. "You can't come in here like this. My pa is gonna be plenty mad."

"Then I'll wait on the porch." She stepped outside.

He ran behind her. "Won't do you no good. He won't talk to you."

With a sigh, Bonnie sat down on the top step. The boy was a handful, all right, but despite his ornery nature, he was cute, though a bit unkempt. He had pretty brown eyes and a sprinkling of freckles on the tip of his nose, but his sandy blond hair, which hung to his shoulders, was terribly shaggy. His overalls were worn through at the knees, and there were buttons missing on his shirt.

He made a face at her, then asked, "Why are you staring at me?"

"Oh, I was just thinking how I'd like to mend your overalls, cut your hair, and clean you up a bit. I'd also like to fix you a good hot meal."

He sneered. "You ain't my ma. You ain't gonna touch me."

"You shouldn't say *ain't*."

"I'll say any damn thing I want to."

Bonnie's brows lifted. "And you certainly shouldn't cuss."

"You can't tell me what to do."

Bonnie ground her teeth together. She was getting nowhere fast. The boy hated her on sight and would have a tantrum if his father hired her. She had wasted her time.

She stood. "All right. I'll leave. But tell your pa if he wants to hire me to look after you, he should let Mr. Hollowell, the blacksmith, know."

Things were looking real desperate, she thought

as she went to the well to draw a bucket of water and fill her canteen for the trip back to town.

"Hurry up and go—now," the boy suddenly hollered around the corner of the cabin. "Git right now."

"Not till I have my water," she said, annoyed. Who did he think he was, anyway, talking to her that way? What he needed was a good spanking. His father was undoubtedly spoiling him, and that was why he was such a handful—and why no one wanted the responsibility of looking after him.

"You better—"

"Luke, who are you talking to?"

Bonnie heard a man's voice and wheeled about. She had been in the process of hauling up the bucket, but, startled, dropped the rope.

Frantically, she quickly leaned over the side of the well and tried to grab it, but it was too late.

The bucket hit the water with a loud splat, the rope trailing after it.

She heard the boy say, "It's a woman, come to steal our water, Pa. I tried to run her off, but she wouldn't go. I told her I'd shoot her, and—"

The man's voice fired back, "You don't talk to people like that, especially women."

Embarrassed by what she had done, Bonnie stared dismally into the black pit that was the well. Thanks to her, the bucket was lost.

"Ma'am, I'm sorry if my boy was rude," the man said as he quickly walked towards her. "My name is Zach Pressley, and you're certainly welcome to all the water you want."

"I dropped the bucket," she said dully.

"Well, I've got another."

"I'm sorry."

"It's all right. What brings you out here, anyway?"

She continued looking down the well. "Seth Hollowell told me you needed someone to take care of your son while you work, but I'm afraid he hated me on sight."

His laugh was bitter. "Don't feel bad. He hates just about everybody on sight."

"Well, I'd be willing to try to look after him. I need work bad, and maybe a place to live even more. My name is Bonnie Craven. I'm pleased to meet you."

Pasting on a smile, she turned—then froze as his face suddenly twisted into a sneer of disgust.

"You!" He spat the word.

"I . . . I beg your pardon?"

And then it dawned.

He *was* the ruggedly handsome man she'd seen the night before at the Wild Horse Saloon. But why was he looking at her as if she was dirt?

"Surely you didn't think I'd hire your kind. What's the matter, didn't you have enough experience to be one of Goldie's girls?"

"One of—" Her eyes went wide as realization dawned. "You think I'm a—a *prostitute*?"

"You were about to try on one of her dresses when I saw you."

Indignant, Bonnie snapped, "And I gave it back to her when I realized what she wanted me to do."

He shrugged. "Well, it doesn't matter. I don't want you here. I'll get another bucket and draw you some water, and then I'll thank you to leave."

He left and returned with the bucket. When her canteen was filled, he walked her to the wagon and offered to help her up.

She waved him away. "I can take care of myself."

Settling in the seat, she took the reins but paused

to try one more time. "Mr. Pressley, I wish you'd give me a chance. I really do need a job, and—"

He cut her off. "It wouldn't work. I'm sorry."

He turned and walked away.

Rejection and disappointment getting the best of her, Bonnie could not resist calling after him, "Well, maybe it's just as well, because it appears to me you're just as rude as your son. Maybe he's not the only one who needs discipline around here."

With a snap of the reins, she set the mule lumbering forward.

She did not look back, did not see how Zach Pressley was staring after her, a thoughtful, bemused expression on his face.

Chapter Four

Zach stood on the front porch, sipping coffee as he watched the sun rise.

It was going to be another hot, dry day, and he needed to get started on his chores while there was still a breath of cool morning air. Yet he continued to brood about the girl, haunted by the hurt, desolate look in her eyes as she turned away.

He knew he had been rude and felt bad about it. After all, she had come a long way to ask him for work.

And something told him she was telling the truth about walking out on Goldie once she found out the kind of job the saloonkeeper had in mind for her.

She was also pretty, and that had set his teeth on edge. Pretty women were trouble, because sometimes they got bored with living in the wild and woolly west and returned to civilization—with another man.

Like Amelia.

What a beauty she had been. Hair soft and golden like corn silk, eyes the color of Bluebonnets, and a smile that had once melted his heart.

But he should have known better than to bring her west. Her wealthy parents said she was used to a pampered life of luxury and predicted that she would never be happy.

They turned out to be right sooner than expected, because halfway to Texas Amelia had wanted to turn back. The only thing that had kept her from it was realizing she was in the family way.

She had been angry and cried that had she known she would never have left home.

From then on, their marriage had been just one miserable day after another. Nothing he did pleased her, and all she talked about was going home to her parents.

He had hoped she would change once the baby was born. Working harder than he ever had in his whole life, Zach built the nicest, best cabin he could.

Nestled near the stream, it was a beautiful place to raise a family, and he harbored dreams of a happy future for them both.

But it had not turned out that way.

After Luke was born, Amelia was even harder to get along with, complaining that his crying got on her nerves. She would whine about how she was having to tend to a baby in the middle of nowhere when she could be back home going to parties and dances and teas.

Zach couldn't think of anything he might have done differently to satisfy her. He supposed it just took a special kind of woman to accept his kind of life.

By the time Amelia finally left, there was no love

between them. If not for Luke, he wouldn't have cared, but the boy loved his mother and cried himself to sleep every night for weeks after she took off. Oh, she'd made noises about taking him with her. Zach had refused, saying if she wanted to go, he wouldn't stop her, but she would never take his son. And they both knew she didn't really want him.

So now it was just the two of them and had been for over a year. The only thing was, Luke could be a holy terror, disobedient and given to tantrums. Zach did the best he could, hoping he would outgrow it. Meanwhile, none of the women he knew in town wanted to look after him, and it was almost dangerous to leave him alone because he got into so much trouble.

When he was older, Zach intended to keep him busy doing chores, but there was only so much a six-year-old could do.

He turned to go back inside, and that was when he realized Luke was standing in the doorway.

"Aren't you gonna go work with the cows today?"

Zach corrected him. "Steers, Luke. They're called longhorn steers. If you're going to be a rancher, you'd better learn the difference, or folks will laugh at you."

"I don't care. I'm not gonna be no rancher, anyway. My momma is gonna come get me and take me to live with her. She told me so."

Zach's heart went out to him. "That might not happen, Luke. It's been a long time."

"She told me she would," he said stubbornly, petulantly. "That's why there can't be nobody but you and me, 'cause if she comes back and finds out you got me a new momma, she'll be mad and leave again."

Zach sighed wearily and held Luke away from him so he could look him in the eye. "Is that why you misbehave when I leave you with anybody? Because you're afraid your mother will be mad if she finds out?"

Luke nodded vigorously. "Uh-huh. Just like yesterday. That woman who dropped the bucket in the well, she wanted to be my momma."

"What makes you think that?"

" 'Cause she said she wanted to fix my overalls and cut my hair and cook for me and make me take a bath. That's what Momma used to do."

"Well, just because a woman takes care of you doesn't mean she wants to be your mother."

As Zach straightened and ruffled Luke's hair, he realized that it really did need cutting. He noticed the worn knees of his overalls, too, but damn it, there just weren't enough hours in the day to do all the chores and still have time to care for the boy the way he should.

Like it or not, he was going to have to find someone to help out. If he had parents, he might be tempted to send Luke to them, but he was all alone in the world.

Maybe, he dared to think, he should not have been so quick to run the girl off.

Bonnie had not had the nerve to tell Seth and Alice how her visit with Zach Pressley had turned out. She could tell they thought she was being stubborn not to marry the man the agent had found for her. But she was determined to find some other way to survive.

Leaving the wagon and mule behind the blacksmith shop, she had wandered around town until it got dark. Then she returned to the alley behind Seth's to once again bed down behind the rain barrel. At least there she felt safe from all the revelry and gunfire that went on during the night.

Her stomach rumbled with hunger. It was becoming a familiar feeling. She had not eaten since breakfast the day before and was starting to feel weak.

She got up and went to the barrel and splashed water on her face. Then she ran her fingers through her hair, trying to smooth it a little. Nothing would make her dress look presentable. It was wrinkled and soiled and looked terrible. But she'd still had neither time nor opportunity to wash her other one.

The sun was high in the sky. She was surprised to have slept so long, but the noise had kept her awake after all until the wee hours . . . along with thoughts of Zach Pressley.

She felt sorry for him and couldn't understand why. Actually she should have been angry for the way he acted. But she had seen such misery and despair mirrored on his face that she could not feel anything other than pity.

She also thought about the little boy. His clothes might need mending, and his hair could use a trim, but despite all that, there was something he needed much, much more.

He needed a hug.

Maybe then some of the anger and bitterness would leave him.

However, her smile as she thought about it was rueful. From the impression she got, he would probably double up his little fists and try to pound anybody who tried to lay hands on him.

And that was even sadder than his father's face.

Leaving the alley, she walked to the main street. A man was sweeping the boardwalk in front of his store, and she approached him.

"For an apple, I'll do that for you," she said, pointing to a bucket of bright red fruit sitting next to the door.

"You would?" he asked, surprised. "You must be real hungry, little lady."

"I am, and I also need a job. I'd work for my food, and—"

"Herman, who are you talking to?" A woman with a face that seemed perpetually frozen in an expression of disapproval appeared in the doorway. Seeing Bonnie, she snapped, "Who are you?"

Bonnie politely introduced herself, then explained, "As I was saying to your husband, I'm willing to work in exchange for something to eat."

"Oh, you're nothing but a beggar." The woman scowled. "Work for food, indeed. Decent women don't have to. How come you don't have a husband? It's easy enough to find one in these parts. Wagonloads of women arrived yesterday, and I hear tell there weren't enough to go around."

Bonnie did not care to discuss it. "Well, if you don't need me, I'll be on my way. Sorry I bothered you."

With an angry glance at his wife, the storekeeper handed Bonnie an apple. "Sorry, little lady. If I could, I'd hire you, but there's not enough work around here."

She accepted the apple eagerly and thanked him. His wife gave an airy sniff and went back inside.

As Bonnie started to walk away, he called softly, "I might know where you can find some work. Dan Foley's dishwasher got himself killed last night. He got drunk and run his mouth to the wrong person."

Bonnie cringed to think she'd be taking the place

of a dead man, but desperation needled. "Where would I find this Mr. Foley?"

"His place is next door to the Wild Horse. You know where that is? Everybody does. It's about the rowdiest place in town, but Dan's is smaller and quieter. He serves up more food than he does liquor. I think you'd like working for him."

Happily, she tossed the apple into the air, caught it, and grinned to say, "I think I would, too, sir, and I thank you for telling me about it."

She nibbled on the apple as she walked along, wanting to make it last as long as possible.

All was quiet. Few people were out and about at such an hour. She only hoped she could find Dan Foley before he hired someone else. He might even have a room she could rent, and wouldn't that be wonderful.

Her hopes were building to the sky but were quickly dashed when she reached Mr. Foley's place to find it was closed. She looked in the window but didn't see anyone.

She jumped at the sound of a woman's voice. "He's gone to see about the burying."

Bonnie frowned when she saw it was Goldie. She was leaning in the doorway of her saloon, a glass of whiskey in one hand as she brazenly puffed on a cheroot.

"You're the little twit who thought you were too good to work at my place, aren't you?"

"I couldn't do what you wanted," Bonnie said quietly.

"Did you ever find a job?"

"As a matter of fact, I haven't."

"So you're wandering around town looking for

anything, right? But you still think my place ain't good enough for you."

Politely, Bonnie responded, "That had nothing to do with it. It's like I told you—I wasn't looking for the kind of work you were offering."

"So you've gone to begging for food." Goldie nodded to the half-eaten apple in her hand.

Coolly, Bonnie said, "It was given to me. I offered to work for it."

Goldie snickered. "So now you've come to see Dan, hoping to get Reuben's job before he's even cold in the ground. Why, besides being a snob, you're a ghoul."

Bonnie turned on her heel. "I'll come back later."

"Oh, wait a minute. I was only joking. And listen, Dan told me if anybody came by wanting Reuben's job to tell them the key was under that flowerpot you see there, and to use it and go inside and have some pie and coffee while they're waiting. Coffee's probably cold by now, but you'll like the pie. Dan's a good cook."

Bonnie was too hungry to turn down the offer of food. "Thanks for telling me."

She got the key and opened the door.

The saloon was small, with only a few tables. A counter ran along one wall, where food was served up, as well as whiskey.

She found the coffee pot, but it was empty. She did not see any pie, either. In fact, there was no food anywhere.

There was a room at the rear. She decided that Mr. Foley might have left food there but found it was only a storage room and an office. Shelves loaded with canned goods lined the walls, and there was a small desk and safe in a corner.

Suddenly a voice boomed, "Just put your hands over your head, and you won't get hurt."

Whirling around, Bonnie saw the man who had managed to creep quietly up behind her. He held a gun, pointed right at her.

He also wore a badge.

"I said, put up your hands."

She did so and tried to explain. "I didn't break in here, sir, and I didn't come to take anything. I'm waiting to see Mr. Foley about a job, and Goldie— the woman who owns the saloon next door—told me where the key was, and—"

Goldie suddenly stepped into view. "Hey, don't you tell lies on me. I saw you nosing around over here, but you didn't see me. You were trying to find a way in, and then you found the key. That's when I sent for the law. You're trying to rob Dan."

Bonnie's mouth gaped open, and she stammered, "But—but that's not true, and you know it. You told me where the key was. And you told me Mr. Foley said anybody looking for the job should come inside for pie and coffee and wait for him."

Goldie asked the deputy with a grin, "Now when have you ever known Dan to give anything away for free?"

The deputy shook his head and laughed. "Never." He nudged Bonnie with the gun. "You're going to jail."

"But you have to believe me," she argued, not budging. "I'd never rob anybody."

"Then what were you doing all the way back here in Dan's office, where his safe is?"

She glared at Goldie. "I was looking for the food she said Dan had waiting. I'm hungry. I have no money. No home. But I'd never rob anybody. All I want is a job."

"Which was offered to you," Goldie sneered. "But you think you're too good to work in a saloon."

"And that's why you did this, isn't it? To get even," Bonnie said.

Goldie snorted and frowned at the deputy. "I thought you were going to lock her up."

"I sure as hell am." He gave Bonnie a hard shove that sent her stumbling forward. "I'm gonna see to it you get something to eat, and a home to boot—behind bars."

A crowd had gathered in the street, and Bonnie hung her head, embarrassed to look at anyone, afraid she might see Alice or Seth.

Goldie had tricked her and now she was going to jail, and there was nothing she could do about it, because no one would believe her.

When the marshal heard her story, however, he allowed that it might have happened just as she said. He knew Goldie and how vindictive she could be when she was riled.

"Does that mean I can go?" Bonnie asked, hope rising.

"Not unless you've got somebody who can vouch for you being so hungry you'd be desperate enough to believe such a wild tale about Dan Foley." He snorted. "Pie and coffee, indeed."

Tired of being treated like a criminal, Bonnie snapped, "Well, I can prove I'm hungry. Just set some food in front of me, and I'll show you how fast I can eat it." She stamped a foot in exasperation.

He scratched his chin and shook his head. "That won't prove nothing. What I need is for somebody to sorta say they'll be responsible for you if I turn you loose. I can't have you going around hungry and homeless. You'll just wind up in trouble again."

Bonnie thought of Alice. She hated to involve her but saw no other way. "Well, there is someone—"

Suddenly, a man called out from the door to the marshal's office. "I can vouch for her. She's just hungry and desperate, that's all."

Whirling about, the marshal demanded, "Who the hell are you and how come you know so much about her?"

Bonnie could not see the man's face but was jolted when she heard his next words.

"The name's Zach Pressley, and I know she's been looking for work, because she came to me and asked for a job . . . which she can have if she still wants it."

Chapter Five

"Did you mean what you said?" Bonnie asked Zach as soon as they left the marshal's office. "Are you willing to hire me?"

"You've met my son," he said pointedly.

"Yes, and I don't think he likes me, but—"

"He doesn't like any woman. He thinks his mother is going to come back for him one day, and if she finds someone else taking care of him, she'll be mad and leave again and not take him."

"Would she do that?"

"No, because I doubt she'll ever return. But Luke refuses to believe that. It ripped him apart when she left, and he hasn't got over it. Maybe he never will. That's why I spoil him, I guess, because he's had a rough time of it."

He started walking down the street.

Bonnie fell into step beside him. "I'm sure it has

to be hard on him." She could empathize because, in a way, she'd been abandoned by her mother, too.

"So what about the other women who went to live with you? Did they just give up and quit?"

He cut her a sharp glance. "You're the first. I've paid women in town to keep him at their homes, but they couldn't handle him. I don't think you can, either, but maybe you'll try harder since it's keeping you out of jail."

She was taken aback by his curtness, and it showed.

At once he was contrite. "Sorry. I didn't mean to be so blunt."

"It's all right, and I am grateful you got me out of jail. But tell me—how come you showed up there, anyway? I don't think it was by accident."

"What makes you say that?"

"Because, in your own way, I think you're as desperate as I am, Mr. Pressley."

Their eyes met and held, and then Zach grinned and said, "Maybe you will succeed where others have failed, Miss Craven. You've got spunk. And I don't think the others really tried, anyway, because they didn't care about Luke. Maybe you will. I sense a caring way about you, despite how tough and hard you try to act."

"It would make anybody hard to go through what I have."

"Then maybe you'd better tell me about it. After all, I've got a right to know about the person who's going to be taking care of my son."

Not about to share the whole story, Bonnie offered a partial truth. "I signed up to come west to take a husband, only when I arrived, I was told he had married someone else."

"I'm sorry."

"I'm not. I didn't want to marry a stranger, anyway, so it didn't bother me at all. The company agent found somebody else for me, but I refused."

He looked at her curiously. "Why did you want to come all the way out here if you knew you'd be on your own? Didn't you think there was a chance you'd find yourself destitute?"

"No," she replied with all candor. "I was determined to find a job and take care of myself. Which it seems I have," she added with a confident smile.

"I'm surprised the company would leave you stranded."

"They offered to send me back east. I didn't want to go."

He pressed on. "Why not? Seems to me that would've been the thing for you to do."

She gave her head a vigorous shake. "I didn't want to go back. There's nothing for me there. The west is my home now. I'll never leave."

"Glad to hear it." He sounded pleased. "Maybe we've both found the answer to our problems."

"Maybe," she said. Then, feeling stranger the more he stared at her, she abruptly turned to business. "I think we should discuss exactly what you expect of me, Mr. Pressley, what my duties will be, and what kind of living arrangements I will have."

He honed in on her latter concern. "You'll have a separate room, of course. I'll move Luke in with me."

"I don't think our living together under the same roof would be proper."

His eyes went wide. "You mean you want me to sleep in the barn?"

"No. After all, it's your cabin. *I* will sleep in the barn."

He stared at her, incredulous. "Wait a minute. I can't let you do that."

"It would be an impropriety otherwise."

He threw up his hands. "Who cares? This is the west. We don't worry about things like that. We can't. We're too busy trying to survive."

"And survive we will," she said primly, lifting her chin. "With you and your son in the cabin, and me in the barn. I'm sure I can find a corner where I'll be comfortable."

"But—"

She cut him off. The sleeping arrangements had been settled. "You still haven't told me exactly what my duties will be."

"All you've got to do is take care of Luke and try to keep him out of trouble."

That, she knew, would be a formidable task.

"I've got my herd of longhorns to look after. Sometimes it keeps me away all day. I can't afford to hire wranglers yet, and Luke's too young to go out on the range with me."

"And my compensation?" She averted her gaze, pretending to be interested in a window displaying ladies' hats. Anything to keep from looking at him. His shirt was unbuttoned to the waist, and the slight view of his bare chest made her feel all warm and tingly.

"You'll get room and board, of course, and then five dollars a month. I think I can afford that."

She was careful not to let her excitement show. The money was more than she had dared hope for. In no time at all, she should have enough to get her to California—if she could last that long.

Because not only would she be challenged by Luke's behavioral problems.

She would also have to deal with the realization of how fast she was becoming drawn to his father.

"He gave you a pretty rough time when you were out here, didn't he?" Zach remarked as they turned from the main road to the path leading to his cabin.

"Well, he made it plain he didn't want me around."

They rode double. She sat in front of him and wished they would hurry and get there, because the delicious feel of his thighs pressed against her was almost unbearable.

"Have you told him you were bringing me back?"

"Didn't know it myself," he replied breezily.

"Then your intention wasn't to hire me when you rode into town this morning?"

"No. I just wanted to find you and apologize for how Luke acted yesterday. And I wasn't very polite myself."

She could not help feeling disappointed that he'd not had another motive, but she told herself she was being silly.

As though he could tell what she was thinking, Zach suddenly, bluntly, said, "In case you're wondering why I haven't signed up to find another wife instead of hiring somebody to look after my son, it's because I don't want one. I never intend to be tied down to a woman again or have a woman feel tied down to me."

"That's entirely up to you," she retorted, somewhat stiffly. "It's really no concern of mine."

"Well, I just thought I needed to make it clear. After all, you came out here intending to wed, and I didn't want you to think I had any notions like that."

Indignant, she snapped, "And I made it clear to you that I've no intention of taking a husband just to have someone take care of me. I intend to do that myself."

"Well, then, we understand each other."

"Yes," she said coolly. "We do."

When they rounded the last bend in the road and the cabin came into view, Bonnie saw that Luke was sitting on the front porch.

As they drew closer, he slowly got to his feet, an expression of rage taking over his face.

"Let me tell him," Zach said.

"As if I want to be the one," Bonnie murmured.

"He's got to get used to the idea."

"And so do I."

With a sigh, he reined the horse to a stop. "Look, Miss Craven, if you're having second thoughts, I can turn around and take you back to town right now. Maybe you should reconsider going back east. The west is hard on a woman, and—"

"And I'm not the sort to turn tail and run when things get rough, Mr. Pressley. Now let's ride on and get this over with, shall we? I'd like to get settled and then cook a hot meal for the two of you. Maybe a full tummy will make Luke warm up to me a little."

Zach chuckled. "Don't count on it. Maebelle Proctor was the last woman who tried to keep him, and she's known as a good cook far and wide. But she said she had to coax him to eat every bite, because he was so homesick."

Homesick, my foot, Bonnie thought, disgusted. What he needed was to be shown who was boss, and if he wanted to go hungry in the meantime, fine. She would be good to him, but he would soon find out the days of coddling and catering to his whims were over.

"What's she doing here?" Luke asked, stomping down the steps with a hateful glance at Bonnie.

Zach dismounted, then helped her down. "This is Miss Craven, Luke. You can call her Miss Bonnie, though. And she's going to stay here and look after you while I'm tending the steers."

Luke cried, "I don't want her to! And we don't need her."

"Yes, we do," Zach said firmly. "We need her a lot. And I want you to be nice to her, or we'll take a little trip out behind the woodshed."

Luke backed away, still staring venomously at Bonnie. "Momma never hit me. She'd never let you, neither. And I'll tell her. I'll tell her if you do, and she'll be so mad she'll hit you for doing it."

Zach held out a hand to him, but he bolted out of reach. "Luke, listen. You can't act like this. I've got to have someone to look out for you, and you know it. What do you want me to do? Sell the ranch and move into town so I won't have to worry about you out here in this wilderness?"

"We can move back east and live with Momma. She wanted to take me with her. You know she did. Only you wouldn't let me go, and now you're bringing this—this witch to try and take her place."

"That's enough. I won't have you calling Miss Craven names. Now get inside."

"Zach, wait." Bonnie started towards Luke. "Let me have a moment or two alone with him, all right? Then you can show me around. I'd like to clean out my spot in the barn before I start supper."

"You aren't sleeping in the barn."

She matched his stubborn tone. "I most certainly

am or I won't stay. I'll not have you move out of your home on my account."

Zach, shoulders slumped, turned away, muttering that he was tired of arguing with both of them.

Luke ran to where a rope hung from a tree limb. Grabbing it, he began to swing to and fro, eyes warily on Bonnie. "You really gonna sleep in the barn?"

"I sure am. You and your pa will sleep where you always have. I just work here, Luke. I'm not going to try to take your mother's place, all right?"

"Sure. Because you can't. And if she finds you here—"

Bonnie interrupted to impress upon him, "I'll tell her the same thing—that I'm here to look after you, and that's all. Now do we understand each other?"

"I don't like you."

Bonnie shrugged. "Well, right now I don't like you, either. So we're even."

He blinked, surprised. "Then why do you want to take care of me?"

"Because I need a place to stay. I also need the money your father is paying me.

"And why should I like you?" she challenged. "You've been nothing but rude to me since we met. There's nothing about you to like for the time being, Luke, but I'm hoping that once I get to know you, I'll find something. Maybe deep down you aren't such a little brat, after all."

He stopped swinging. "I'm gonna tell my pa you called me a brat."

"Go ahead. I imagine he knows it better than I do."

She started walking away, and he yelled, "Where are you going? I don't want you going inside my momma's house."

"Well, that's too bad. I work here now. And you can't keep me out."

"My momma can." His voice broke. "You just wait. She'll fix you good . . ."

It was all Bonnie could do to keep on going when everything in her wanted to turn around and run back and gather the angry little boy in her arms and tell him he had no reason to hate her. She meant him no harm. All she wanted was to give him the love his mother had denied him.

Just as her own mother had denied her.

She knew the pain of rejection.

And wished she could make it go away . . . for both of them.

Zach was nowhere around, so Bonnie decided to go exploring on her own.

Though she knew nothing about construction, she could tell the cabin was well-built, as Seth had said.

The middle room had an area for cooking, but the sight of the cookstove brought back memories of how excited her mother had been over the one in Nate's kitchen.

"I had it shipped from back east."

Bonnie turned at the sound of Zach's voice. She had not heard him come in.

"I thought if I could give Amelia nice things, it would make her happy."

"Well, it should have," Bonnie said incredulously. "Any woman would be tickled pink to have a stove like this. I don't claim to be a good cook, but I can't wait to try it out."

She glanced about. Two rockers were positioned in front of the fireplace. There was a worn, but comfortable-looking sofa, and a long table with benches on each side. She noted that the curtains at the windows were limp and faded.

He saw her staring and said, "I'm afraid I haven't had time to keep the place up since she left, and she didn't do such a good job when she was here."

"I'll get to everything when I can. Just give me time."

"How did it go with Luke?"

She did not mince words. "He's a very angry little boy. I can understand why no one wants to keep him."

His mouth curved in a sad, knowing smile. "Changed your mind already?"

"I told you, I'm not the kind to give up without a fight."

"Good. Now let me show you around."

"I'm doing pretty well on my own. Is that your room?" She pointed to a door.

"No. That's Luke's. And I wouldn't go in there if I were you. That would really get things off on the wrong foot."

"Too late," she quipped. "They already are. But I'll heed your warning just the same. And that"— she gestured to the room opposite—"must be yours. I won't go in there, either."

"Of course you can, because that's where you'll sleep. I've already made myself a place in the barn."

She was quick to argue, "No, I'm not going to let you do that, Mr. Pressley. It's not right. This is your home, and—"

"And that gives me the right to make the rules, Miss Craven," he said adamantly.

"Besides," he added jovially, "it will give me a chance to see how bad the roof leaks when it rains.

I'm afraid I've been neglecting things around here to tend the cattle."

She knew his mind was made up and there was no point in arguing. She also wanted to seize the opportunity to ask why the cattle required so much attention. "I thought all they had to do was wander around and eat grass."

Amused, he explained, "That's the problem—they wander. And I have neither the money nor the help to fence two square miles of rangeland. I spent almost everything I had to buy them, and I can't risk losing them. But unfortunately, my land doesn't have as much grazing as farther north, and that's where they head. I have to keep driving them back."

"So that's why you have to be away all day."

"And also why I've let things go around here. I'm out from daylight to dusk most of the time. But they've started herding a bit closer to home, so maybe it won't be so bad. I'd like to be able to ride in once in a while to see how you're getting along with Luke."

She laughed. "Oh, I'm sure if you just cup your ear in this direction, you'll hear him. He's quite vocal in his objections to me, I'm afraid."

He was silent for a moment, and Bonnie fought against squirming beneath his deep, thoughtful gaze. Finally, he said, "You just might be able to cope with him, after all, Miss Craven. I truly hope so.

"Now, then," he said brightly, the strange tension disappearing as quickly as it had come, "I'll show you around outside."

Bonnie found the place as lovely as the first time she had seen it. Quiet and tranquil, the yard sloped down to a lazy, meandering stream. Ducks played on the bank, and Zach explained that he had bought them from a farmer and brought them out to entertain Luke.

Bonnie thought how a weeping willow tree planted near the stream would make a nice picnic spot. There were also lots of wildflowers blooming that could be transplanted to window boxes, but it was a waste of time to think about things like that. First of all, she had come to do a job, not plant flowers. And she didn't plan to be around long enough to care how the place looked, anyway.

Still, she could not deny that it felt nice . . . cozy . . . to walk along beside Zach. He spoke in low, almost reverent tones as he showed her around. His love and enthusiasm for his home was obvious. But that was not what she found so unnerving. It was how easily they seemed to drift together, and she thought how natural it would be to just slip her hand in his, as though they were a couple, intimately discussing their world . . . their future.

"So this is the barn," she said too suddenly, too loudly, as she fought against such silly fantasies. "I hope it doesn't rain. You know, I really don't feel good about this, Mr. Pressley. I wish you'd reconsider."

"What *I* wish is that you'd stop calling me Mr. Pressley. And I'd like to stop calling you Miss Craven. It's Zach and Bonnie, all right?"

"As you wish," she murmured, liking the way he spoke her name. In fact, there were many things she liked about him, and she told herself to be wary, lest she do or say something that might jeopardize her job.

* * *

Unfamiliar with the stove, and not having much experience cooking anyway, Bonnie's attempt to make supper was a disaster.

The dried apples she found in a cabinet that she used to make a pie were far too salty. The crust was mushy and fell apart, and the biscuits also had too much salt, as did the beans and bacon.

Zach remarked that she apparently liked salt, but she said it wasn't that. She couldn't understand what had happened, because she hadn't used all that much.

And then she saw a mischievous gleam in Luke's eyes and knew he was responsible. But she didn't say anything, afraid Zach might think she just wanted to put the blame on someone else for her own mistakes. She resolved to be more careful in the future and to keep an eye on Luke around the food she prepared.

Bonnie had difficulty falling asleep. Lying in Zach's bed was provoking all sorts of strange, sensual thoughts she'd never before experienced.

Her own heat rising, she imagined what it would be like if he were there beside her to take her in his arms, then scolded herself for allowing such brazen musings.

Still, she could not help thinking that she might wait a while to go to California, even when she had the money saved.

After all, Luke needed her.

And maybe, one day, Zach might decide that he did, too.

Chapter Five

Bonnie overslept, waking to find Luke staring down at her with a smirk on his face.

"My pa had to ride off without his breakfast. He didn't want to wake you up . . . said you were tired and to let you sleep. My momma always fixed his breakfast. Mine, too."

Sure she did, Bonnie thought. From what little she knew, Amelia seemed the kind to expect to be served in bed and wouldn't give a toot whether anybody else got anything to eat or not. Any woman who could walk away from her own child—

Something Luke was saying caught her attention.

"I was hungry. So I made my own breakfast, 'cause you're so lazy."

"And what did you make for yourself, Luke?"

He had that gleam in his eye again.

"Pancakes. Lotsa syrup."

He took off running, and Bonnie leaped out of bed to follow right behind him.

But before she reached the kitchen corner, she knew what she would find.

Pancake batter dripped over everything, along with syrup and butter and eggs and anything messy Luke could think of to drag out.

He watched her to see how she would react, rocking back and forth on his heels. "Pa made himself some coffee and left the fire going, so I was able to cook. They were good, too. Not salty like everything you make."

Bonnie, hands on her hips, stared down at him. "We both know you put extra salt in the food when I wasn't looking. Just like we both know you deliberately made this mess for me to clean up. But you forgot one thing."

Some of the gleam faded. "I don't know what you mean."

"Well, you're going to find out, because you're going to clean it up. Every bit of it."

He stomped his foot. "No, I won't. That's what you have to do. That's why you're here. To take care of me."

"To take care of you but not clean up messes you deliberately make."

He smiled. "You can't make me."

She pursed her lips as though considering that fact, then smiled. "You're right. I can't. But what I can do is leave you here when I hitch up the wagon and go out to find your pa and take him his lunch."

"You don't know where he is."

"I can find him. He told me last night when he was showing me around that he'd left the herd grazing a mile or so upstream. He even told me about how the stream widens out up there, and how he goes swimming. I thought you'd like to do the same after we had a picnic. I was going to kill a chicken and fry it and maybe bake some cookies."

His lower lip jutted out.

"I also thought maybe you'd like to do some fishing."

His eyes widened. "You know how to fish?"

"I sure do. I used to live by a river, and many an evening I'd catch supper for me and my mother."

He frowned. "My pa said he'd teach me to fish when he had time."

Bonnie could not resist goading, "But he never has the time, does he? He has to try and keep the cattle on his range so he won't lose them. So I guess it's up to me, and I'm not taking you anywhere till you clean up this mess."

She turned on her heel, went back to her room, and closed the door.

For a long time, she sat on the edge of the bed and listened for sound from the other room.

Then, at last, she heard it—dishes rattling.

It took quite a while, but finally Luke pounded on her door. "I did it. I cleaned it up. Now you gotta take me on a picnic—and fishing, too, like you said you would."

She let him in. "That's right, and I always keep my word. So now you can help me with the chicken."

He did so but pouted the whole time over having to help.

Bonnie had to constantly struggle to keep from smiling. No doubt it was the first time the boy had been made to give in on someone else's terms, and he didn't like it one little bit. The other women who had attempted to deal with his tantrums had likely had one themselves in response.

At last the chicken was fried crisp and golden, and the cinnamon cookies turned out beautifully.

"So let's go," Luke said petulantly. "I'm hungry, and I want to get started fishing. But I don't think you know how, anyway," he added with a smirk.

Bonnie matched it with one of her own. "Well, I guess there's only one way to find out, isn't there? But we aren't going anywhere till you sit down in that chair so I can cut your hair. You look like a shaggy dog."

Immediately, he put both hands on top of his head and cried, "No, you aren't! I never let anybody cut my hair but my ma or my pa. You aren't touching it."

She went on as though he had not spoken. "And after that, I'm going to scrub your face."

He doubled up his fists. "No, you won't."

"Very well." She picked up the picnic basket, the contents covered with a red-and-white checkered cloth. "I'll see you when I get back."

"You—you can't leave me," he sputtered. "I've got to go, too. You're supposed to tend to me."

"Tend to you, indeed," she scoffed. "Luke, we both know you're very capable of looking out for yourself, but you've made your pa think otherwise to get attention.

"Yes," she continued, walking towards the door, "I most certainly am going without you. I'm going to eat the chicken and the cookies, and then I'll do some fishing. You can stay here and make a mess or get in any other kind of trouble you want. I don't care."

"I'll tell my pa!" he screamed.

Sweetly, she retorted, "You don't have to. I'll tell him myself when I see him."

Zach saw them coming and waved heartily.

Bonnie Craven, he decided, was an amazing woman. As the wagon drew closer, he could see that not only had she given Luke a haircut, but he looked cleaner than he had in a long time.

He was warmed by the sight—and not merely because his son appeared to be well cared for. It had to do with Bonnie, her zest and spirit drawing him to her.

He also liked the way she seemed to delight in just being alive. When he had shown her around the night before, she had marveled at each and every little thing. And when they'd heard the mournful wail of a coyote in the distance, she had laughed out loud like a little girl, clapping her hands and saying she'd never heard one before and oh, did he think she would ever actually see one?

Amelia, he frowned to recall, had complained not only about the coyotes but about everything else as well.

Bonnie had said she couldn't wait to gather eggs from the hen house.

Amelia said it was a dirty, smelly chore and refused to do it.

Bonnie had scooped up a baby chick and cooed to it, loving the feel of its downy yellow feathers.

Amelia would kick them out of the way.

There were so many differences in the two women, and Zach had lain awake a long, long time the night before, daring to wonder what it would have been like had he married someone like Bonnie.

Maybe things would have worked out.

And maybe he would not now feel so lonely and desolate and too filled with bitterness to ever think of marrying again.

Women could not be trusted.

And Bonnie Craven was a woman.

She might pretend to like his world, but he knew she would likely run away once she became bored. Civilization would beckon, and she would be gone.

But he'd be damned if she'd take his heart with her.

"Now that's a sight to behold," he said when Bonnie reined in the horse. "How'd Molly do?" He nodded to the mare.

"She was a sweetie." Bonnie jumped to the ground and gave her a pat on her rump. "I think I'd like to ride her sometime if you have an extra saddle."

"You can ride?" he asked, surprised.

"Not very well, but—"

Suddenly Luke interrupted to protest, "You aren't using my momma's saddle." He whirled on Zach, angry tears brimming in his eyes. "You tell her, Pa. You tell her she can't use it."

Zach dismounted and put a firm hand on his shoulder. "There's nothing wrong with it, son. Now I want you to stop this."

"And she wouldn't feed me till I let her cut my hair," he wailed, hands running wildly through it. "See how it looks? Awful. Not like Momma did it, at all."

"It looks better," Zach said firmly. "And I like your face clean, only it's time you learned to wash it without having to be told."

"Oh, he will, or like he said"—Bonnie winked and grinned—"I won't feed him. He'll be a skinny little ragamuffin with hair hanging all the way to the ground."

Zach laughed, but Luke stuck out his tongue at her.

Zach gave him a sound smack on his rear. "Stop it. You're going to learn to behave, and I mean it."

Undaunted, Luke continued to rail, "She wouldn't cook my breakfast, neither. I begged her to. I beat on the door and told her I was hungry, but she wouldn't get out of bed, so I made it myself, and then she said if I didn't clean everything up she was gonna leave me home today and hope I fell down the well and drowned."

Disgusted, Bonnie shook her head and busied herself setting out lunch. A cottonwood tree offered shade, and she spread the checkered cloth on the grass.

"I don't think Miss Bonnie did all that," Zach said to Luke as he steered him to sit down. "And it's all right if she didn't make your breakfast. She was real tired, and I wanted her to get some rest.

"And you didn't have to do all this," he said to her, "but I'm glad you did. I can't remember the last time I had fried chicken. I'm afraid my specialty is beans and bacon."

Luke stared glumly from one to the other as he munched on a drumstick.

"I was glad to do it," Bonnie said. "It's been a long time since I cooked, but I enjoyed it."

"Did you come from a large family?"

"No. I was an only child. My father died a few years ago. Times were hard. Then my mother remarried, and"—she gestured as though it were all quite simple—"I decided to make a new life for myself."

Zach reached for another piece of chicken. "Well,

I'm real glad you did, but you were only hired to keep an eye on Luke."

"Ah, you mean I don't have to do any chores?" She pretended shock. "I don't have to fry chicken and bake cookies? Well, then. I guess I won't bother to catch us some fish for supper, either."

Zach held up a hand in protest. "Wait a minute. On second thought, I believe I forgot to mention I was hiring you on to cook, too."

"Of course you did," she said, her tone soft as their eyes met and held. The warm glow he so easily provoked was descending, and she stammered, "I . . . I like taking care of . . . of both of you."

Something passed between them as fragile and delicate as a spider web drifting in the breeze.

It was a magical moment, crystalized and pure as the water rushing in the stream below them.

Zach told himself to pull away, not to let himself fall under her spell. No matter that her hair shone like fire in the sunlight filtering through the cottonwood leaves, and her face was as radiant as dew on the first petals of a bluebonnet.

Neither should he allow his gaze to be drawn to her voluptuous bosom, straining against the bodice of her worn muslin dress. He would buy her a new dress, he thought, as soon as he got back to town. She had nothing. He'd seen that. But he would look out for her, because she was trying to do a good job, and—

"You said you'd take me fishing!" Luke screamed.

He had leaped to his feet to stand right in the middle of the picnic spread, stepping on cookies and smashing them, sending chicken rolling off the cloth and into the dirt.

The jug of lemonade Bonnie had so carefully prepared turned over, soaking everything that was left.

"Now look what you've done," Zach said, exasperated. "You've ruined everything."

"No, *she has.*" Luke pointed a finger at Bonnie, his face red and tight with fury. "She tricks me and tricks you, too, and you believe her. You never believe me. Nobody does except my momma . . ."

Breaking into sobs, he ran away, toward the longhorn steers grazing in the distance.

Bonnie was about to go after him, but Zach held her back. "Let him go. He'll pout for a while and then get over it."

"But I want to tell him I *am* going to take him fishing." She stared after Luke, brow furrowed. "I'm afraid I may have been a bit too hard on him." She told him everything that had happened that morning.

"Sounds to me like you did the right thing. No one else has ever thought of handling him that way, and I can see already that you're the best thing he's had in his life for a long, long time. I hope you stay, Bonnie."

And for more reasons than one, he thought, because no matter how hard he fought against it, she was able to stir emotions he thought buried so deep inside they would never surface again.

She continued to watch Luke. "I'd like that," she said quietly, then, "He loved her a lot, didn't he?"

"Yes, and I guess in her way she loved him, too, but not enough to stay and be a mother to him."

"I suppose you miss her, too."

"Not really. By the time she left, we had grown so far apart, I guess it was a relief. For the first time in years I had peace. But . . ." He sighed. "I shouldn't make it sound like everything was her fault. Maybe I didn't try hard enough to make her happy."

"I doubt that. You seem the kind of man"—She paused, then finished—"who would try his best.

"Now then," she said, almost too brightly, "it's time I cleaned up this mess and got that moody little boy back here if we're to catch enough fish for our supper."

"You really do know how, don't you?"

"Like I told him, there was a time in my life when I had to fish or go hungry. And, yes, I'd like to show him how. Every little boy should learn."

"That's one of the things I've never found time to do," he said regretfully. "I'll have to make it up to him real soon. We'll all go one day. Now I'd better go ride herd on those steers before they think I've forgotten about them and start to ease off."

Bonnie watched him walk toward his horse, liking the swing of his hips in the tight-fitting denim pants.

She also liked how his shirt stretched across his back, muscles rippling as he moved.

His hair was damp with sweat and clung to the back of his neck; his sleeves rolled up to his elbows. Once more she found herself wondering what it would be like to have his arms around her, and—

She leaped to her feet and started furiously gathering up the mess Luke had made.

Such thoughts were dangerous.

After all, Zach Pressley was not interested in a wife.

She wasn't interested in a husband.

And anything in between was asking for trouble.

*   *   *

Deciding to let Luke pout, Bonnie went about the business of making a fishing pole. She had found string and hooks in the tool shed before leaving, so after breaking off a narrow branch of the cottonwood tree and peeling off the twigs and leaves, she was ready.

She had been sitting on the bank for perhaps a half hour when she heard the sound of someone creeping up behind her. Without looking around, she said, "Your pole is ready, Luke. Put the line in the water like mine, and when you feel something tug, give it a hard yank."

"Maybe I don't want to," he said, sitting down a ways from her.

She shrugged. "Then don't."

A few moments later, she caught a nice-sized fish, and before she even had the hook out of its mouth, Luke had picked up his pole and put the line in the water.

There were several misses, but when he finally caught one, Bonnie didn't know who was thrilled more.

"See?" she beamed, patting him on the shoulder. "I knew you'd learn fast."

His proud grin did not leave his face, but she felt him cringe at her touch and drew her hand away.

It would take time, but she dared hope they were on their way.

Luke monopolized the conversation at supper, bragging about the fish he caught and saying over and over how he couldn't wait to tell his mother about it when she came for him.

Bonnie did not miss the tight, strained look on Zach's face as he picked at his food. No doubt he would be glad when Luke stopped wasting time on false hopes.

When they finished eating, Zach excused himself, saying he was tired and needed to be up early, so he was going to bed.

"I don't want you to go out to the barn," Luke cried, banging his fists on the table. "You're supposed to sleep in my momma's room, like you always have." He pointed at Bonnie. "Make *her* go to the barn, and then maybe Momma won't be so mad when she comes back."

"Wait a minute," Bonnie said, not about to be portrayed as the villain. "I offered to sleep in the barn, but your pa insisted he wanted to."

"That's right," Zach concurred. "And I don't mind. Now stop fussing about it and help Miss Bonnie clean off the table."

"No." He scrambled from the bench and headed for his room. "I'll help my momma, but I won't help her."

"Sometimes," Zach said wearily, "I think maybe I should just take him out behind the woodshed and beat the meanness out of him."

"You wouldn't do that," Bonnie said—and meant it. As little time as she had known him, she was confident Zach would never beat his son. He might wallop his backside a time or two, but that would be the extent of his punishment.

By the time she was ready to go to bed, thunder was rumbling and streaks of lightning split the sky.

A bad storm was about to strike, and she worried about Zach sleeping in the barn with a leaking roof.

There was also a cold, strong wind blowing, so she went to the chest in the corner and took out two quilts. She had not seen what kind of bed he had made for himself out there, but she knew he would appreciate extra covers should the rain blow in.

Stumbling in the wind, lightning opening the darkness to show the way, Bonnie went to the barn and shoved the big doors open.

"Zach, I brought some extra covers for you," she called. "It's storming, and I thought you might need them."

"I'm here."

The voice came from only a few feet to her left.

"Welcome to my stall," he said, getting up.

Another streak of lightning erupted, and she saw that he was smiling, obviously pleased she had come.

"I'll just leave these here."

Dropping the quilts, she took a step backward, but just then a strong gust of wind caught the door. It slammed into her, propelling her forward—and into Zach's arms.

Time stood still.

The storm continued to light up the sky, and thunder echoed all around.

Bonnie did not move.

Neither did Zach.

And in the brief flashes of light, they could only look at each other in wonder . . . and lust.

Suddenly, he covered her mouth with his and kissed her long and deep, arms crushing her tightly.

She reveled in the moment, never wanting it to end.

When, at last, he let her go, he started to say something, but Bonnie was not waiting to listen.

Embarrassed by how she had so willingly accepted his kiss, his caress, she fled into the night.

And the storm exploding above was nothing compared to the one she now felt in her heart.

Chapter Seven

After that night in the barn, Bonnie knew nothing would ever be the same.

No man had ever kissed her before, but she had welcomed it, kissing Zach back and clinging to him.

The next morning, he had not come to the house, instead going straight to the range. She found herself washed with relief, not sure she could have faced him just yet. She needed time to compose herself, feeling as though her insides would never stop churning.

When he had pulled her into his arms to hold her tight against him, it had been everything she thought it would be. She felt wanted, protected, and cherished.

And when he had let her go, the emptiness of her world, her very soul, came flooding back.

Afterward, her first impulse had been to leave, but she knew it would be best to wait until she had the means to do so. Till then, she would have to resist the feelings Zach had ignited.

In the days that followed, Luke continued to be a holy terror. Over and over, he told her how he wished she would leave.

"I don't want you here. I've got my pa. And you'll never take my momma's place."

"I'm not trying to," she told him as she had so many times before. "I just want to take care of you."

"And you make my pa sleep in the barn."

"I offered to bed down there. He knows he doesn't have to. He's just being a gentleman."

Luke had sneered. "No, he ain't. He just don't want to be in the cabin with you, that's all. He knows when Momma comes back, it'll make her mad."

He continued to whine and complain. Bonnie tried to ignore him. Yet she supposed listening to him was better than foolishly daydreaming about Zach and his wonderful kiss. It had been impulsive, and Zach was probably as embarrassed as she was.

One night, a week after the incident in the barn, she spent all afternoon making a pot of delicious stew. This time she was careful to make sure Luke did not have a chance to add extra salt.

The sun was going down when she went out on the porch to wait for Zach to ride in. He seemed later than usual.

"Pa's always back by now," Luke said. He had followed her to sit on the steps, while she took one of the rockers. "It's because of you. He told me he didn't like you."

Then why did he kiss me? she felt like saying as she eyed him coldly. Even when he annoyed her, she could not help thinking what a cute little boy he was and how she wished she could find a way to win him over.

"He only let you come here 'cause he felt sorry for you. He told me so. He said you was starving, and we had to take care of you."

Hearing that did not bother her. If Zach thought saying that to Luke would help him accept her, fine.

"Well, I think it's real nice of him, Luke, and I'm sorry you don't feel the same way."

"Oh, I didn't mind him feeding you," he said matter-of-factly, "but it seems to me you'd be full by now, so why are you staying?"

"Because I'd miss you if I left," she said . . . and meant it. Despite how he acted, she had grown fond of him. If given time and inclination, she was sure she would even love him as though he were her own child.

"I don't believe you," he mumbled.

"Well, it's true."

Leaning back in the rocker, she closed her eyes. There was a cooling breeze as the sun sank lower, and it was a pleasant, dreamy time.

She wished Zach were there to share it with her and imagined how it would be.

He would take the rocker next to her, and they would sip lemonade as he told her how his day had gone on the range. Then they would go inside and have supper. And afterward, they would walk along the banks of the stream, holding hands as they shared hopes and dreams and became one spirit, one love.

At last, they would go to bed, and he would take her in his arms, only this time the kiss would not stop. It would go on and on, leading to deeper caresses, with passion soaring, and then he would take her, again and again.

A girlfriend had told her what it was like. Sue Ellen Whaley had been only fifteen when she married Johnny Barnes, and she had confided everything that had happened on her wedding night.

Bonnie had been the same age, and she had flushed with embarrassment to think of such things and wondered how Sue Ellen could do them and sound so happy about it.

Now, however, Bonnie could understand, because she shamelessly imagined Zach doing the same things to her.

She did not mean to fall asleep, but in the peaceful setting, she drifted off.

The dream descended, wrapping about her like a velvet cloak. Warmth seeped through her flesh and into the very marrow of her bones. Then Zach appeared, and she eagerly opened her arms to him. First he kissed her lips, then trailed his tongue down her throat.

Her breasts tingled in anticipation, and when his mouth finally found and closed about a nipple, her back arched, wanting to give him as much as she could.

His hands were sliding down her hips to hold her tight against him. She could feel his hardness, and it was everything Sue Ellen had said it would be, because it was exactly as Sue Ellen had described what Johnny had done to her.

"Bonnie, wake up. Where's Luke?"

She opened her eyes and sat up straight, hands gripping the arms of the rocker.

There was enough light left in the day that she could see the worry on Zach's face.

"He's not inside. I've looked. And he doesn't

answer when I call him. How long have you been asleep?"

"I . . . I don't know, but it couldn't have been too long."

"I've got to find him before it gets any darker."

His voice had a slight edge, and she sensed that he was annoyed with her.

She followed him down the steps. "I'm sorry, Zach. He was right here. He couldn't have gone far."

"A little boy doesn't have to go far to find danger around here. This is the wilderness, remember?"

His tone was sharper, and she knew then she had not imagined his irritation.

"I said I'm sorry. I didn't mean to doze off, but he knew not to wander away. I've told him over and over he's to stay where I can see him, and he's been pretty good about it, because he likes to try and annoy me in other ways."

"You know how headstrong he is. He was probably waiting for a chance to sneak off."

"I'm sorry," she repeated.

"I'm not blaming you. He's the one I'm angry with. Now let's get busy and try to find him."

Together, they searched the barn, then headed for the stream.

"He can swim," Zach said, "but if he slipped and fell in, he could be hurt."

They walked along the bank for a while, until Zach said it was useless to continue when they could no longer see because of darkness. "Let's go back, and I'll get a lantern and try again. If I still can't find him, I'll ride over to Ben Toomy's place. He's my nearest neighbor, and he's got wranglers who can help."

"Has he ever done anything like this before?" Bonnie was shaking. If anything had happened to Luke, she would blame herself regardless of what Zach had said.

"No. He's just been mischievous, always getting into things he shouldn't. But he's never wandered off. Since Amelia left, he's actually seemed afraid of the dark."

"What about the women who kept him in town? Did he ever run away from them?"

"No. Again, he just misbehaved. This isn't like him at all."

When they reached the cabin, Zach left her to go to the barn for the larger lantern he kept there.

Bonnie sat down to wait, nervously running her hands up and down her arms. She was scared. There were just so many horrible things that could happen to a little boy. Oh, why had she fallen asleep? It was her responsibility to look after him, and she had failed miserably.

Still, she attempted to soothe her guilt by thinking how it was impossible to watch him every minute day and night. What if he got up early and sneaked out of the house? She could not tie him to his bed or lock him in his room. So maybe she was being unduly hard on herself.

Zach returned with the lantern. "You stay here in case he comes back."

He turned to go but froze when he heard a soft moan.

Bonnie heard it, too.

"Pa . . . Pa, help me. I fell . . ."

They ran down the steps together, rushing around the side of the cabin.

Zach held the lantern high, then saw Luke sprawled

under the porch. "Good God, he's been here all the time."

Bonnie took the lantern while he gently pulled Luke out.

"How did you get under there?" Zach asked after carrying him inside and laying him on the sofa.

"I fell," he said, gasping for breath. "I went to pick some flowers for Miss Bonnie, but I stumbled and fell, and the next thing I knew I woke up.

"Didn't you hear me?" He looked at Bonnie with wide, innocent eyes. "I screamed when I fell. I yelled for help. Why didn't you come?"

"Miss Bonnie was asleep," Zach explained carefully. "That's why she didn't hear you. If she had, you know she'd have been right there."

"Yeah . . . sure . . ." He turned his head and stared up at the ceiling. "But Momma would've been there. She wouldn't have gone to sleep when she was looking after me."

Zach felt his arms and legs. "Do you hurt anywhere? Did you hit your head when you fell?"

"No. I guess I landed on my tummy and couldn't breathe, and that's why I went to sleep."

Without taking his eyes off Luke, Zach explained to Bonnie, "He did that once before. He was running and tripped and had the wind knocked out of him. He was so dizzy, he passed out. That's what must have happened, only I'm surprised he was unconscious for so long."

Bonnie wasn't.

Because she did not believe for one minute that Luke had been unconscious.

Neither did she swallow his story about having fallen in the first place, much less that he had gone to pick flowers for her. It was all an act, meant to make her look incompetent. And the whole time they had been searching for him, he had been hiding under the porch, probably laughing his head off.

"I'll put supper on the table," she said, leaving them to go to the stove and begin dishing up the stew.

Zach asked Luke, "Do you feel like eating?"

"I guess so," he answered thinly. "If she didn't use too much salt like she did the other time."

Zach laughed and ruffled Luke's hair. "That was a mistake. And people learn from their mistakes. You don't have to worry about Miss Bonnie putting in too much salt, and we don't want to have to worry about you wandering off by yourself after dark, okay?"

"Yes, Pa," Luke said sweetly, sitting up to put his arms around Zach's neck.

Zach hugged him. "That's my boy."

Over his father's shoulder, Luke looked at Bonnie.

She could not see the lower part of his face to know whether he was smiling.

She did not have to.

His triumph shone in his eyes.

Later, after they had all eaten and Luke had been put to bed, Bonnie started for her room, but Zach asked her to go with him to sit on the porch for a spell.

Heart pounding, she could not refuse.

They sat in the rocking chairs, side by side, and she squeezed her eyes shut and commanded herself not to drift from reality to fantasy, not to imagine they were husband and wife, sharing quiet moments before bedtime.

"I just wanted to tell you again," he began, "that

I don't blame you for what happened to Luke. It wasn't your fault."

"I shouldn't have fallen asleep," she retorted lamely.

"You had every right, Bonnie. You shouldn't have to be on guard around the clock. I think you're doing a wonderful job. I want you to know I'm pleased and hope you stay with us a long, long time."

There was a moment of awkward silence. Then Bonnie said, "I appreciate your talking to me about it, Zach. I was worried you might be upset with me. Now we'd better get to bed."

"Wait, please. There's something else . . ."

She had started to get up but sat back down, apprehension creeping up on her.

"I've been wanting to talk about that night in the barn. I don't want you thinking that when I hired you I had anything like that in mind . . . that I thought you would . . . Oh, hell," he cursed, frustrated. "I'm not saying it right, but I've never apologized for kissing a woman before, and—"

"And you don't have to now," she blurted out, then gasped to think that might sound brazen. She began talking fast, the words tumbling out on top of each other. "It was an accident. Neither of us meant for it to happen, so let's try to forget it, and I really need to go to bed. Good night." She ran inside before he could try to stop her.

Zach stared out into the darkness for a long time before finally heading for the barn.

Maybe Bonnie could forget the kiss, but he wouldn't. Remembering the feel of having her in his arms, his lips pressed to hers, would haunt his dreams for many nights to come.

But she wasn't the sort to bed for the hell of it.

She was the marrying kind.

And he wasn't.

Not anymore.

Not since Amelia.

Which meant he was going to have to get a rein on his emotions, because what he was feeling for Bonnie went beyond lust.

Chapter Eight

Bonnie was determined to stop having fantasies about Zach, but it was hard. He occupied her every waking moment and monopolized her dreams at night.

To get her mind on something else, she worked harder than necessary. He had never asked her to do anything but care for Luke, but she found things to do. She fed the chickens, gathered eggs, learned to milk the cow, and even weeded the garden.

Zach was appreciative but told her it wasn't necessary. "I'm sure Luke takes up enough of your time."

Actually, that was true, because the boy seemed to have dedicated himself to making her life miserable. However, he was cunning enough not to be so bold around his father.

She had been there three weeks when Zach told her they would be going to church the last Sunday of the month. The circuit rider came then, and he always tried to go, feeling it was good for Luke.

Bonnie was thrilled, especially when he told her the ladies took food to be shared by all after the services. She had missed being around people and assured Zach that she would have a nice basket packed for their contribution.

The only thing that dimmed her joy, however, was not having anything nice to wear. Even though she regularly mended and patched her two dresses, they were sadly worn and faded. She supposed that if she asked Zach, he would give her an advance on her salary in order to buy something, but she knew nothing about his financial situation. He might not have any money just then, and she didn't want to embarrass him. So she washed the dress that was the least shabby.

"Don't tell anybody you're my momma," Luke warned her on Saturday. "If you do, I'll tell 'em you ain't."

"*Aren't,*" Bonnie patiently corrected. She was spreading chocolate frosting on the cake she'd made. Luke was standing on the bench beside the table, watching.

She continued, "And I'd never tell people that, and you know it. You're just being nasty, Luke."

He stuck out his tongue. "Am not. You want everybody to think you're my momma. I know you do. But you aren't, and you never will be."

"Maybe not, but I still like taking care of you."

"No, you don't. You just do it 'cause you ain't got nowhere else to go."

Bonnie sighed and reached deep within herself to muster the inner strength that it took to cope with a little boy bent on being difficult. "We've talked about this before, Luke, and I've explained many times how that's only partly true. Yes, I didn't have anywhere else to go when your father hired me, but that doesn't stop me from enjoying taking care of you."

He grunted. "You're just saying that."

"No, I'm not."

"Why would you want to look after me when you know you can't never be my momma?"

"I don't have to be your mother. I can be your big sister."

Seeing his eyes narrow as he thought about that, Bonnie knew she had stumbled onto something. If he could find a place for her in his life that did not compete with the one he held for his mother, it might be a solution to the problem.

"Yes, your big sister," she persisted. "You see, I was an only child and never had any brothers or sisters. But I always wanted to. So you're like the little brother I never had."

"Boys don't need sisters. They have mothers, like I do."

"But she isn't here right now, Luke," she carefully reminded him. She could have told him how it was likely his mother would never come back, but that would only hurt him. And even though he needed to accept reality, it was something he would have to do on his own.

He sighed as though it was nothing to worry about. "Well, she'll come back when she gets over being mad with Pa. That's why you can't stay."

She swirled the thick chocolate on top of the cake. "But you need me to look after you until she does." She'd said the same thing over and over, and though it never did any good, she knew of no other way to respond to him.

"No, I don't," he said, eyes stormy. "I don't need nobody."

"What about your pa?"

He shrugged. "I'm mad at him 'cause my momma is."

"And why is that?" He had never said anything about the problems between his parents before, and she wondered how he felt.

"She wanted to go home, and he didn't."

"But this is your home now. You wouldn't want to leave your father here all by himself, would you?"

He thought about that, then solemnly shook his head. "It's best she comes back to stay, but she won't as long as you're here, and I'll be glad when you aren't."

When Bonnie had first arrived, such candor had been upsetting. But she had heard it so often, over and over, that it no longer bothered her. "Well, I wish you didn't feel that way, especially when I want you for my little brother."

He ran a finger across the side of the cake, digging out frosting so he could lick it off.

Bonnie lightly rapped his hand with the back of the smoothing knife. "Don't do that."

He grinned. "Why not?"

"Because it's not nice. Besides, I don't want smears on it. This is my first cake to take to the church picnic, and I want it to be perfect. So leave it alone. You can lick the bowl."

"Don't want to. It's not good." He scrambled down from the bench. "Momma would've let me have all the chocolate I wanted, and hers was better than yours."

She felt like saying that *Momma* probably never baked a cake in her life. From all she'd heard, it didn't sound as though Amelia had enjoyed being a homemaker.

Repairing the damage from Luke's poking finger, Bonnie then put the cake in the pantry so he wouldn't be tempted to do the same thing again.

Keeping a watchful eye on him as he played quietly on the front porch, Bonnie sat in the bedroom, mending another hole in her dress. Zach had gone to town for supplies, and she was waiting for him to return before making supper.

At last, Luke's delighted squeal announced Zach's arrival. She almost went out to meet him but decided against it. That was something a wife would do, and she was just hired help.

She continued her mending, and a few moments later there was a soft, almost hesitant, knock on the door. "Yes, come in," she called, making her tone nonchalant, as though she weren't fighting to keep from shaking with excitement to see him.

He opened the door and poked his head inside. "Can I interrupt for a minute?"

Glancing up, she saw a mysterious smile on his face.

"Of course. I'll be done here in a minute and then I'll help you unload the wagon."

"No need. I can handle it. What are you doing, anyway? Mending again? Don't you get tired of that?"

She made her voice bright. "No, because I enjoy sewing. Besides, it's going to look as good as new when I finish with it."

"As new as this?"

He held up the green-and-white gingham dress he had been hiding behind his back.

Bonnie leaped to her feet, her mending falling to the floor. "Oh, Zach, is that for me?"

He glanced about as though looking for something,

then said, grinning, "Well, I don't see any other ladies around here, and I sure as heck don't plan on wearing it. So I'd say it must be yours."

"I . . . I don't know what to say." She took it from him and held it at arm's length to marvel. It was the most beautiful dress she had ever seen in her life.

"I hope it fits," Zach said. "I had to guess the size, but it looked like you."

"It will be fine . . . and I thank you," Bonnie stammered, swept with emotion. "But you shouldn't have. And I'll pay you when I have the money, I promise."

"No, you won't," he said simply. "It's a present."

"But you don't have to give me presents."

"Yes, I do. It's your birthday."

She couldn't help but laugh at the impish look on his face. "You don't even know when my birthday is."

"No, but everybody has one, so it has to be sometime. Early or late, it's for your birthday, and that settles it."

He went to finish unloading, and Bonnie could only stand there, rocked to the core with wonder. Then she reasoned he had only done it because he was ashamed to be seen with her otherwise. After all, she would probably have been the dowdiest woman at the picnic. Still, she was deeply moved by his generosity.

Sunday was a beautiful day, all blue and golden with cooling breezes, perfect for a picnic.

Luke was quiet and sullen, saying little as the three of them rode in the wagon to church. Bonnie was sure it had to do with her new dress, because his face had gone tight with anger when he saw her wearing it.

She had expected him to say something about how his mother would have worn something much prettier, but he'd been careful lately to behave in front of Zach. She knew it was part of his act but dared to hope he might be resenting her a little less as time went by.

Everyone was cordial and polite as Zach introduced her, explaining that he had hired her to take care of Luke.

It was obvious that Zach was well-liked. Not for the first time, Bonnie found herself wondering how Amelia—or any other woman—could have deserted him and their child.

After the service was over, Zach joined the men to talk about their crops and cattle while the ladies made ready to serve lunch.

Bonnie was pouring lemonade when Maebelle Proctor, one of the women who had once kept Luke, bluntly informed her, "Some of us have been talking about how nice it would be if you and Zach got married. Zach doesn't need to raise his son alone, and I guess you know you can't just go on living with him. It doesn't look nice."

"We aren't living together, Mrs. Proctor," Bonnie was quick to advise her. "And I am well aware how it would look if we were. So Zach sleeps in the barn, and Luke and I sleep in the cabin."

Maebelle exchanged skeptical glances with some of the other women who were watching and listening to their conversation. "Well, I'm sure it's like you say it is, my dear, but as The Good Book says, one must avoid the appearance of evil."

"And I agree," Bonnie responded pleasantly, "and

I see nothing that could appear evil when we don't sleep under the same roof."

"I suppose so, but I still think—as others do," she emphasized, "that it would be best if you two got married."

"Well, I appreciate your concern, Mrs. Proctor, but Zach doesn't want to get married, and neither do I."

Maebelle smiled. "But it's the thing to do out here in the west. A woman needs a man."

"Not necessarily. Not if she can take care of herself."

Bonnie moved away, anxious to end the conversation, and went to get the cake from the wagon.

She was lifting out the box when Louise McGuffey, a woman she really liked and hoped to call friend, came to tell her to hurry. "Preacher Barnes is ready to say grace, and we always get in a circle and hold hands while he does."

It sounded like a nice gesture to Bonnie. Hurrying over to the dessert table, she quickly took out the cake, set it down, and hurried to where everyone was gathering.

To her surprise and delight, Zach reached out to take her hand, pulling her into the circle to stand next to him.

As Preacher Barnes prayed over the food, Bonnie prayed Zach would not notice how shaken she was by his nearness, as well as his touch.

Afterward, he lingered to say, "I'll round up Luke and keep him with me while you help serve with the ladies, and then we'll eat together, all right?"

"That . . . that would be nice," she managed, feeling her face grow warm. *It doesn't mean anything,* she told herself as she walked away. *He's only being kind because I'm a stranger here.*

She scooped endless spoonfuls of potato salad onto platters, and after a while, felt that the line had thinned enough that she could slip away to join Zach and Luke.

"I brought extra fried chicken and some more hot biscuits and honey."

"Well, I've already tried a biscuit, and they aren't as good as the ones you make," Zach said. "I'm afraid you're spoiling me with your cooking, Bonnie."

"Momma cooked!" Luke all but shouted.

Hesitantly, Zach responded, "Well, yes, she did, sometimes, but Miss Bonnie cooks *all* the time."

Luke scowled. "When my momma comes back, you'd better not tell her she cooks better'n her. If you do, I'll say it's a lie."

Zach began, "Now, Luke—"

Someone screamed.

Like everyone else, he and Bonnie scrambled to get up and run toward the sound.

"Who—who made this wretched cake?" Maebelle Proctor was darting angry glances at the women gathering about. "I want to know, because I never intend to eat another bite of anything she cooks."

Bonnie's heart dropped to her toes.

The cake Maebelle was pointing to was hers.

"What happened?" Zach asked warily.

Bonnie knew he had recognized it, too.

Maebelle cried, "It's got bugs in it. Nasty, nasty bugs. Just look."

Upon closer scrutiny, Bonnie saw what she had failed to notice in her haste to join the prayer circle. The frosting on one side of the cake was messy, as though someone had tried to patch a hole.

Maebelle saw the wretched look on her face and coldly demanded, "Is this your cake?"

Bonnie nodded, feeling sick. The slice of cake Maebelle was holding had several dead bugs sticking out of it. "I don't understand," she said feebly. "They weren't in there when I baked it, and—"

Maebelle shook her head in disgust, slammed the plate down, and walked away.

The others also left, murmuring among themselves.

Zach tried to comfort her. "Maybe they were in the flour, and you just didn't notice. Don't worry about it. In time, they'll forget about it."

Bonnie did not think so. All she wanted right then was to escape the condemning eyes. "I'd like to go home now, Zach, if you don't mind."

He squeezed her hand. "I understand. I'll go round up Luke."

Luke.

Of course—Luke was responsible. It was his way of getting back at her for the way she'd chastised him for putting his finger in the frosting earlier. He had later stuffed the bugs in and smeared chocolate over the hole, and she hadn't noticed.

She did not say anything when Zach brought him back.

Neither did she say a word on the ride home.

It was only later, when Zach had changed into his work clothes and gone to check on his steers, that she quietly told Luke that she knew what he had done.

"It was a terrible thing, Luke. I'm ashamed of you and hurt that you could do it."

He was sitting on the porch, playing with the slingshot Zach had carved for him. He was good with it, too, able to hit anything he aimed at.

"You can't prove it," he said.

"I don't have to. We both know you did it."

"Pa won't believe you."

"I don't plan to tell him."

He put down the slingshot to give her a puzzled look. "How come?"

"Because I don't want to hurt him like you've hurt me."

He shrugged.

"Luke, you've not only embarrassed me, but what if someone had eaten the bugs and got sick? Wouldn't that make you feel bad?"

"Nobody did."

"But how could you do such a thing? Do you hate me so much? Good heavens, Luke, I try so hard to be good to you, to make you happy. And I've told you over and over I'm not trying to take your mother's place. You can be my little brother, and—"

"I don't want to be your brother!" he shouted, face turning red. "And I don't want you for my sister *or* my momma."

Scrambling to his feet, he ran down the steps and disappeared around the corner of the cabin.

Tears filling her eyes, Bonnie went after him.

After all, it was her job to take care of him, no matter what he did—no matter how much he hurt her.

Chapter Nine

Luke did not want any supper.

Neither did Zach.

They both claimed they weren't hungry, but Bonnie was sure there had to be another reason. After all, lunch had been ruined when the bugs were discovered in her cake, as they had promptly left without eating.

She knew it would do no good to coax them, so she went about her business of tidying up.

Luke went to bed without being told, and since Zach had disappeared out the front door some time ago, she decided to sit on the porch for a few minutes before turning in herself.

Stepping into the night, she felt her way to the closest rocking chair and sat down.

Fireflies danced in the shadows, and the air was soft and sweet. It was her favorite time of day, and she longed to be able to share it with someone . . . like Zach.

Suddenly, the rocker next to her creaked, and she jumped, startled.

"It's a nice night, isn't it?" Zach murmured softly.

"Yes . . . beautiful," she managed to say over the excited rush of feeling to find him beside her. "I thought you'd already gone to bed."

"I was waiting to talk to you. I know you're upset about the cake, and I just wanted to tell you again not to worry about it."

He continued, "The bugs had to have been in the flour. You probably used an old sack. But I threw out everything in the pantry. I'll go into town tomorrow and buy more."

She ached to defend herself but since she could not prove Luke was responsible, she murmured instead, "I'm so sorry. I know it must have been terribly embarrassing for you."

"No, because it was an accident. And I think Maebelle was wrong to get so hysterical about it. But tell me, did you have a good time otherwise?"

"Yes, I really did. Everyone was nice, and I felt right at home."

"That's good," he said, more to himself than to her. "I'm glad you like it here, because I don't know what I'd do without you now that I've got used to having you around."

"Well, I'm afraid Luke doesn't share your feelings and never will."

"He would if he'd accept the fact that his mother is never coming back." He muttered an oath. "Sometimes I feel like writing and asking her to get in touch with him and tell him that so he'll stop clinging to false hope."

Bonnie dared ask, "Do you miss her?"

He gave a disgusted snort. "Not in the least."

"Then you don't still love her?"

"Sometimes I don't think I ever did. I was in love with a dream, the thought of having someone to make a home with, a future, but I should have known better than to think her kind could ever be happy in this godforsaken wilderness."

Bonnie was quick to dispute that view. "That's not true. It's beautiful here, and any woman should be proud to call it home and have a child like Luke and—" She caught herself, about to add, *and a man like you.* But that would be revealing secret thoughts, emotions, that had to remain hidden.

They both fell quiet; then, after interminably long moments, the rocker creaked as Zach stood. "I guess I'd better go and let you get to bed."

She also rose. "Yes, I suppose so."

Neither moved.

Then, suddenly, Zach reached out and found her in the darkness to take her in his arms.

It felt as good as she had dreamed about, as it had the other time, in the barn. Only this time, when his mouth claimed hers, she clung to him tightly, never wanting him to let her go.

The rest of the world faded away as Bonnie melted against him. Nothing else mattered except the consuming rage of desire that swept over them like a mountain river run wild.

Zach began to trace her lips with the tip of his tongue. It sent shivers racing up and down her spine.

She could feel the pounding of his heart, hear his ragged breathing.

A strange rippling went through her belly, and as

Zach slid his hands downward to cup her buttocks, Bonnie swayed dizzily.

"God, woman, tell me to stop," he groaned, lowering his mouth to her neck as he crushed her against him. "Tell me to stop before it's too late."

Shivers of excitement shot through her like the blast of a gun. He had danced one hand upward to caress her breast, and she could feel her nipples grow hard.

"I can't . . ." she whispered huskily, her body arching into his, bringing her stomach into contact with the hardened length low on his abdomen. "God help me, but I can't . . ."

With a fierce groan, he lifted her in his arms and carried her inside to her bedroom, closing and locking the door.

She had left the lantern turned low, and the room was bathed in a soft glow.

He laid her gently on the bed. "I want you," he whispered, eyes burning into hers as he stripped off his shirt.

He leaned to kiss her again, then opened his trousers.

". . . must have you . . ." he said throatily, and then he was beside her on the bed, helping her to lift her dress over her head, stripping her of her undergarments to render her naked and vulnerable. "I want to touch you all over . . . feel you all over, but I can't wait, and I don't want to hurt you."

Bonnie thought her body would explode with the raw pleasure that coursed through her as he leaned down and took her breast in his mouth. The heat of his licking, suckling tongue scalded her flesh and rocked her to her toes.

His hand squeezed her other breast simultaneously, fingertips and open palm evoking a pleasure as heated as that which he was giving her with his mouth.

As he took her nipple between his teeth, she could not hold back the shuddering moan of ecstasy.

"Now . . ." He reached to spread her thighs. "Let me have you now, before I die from wanting you so bad . . ."

He positioned himself above her, and she reeled to think of the power in his muscled chest, the strength in his broad shoulders.

She buried her fingers in the soft mat of dark hair at the center of his chest.

He slipped his leg between hers, and she tensed.

"It's your first time, isn't it?" he whispered, the heat of his breath teasing her nipple as he continued to suckle and lick with his tongue.

She nodded, panting with want as her hands slid to his shoulders to cling tightly.

"You have to relax and open up for me. I'll try to be gentle."

She tried but her body refused to yield. Her thighs were stiff, her spine rigid.

He moved his leg farther between hers, spreading them wide.

"I won't hurt you more than I have to, Bonnie, but there will be a little pain. Please, relax . . ."

She gasped as his hand slipped between her legs, and when she felt his finger plunge inside her, she winced at the quick, sharp pain.

"Easy . . . it shouldn't hurt long . . ."

He withdrew his hand, and then she felt the pressure of him entering her. But he was so tender and gentle that in moments she found herself arching toward him once more, wanting him to answer the gnawing hunger within her.

He sank deep inside her, and she cried out, but he covered her mouth with his to smother the sound.

And then the pain receded, replaced by pleasure so deep and wondrous that she felt nothing else.

She bent her knees, raising her legs to lock her heels in the small of his back. Her need was urgent, nearly frantic, and she wanted him deeper, harder, inside her.

"Am I hurting you?" he lifted his mouth from hers to ask.

For answer, she dug her fingers into his buttocks and held on tightly, clinging to him and wanting more. He had awakened a primal need that demanded to be fed, or surely she would die then and there in the wild throes of passion and longing.

And then her eyes went wide as she felt a pulsating wave start deep within her. It spread like liquid fire, and she could hardly breathe as the quickening intensified.

When it reached a peak, she cried out, frightened of the raw, wild sensation that swept over her.

Then Zach moved even deeper and faster, finally pitching his body forward to empty himself into her in quick, powerful thrusts.

Finally, he rolled off her to collapse beside her.

Bonnie lay still, her breath deep and harsh as she tried to grasp the enormity of what had just happened. She did not want to speak or move. All she wanted was to feel him next to her.

Suddenly, he rolled to his side to wrap her in his arms and nestle her close. His body, like hers, was slick with perspiration, and she reveled in the feel. Never had she felt so close to a man . . . and never had she wanted to. But amidst the glory of the wonder just shared, she was plagued with worry that nothing would ever be the same between them again.

Zach was the first to speak, his voice caught on a sigh. "I hope you aren't upset with me, Bonnie. I didn't mean for this to happen, I swear, but I've wanted you for so long . . . maybe since the first time I laid eyes on you."

She burrowed her face in his shoulder, not trusting herself to speak for fear of saying the wrong thing. Zach was merely a man in need of a woman, and she supposed she should adopt the same attitude over her longing for him.

But she could not.

Because the reality was that she had fallen in love with him.

He raised himself on one elbow to gaze down at her. His brow was creased with worry over why she had not spoken. "Did I hurt you? Is that why you're so quiet?"

"No," she answered, though it was only partly true, because it was not her body that was aching. It was her heart. "I'm all right."

"Then what's wrong?"

She wasn't about to tell him, because to do so would ruin everything. Instead, she said, "We shouldn't have let it happen. It isn't right."

"What's not right about it?" he challenged softly. "You're a woman. I'm a man. It's only natural. After all, even if I do sleep in the barn, in a sense we still live together."

"But it's still wrong."

"Who's to know?" He trailed a finger down her cheek. "You're a beautiful woman, Bonnie, and I should have known that sooner or later I'd have to have you. But believe me when I say that if you had pushed me away, I wouldn't have forced you. And if it happens again, it has to be because you want it too.''

"It ... it can't happen again," she stammered, pulling away from him. Suddenly she was terribly self-conscious and reached to pull the covers over her nakedness. "I think you'd better go now. Luke might wake up, and it wouldn't do for him to find you here."

"I'll go," he said hotly, tensely, as he drew the covers away from her. "But only if you really want me to, Bonnie. Only if you tell me to stop ... this ...''

Helplessly, she could only yield to that which her body demanded ... as did her heart.

She had fallen asleep in his arms, only to awaken sometime during the night to find him gone.

After that, she could not go back to sleep as she relived the glory of their lovemaking amidst concern over the future.

More than ever, Bonnie felt she ought to leave as soon as she could afford to do so. She did not want to become trapped in an immoral relationship that could only end with her heart being smashed to bits.

Worse, she worried over the possibility that she might get pregnant. And what then? Zach had made it clear he never wanted to marry again, and if he offered out of duty, pride would force her to refuse.

Finally, as the first pale fingers of dawn crept through the windows, she had still not resolved anything. Because even with all the problems she faced, she was sure of two things—she loved Zach and she did not want to leave him.

* * *

At midday, Zach did something unusual. He rode in for lunch.

"Don't go to any fuss," he told Bonnie. "Anything will do. Crackers and beans will be fine."

Actually, crackers and beans was all she could come up with on short notice. She had been weeding the garden, and Luke had been giving her a particularly hard time. He complained about working in the sun and whined that he wanted to go swimming in the stream. When she refused to give in, he had thrown a spider on her, which nearly gave her a heart attack, because she was scared to death of spiders.

Luke played with his food, refusing to eat, and finally Zach surprised him by telling him to go on outside and play. Normally, he made him sit at the table until everyone was finished.

Suddenly alone with Zach, Bonnie felt unease creeping over her. She wondered if he would pretend nothing had happened, tell her it never could again, or let her know he intended to have her any time he pleased.

She did not have to wonder long.

"I sent him away so we could talk," he said.

She pushed her plate away. It had been all she could do to force herself to eat. "Very well. What is it?"

His hand snaked across the table to close over hers. "You know darn well what it is, Bonnie. It's about last night. I have to know if you hate me."

She blinked. "Hate you? Why, I could never hate you, Zach. How can you think such a thing?"

He withdrew his hand to run his fingers through his hair in misery and frustration. "Because I didn't intend for it to happen, and I don't want you thinking that's why I hired you.''

"I don't think that at all.''

His furrowed brow eased. "Then how do you feel about it?''

She slipped her hands under the table to clench them tightly in her lap, lest he see how they had begun to tremble. She had to pretend nonchalance, or he might realize how she actually felt toward him, and that would never do. He would think she was hoping to rope him into marriage.

She swallowed hard and took her time framing her response. Finally, she said, "I think it was nice, but we have to be careful. If Luke found out . . .'' She shook her head to think of such a horror.

"He won't,'' he said with confidence. "He didn't hear me leave. But maybe you could come out to the barn tonight to be on the safe side. Then if he hears you come in, he'll think you were just out walking.''

She nodded, pulses quickening. *He wanted her again,* and for the time being, she was not going to worry about the right or wrong of it . . . because she wanted him, too.

"I like you, Bonnie,'' he said huskily. "I've grown real fond of you these past weeks. And I hope you feel the same about me.''

"I do,'' she said thinly, wondering what he was leading up to.

He continued, "But I don't want you thinking that I expect . . . anything.''

She was not sure what he meant, and then it dawned with a stab to her heart. He was trying to tell her that he neither expected nor wanted marriage. All he did want was for them to share the ecstasy they had the night before, enjoying each other's body to the fullest for as long as she was there.

Finally, she was able to say, "Well, I feel the same. I don't expect anything, either."

She wondered why he looked disappointed. He nodded and slowly said, "Well . . . good. We understand each other, and nobody will get hurt."

Zach was having a hell of a hard time pretending he gave a damn about anything except making love to her every chance he could.

Hell, she had come all the way to Texas, determined she would take care of herself. She had also made it clear that she did not want a husband. So he was not going to make a fool of himself by asking her to marry him.

"Well, I guess I'd better get back to the garden," she said, getting up from the table.

He wondered why she avoided meeting his eyes, then decided she was probably feeling real self-conscious around him. After all, she had been a virgin.

And that reminded him to ask, "How do you feel? Are you sore? I tried to be gentle."

"I know you did. And I'm fine, really."

He also got up and went around the table to take her in his arms. "Will you come to me tonight? I know a bed of straw isn't much, but it's safer there."

"I'll try."

Hugging her to him, he pressed his lips to her forehead. "I'll be waiting. Make it a quick supper, all right?"

* * *

After he left, Bonnie sank into the nearest chair.

Dear God, how could she go on this way? Sooner or later he was going to realize that she was in love with him, and that would ruin everything.

Lost in thought, she did not hear Zach return until he was towering over her, gray eyes hooded with anger.

"Bonnie, Luke just told me why he didn't want any lunch."

She was confused over his apparent anger. "What did he say?"

"That you put a spider on him in the garden to punish him for complaining about having to work in the hot sun."

She leaped to her feet. "I did no such thing. *He* put a spider on *me*."

"He was sitting on the steps crying. At first, he wouldn't say why, not till I agreed I wouldn't tell you."

"So now you're telling me after you promised him you wouldn't, and you're looking at me like you want to strangle me. What exactly is this all about?"

"I wanted to ask you about it."

"Zach, for God's sake, you should know me well enough by now to realize I would never treat a child like that, even one as mean-spirited as Luke. And I resent your thinking otherwise. I also resent your feeling the need to ask me about it. Luke is lying, and if you want to believe him, go ahead."

At once, he was contrite and tried to take her in his arms, but she pushed him away.

"Bonnie, I'm sorry. You're right. I should have known better. It's just that sometimes he can be so pitiful and sound so honest. And the fact is, I do cater to him because I feel sorry for him."

She gave her hair a toss, and, with hands on her hips, looked him straight in the eye and said, "Well, maybe it's time you felt sorry for yourself, Zach, because you let a six-year-old boy run your life."

"Sadly, I guess you're right. Again, I'm sorry. Please don't let this make any difference between us."

This time, she allowed him to put his arms around her and draw her close, because her heart was aching to see him so forlorn and tormented.

And then he kissed her, long and hard, until they were both breathless and trembling with need.

"Tonight," he whispered against her ear. "It can't get here soon enough."

He let her go, and for the briefest of seconds, Bonnie thought she saw movement behind him. A flicker of a shadow and then it was gone. She told herself it was her imagination, because she was so worried that Luke might see them. But when she walked with Zach to the door, Luke was out at the tree rope, swinging listlessly to and fro.

Zach went to his horse, mounted, and rode away.

Bonnie watched him ride out of sight, then went back inside.

She would have liked to go to Luke and tell him she knew how he had lied, then turn him over her knee and give him the spanking he deserved. But it wouldn't do any good. The boy was determined to get rid of her, one way or the other.

And that bothered her deeply, because she was starting to realize, despite everything, that she wanted to stay forever.

Chapter Ten

It became a ritual for Bonnie to sneak out every night after dark to meet Zach in the barn. They would make wild, sweet love, then fall asleep in each other's arms. And just before dawn, she would leave him to return to the cabin as quietly as she had left it.

She might have been happy had she felt there was any chance Zach might one day love her and Luke would eventually accept her as part of his life.

Zach never spoke of the future, at least not of one with her in it. He talked about his plan to add to his herd of longhorns, intending to be a rancher on a large scale.

As for Luke, his making up the story about her putting a spider on him appeared to have been the beginning of habitual lying, more than just the occasional fit to make him look like an angel and her like a villain.

When Bonnie was alone with him, he was very quiet,

speaking only when spoken to. He no longer got into mischief, instead spending all his time brooding. Sometimes she would catch him staring at her with a strange look in his eyes. Not with hostility, as in the past, but instead with something she could only define as fear. That bothered her deeply as she wondered if he might actually be starting to believe his own lies and was frightened of her.

Then one evening when Zach rode in from the range, Luke was waiting at the road to tearfully show him a bruise on his leg. Bonnie, he wailed, had hit him with a stick because he told her he did not feel like pulling weeds in the garden. It had hurt so bad, he moaned, that he could hardly stand on it.

He had also said he got sick to his stomach because of the pain and the heat, but she made him keep working anyway. In addition, she had threatened that she would throw him down the well if he told on her, and say he fell in.

Zach had related it all to her that night when she went to the barn, and she was so distressed that she could not respond to his later attempt to make love to her.

She had pointed out to him that Luke was not limping when he came in the house for supper. Zach said Luke had a story for that, too, claiming she had also threatened to throw him down the well if he acted as if he was hurt.

"I don't understand it," Zach had said. "All the other times I had someone look after him, he just threw tantrums and misbehaved—like he did when you first came. Now it's getting serious. I don't like him lying."

Bonnie didn't, either, for fear that sooner or later he would come up with a story Zach might believe.

She had decided then and there that even though Luke would feel that his father had betrayed him when he learned that Zach had told her about his lies, it was time to confront him.

The next afternoon she sat on the porch shelling peas while Luke swung aimlessly from the tree rope. Making her voice firm, she called to him. "Luke, come over here. I want to talk to you."

He kept on lazily swinging, clinging to the rope, his bare feet scuffing the ground.

She set the pan aside. "Luke, did you hear me? Please don't make me come get you."

He let go of the rope and walked to the porch, head down, shoulders slumped.

She waited until he sat down on the bottom step to begin. "I know about the lie you told your father yesterday—how you claimed I hit you with a stick."

He showed no reaction as she spoke. He had pulled his knees to his chest and propped his chin on them, staring straight ahead in silence.

"I know about the other lies, too—how you told him I threatened to drop you down the well. This is serious, Luke. You can't tell lies like that about people who love you."

She gasped softly to hear her own words. She had not thought about it before, but the truth was she did love him. True, he was not a likeable child, but she had never encountered one who needed loving more.

Still he said nothing.

Her ragged sigh came from the pit of her soul. "This can't continue."

Suddenly, he whirled about to glare at her and scream, "Why don't you go on and leave, 'cause if you don't, I'm gonna shoot you, and this time I mean it."

He jumped up and took off running.

Bonnie leaped to her feet, the pan of peas spilling everywhere.

Cold chills ran down her spine as she watched him disappear around the side of the barn.

With legs shaking, she lowered herself back to the chair.

Dear God, it was more serious than she had thought. The child had threatened to kill her, and in his confused state he might actually try to do it. After all, there was no way of knowing the extent of the damage done by his mother's abandonment.

She had rarely gone into Luke's room. And on the occasions when she did, to change his bed and tidy up, he always stood right inside the door, watching every move she made.

Above the door was the rifle Zach had given him for his birthday when he turned six. Bonnie had thought him much too young to own a gun, but Zach had explained how it was necessary for boys to learn to shoot at an early age, especially in the west. However, Luke was not yet allowed to use the gun by himself. That was why Zach had put it in a rack where he couldn't reach it.

But Bonnie knew Luke had sense enough to pull up a chair to stand on if he wanted to take it down, and after what he had just said, she was taking no chances.

She took down the rifle and hid it under her mattress. As soon as Zach got home, she intended to tell him what she had done and why.

But he wouldn't be back for hours, and she had to deal with Luke in the meantime.

She followed him but was not surprised when she didn't find him. Neither did she expect him to respond when she called him.

There was nothing she could do but go back to the cabin and wait for him to show up, or for Zach to return and go look for him.

As the afternoon passed, Bonnie did a lot of soul-searching.

She felt that she had done everything she could to make Luke see that she truly cared about him. She had let him know she was not trying to take his mother's place.

But now it all seemed so futile. He really and truly despised her and apparently would stop at nothing to get rid of her.

She thought, too, about her love for Zach. Her prayer had been that a miracle would happen and he would love her, too, and they would get married and be a family, the three of them. With a warm glow, she also mused over how she had dreamed about having children with Zach.

One night after they had made love, and they had been talking about Luke's refusal to accept that his mother was likely not coming back, Zach had mentioned that perhaps he should tell him about the divorce. Amelia's father had written to let him know it was taken care of and he was free. Zach had not let Luke know for fear of how he might react.

Bonnie had gingerly suggested that he should tell Luke, hinting it was time the child was forced to face reality.

But Zach had seemed reluctant and had not brought up the subject again.

However, learning he was free to marry if he chose to had a profound effect on Bonnie as she dared wonder if he might care for her enough to change his mind about taking another wife.

She knew he was fond of her. He let her know in dozens of ways that he cared, like sometimes taking the time to pick a bunch of wildflowers and, when he rode into town, always bringing back something for her—a scarf, a new bonnet, material to make a dress.

But he never spoke of love and neither did she.

At last, Zach came home. She did not get up to meet him, half expecting Luke to pop out of the tumbleweeds on the road to tell him yet another horrific lie.

She returned his wave of greeting with little enthusiasm, dreading what was to come.

"How did things go today?" he asked when he fell, exhausted, into the chair next to her. "Did Luke behave himself? Where is he, by the way?" He glanced around, noticing for the first time that Luke wasn't there.

"He ran away several hours ago," she said dully. "I looked for him, called him, but he wouldn't come. Perhaps you'd better try to find him."

Zach sat up straight to stare at her incredulously. "He's been gone how long? Jesus, Bonnie, you're supposed to watch him. What happened?"

"I confronted him concerning his lies about me."

"But we agreed—"

She held up a hand, jaw set, mouth a thin line of resolution. "No, Zach. It was your decision not to let him know you told me about his accusations. Not mine. I went along with it to keep peace, but I finally realized something had to be done. It isn't right for a child to get away with something like that.''

He thought about it for a moment, then conceded, "You're probably right, but I wish you'd waited and talked to me about it first.''

"I couldn't. All of a sudden I had to say something.''

"So what happened?"

"He threatened to kill me.''

Zach stared at her in wonder for a few seconds, then burst into laughter. "I don't believe it. You must have misunderstood him. Luke's just a little boy—a very troubled little boy and understandably so after what he's been through. But he'd never threaten to kill you or anybody else.''

Bonnie felt irritation bristling. She did not like him taking the situation so lightly. "He's a very *strange* little boy, Zach, and quite frankly, I think he's capable of just about anything.''

"And I think you're wrong." He got to his feet. "I'm going to find him, and then I think it's time the three of us had a talk.''

"Yes," she agreed at once, matching his sharp, tense glare. "Actually, it's past time. You've let him get away with far too much, Zach.''

"Maybe I have," he said tightly as he stalked from the porch, "but the least you could have done was keep an eye on him till I got home, like you're being paid to do.''

Paid to do . . .

The phrase bounced around inside her head like a ball with spikes, stinging, stabbing, hurting.

Did he also consider that her sneaking out to the barn every night like a wanton whore was part of what she was being paid to do?

Maybe he did, because it suddenly appeared that he had no regard for her beyond that of a hired hand.

There had been no tenderness in his tone, no understanding.

Only contempt and anger.

And she deserved neither.

Zach returned a short while later with Luke in tow.

"He was hiding in the barn, scared to come back to the cabin," he said as Luke darted past Bonnie and ran inside.

Resentment rose inside her, but she swallowed against it to calmly say, "He had no reason to be afraid. When are you going to realize it's all an act?"

"Maybe that's true, Bonnie, but if you'd try to understand—"

"That's what I've been doing for weeks—trying to understand. About the extra salt poured in the food, the bugs in the cake, spiders down my back—everything. Because I firmly believe he was responsible." She shook her head briskly. "But I can't, Zach No matter how hard I try, I can't understand why he hates me so.

"And I have fears, too," she rushed to emphasize. "Fears that sooner or later he's actually going to be able to make you believe one of his lies. And I can't bear for that to happen, because—"

She had been about to break her most solemn vow, about to say that she could not stand the thought of him turning against her, because she cared for him so deeply. He had, in days past, begun to gaze at her with something akin to adoration, and her heart trembled to imagine antipathy in his eyes instead.

But she did not reach that point of no return, because just then Luke burst through the door and onto the porch to scream, "She stole my gun, Pa! She stole my gun, 'cause she's gonna shoot me with it."

He threw himself against Zach in near hysteria.

"Make her go away. Make her leave, Pa. Make her leave before she kills me. . . ."

He clung to Zach, sobbing, and over his head, Zach's eyes met Bonnie's as he asked, "Well, you wanted to confront him about his lies. So did you do what he says or not?"

She did not hesitate to confirm, "I certainly did. After he threatened me, I took the gun and hid it."

"See?" Luke wailed. "She did steal it."

Zach asked him, "Did you threaten to shoot her, son?"

Burrowing his head on his father's shoulder, Luke's denial was barely audible. "No, Pa. I didn't. I swear I didn't. You gotta believe me."

"Well, go to your room for now. We'll talk about it later."

"Will you get my gun back?"

"We'll see. Now run along."

Again, Luke hurried inside without so much as a glance in Bonnie's direction.

When they were once more alone, Bonnie knew it was time for her to admit defeat.

Luke would never accept her.

And Zach could never love her.

And it was best to leave before Zach came to hate her as Luke did.

Zach gave a weary sigh. "I wish you hadn't done that. That rifle was his most prized possession. He lives for the day he'll be old enough to shoot so he can go hunting with me. I'm afraid your taking it has just made things between you two worse."

"Things couldn't *be* any worse," she snapped. "And I've been doing a lot of thinking and decided I don't want to work here anymore."

He was quick to protest, "Wait a minute. I know you're angry and upset right now, but—"

"My mind is made up. I quit."

He shook his head in disbelief. "But you've nowhere to go."

"You owe me a month's pay and more. I can get by till I find work. There are other places to look besides Houston. Besides Texas, too."

She added the lie, "I'm afraid I don't like anything around here anymore. I'm ready to leave."

Zach reeled as though he'd been slapped.

"So if you'd be so kind as to lend me the mare to ride to town, I'll go tomorrow morning. I'll leave her at Seth's, and you can get her the next time you're there."

"If that's what you want," he said tightly.

"Yes," she lied again. "It's what I want. Now I'm going inside to give Luke his gun back, fix your supper, and pack."

After she left him, Zach sat for a long time, frozen in anger and disappointment.

He might have known she would eventually leave.

Like Amelia.

But with Bonnie it was different.

He cared if she went.

But oh, God, how he wished he didn't, because somewhere along the way he had fallen in love with her.

And when she went, she would take his heart with her.

Bonnie set out food for Zach and Luke's supper, then went to her room to spend her last night there.

As when she had left Philadelphia, it did not take long to pack, for she took only what she had brought with her. Everything Zach had given her she left behind.

The night passed with agonizing slowness. She slept little.

When dawn finally came, she looked out the window and saw that Zach had left the mare tied in front of the cabin.

She dressed quickly, picked up her satchel, and started out. Then she paused.

With tear-filled eyes, she looked around for one last time at the place she had wanted so fiercely to call home.

"Fool," she whispered to herself. "You were nothing but a fool to think you could ever win Luke's love . . . or Zach's."

She was almost to the porch when she heard movement and turned to see Luke standing in the door to his room.

"Where are you going?" he asked, eyes wide.

"I'm leaving," she replied. "That should make you happy."

She continued on, but he followed after her to petulantly say, "You shouldn't have stolen my gun."

"I put it back."

"You shouldn't have tried to take my pa away from me, either."

She turned to look at him in wonder. This was

something she'd not heard before. "What makes you say a thing like that?"

"I saw you kiss him."

So her suspicion had been right, she realized with a start. That day in the kitchen corner when Zach had kissed her and she thought she saw movement—a shadow—it had been Luke.

"Yes, I kissed him," she admitted. "But that doesn't mean I was trying to take him away from you."

"Yes, you were. And then I wouldn't have nobody, 'cause my momma's not coming back."

Bonnie could not stand it. Dropping her satchel, she went to him and bent down to say, "Listen to me, Luke. If your mother doesn't come back, you still have your father. He loves you very much. And no woman is ever going to come between you, because even if he were to get married again one day, you still have a place in his heart no one else can ever fill. Remember that, so the next time you won't worry about it and drive someone away."

She turned and left, knowing if she didn't she would break down and cry.

She tied her bag to the saddle, mounted, reined about, and started down the road.

Only then did she let the tears flow.

It was all so sad, but there was nothing she could do.

Maybe Luke was starting to accept the fact that his mother wasn't coming back, but he had yet to stop being afraid another woman would take his father from him. Perhaps one day when he was more mature, he could change.

But until then, he would be a formidable foe should any woman try to come into their lives.

The mare slowly plodded along. Bonnie was in no hurry, and she was too deep in thought to care anyway.

But rounding the bend in the road that took the cabin from view, she thought she heard someone cry out.

She kept on going.

She'd had little sleep. Her nerves were raw. It was easy to imagine things.

But she did not go far before she pulled back on the reins to think about it.

It had sounded like Luke, calling her name.

But no, it couldn't have been. She was doing what he wanted—getting out of his life and his father's. He had no reason to call her, to torment her any longer.

And she felt no guilt over leaving him alone. Zach knew she was leaving. He could have stayed home to look after him. Luke was no longer her responsibility, so there was no need to worry.

Still, she felt uneasy, finally deciding she would have no peace until she turned back and made sure that everything was all right.

Rounding the bend once more, she saw Luke lying in the road and felt panic rising in her.

Kicking the mare into a gallop, the panic became terror as she drew closer and saw the blood.

It was pouring from his leg like water from a downspout.

His face contorted with horror he gasped, "I . . . I fell. And . . . and cut my leg on a rock. It won't stop bleeding."

Bonnie jumped to the immediate conclusion that he had been staging another of his lies. No doubt he planned to say she was responsible for his injury in case Zach had any second thoughts about her leaving. By accident, however, he had really hurt himself.

But his next words erased her suspicions, jarring her to the marrow of her bones as he said in wonder, "You . . . you came back. You didn't leave me like she did."

"*Like she did?* You mean your mother?" Bonnie tore at the hem of her dress to make a bandage.

He nodded, crying. "I didn't want you to go, but I knew you was gonna, so I told you to."

Quickly she wrapped the cloth around the wound, then lifted him in her arms and started running as fast as she could for the cabin. She needed more bandages, and dear Lord, she hoped she remembered how to make stitches with horsehair as her mother had once taught her to do so she could close the deep cut.

As she hurried, Bonnie was moved to realize that, all along, Luke's real problem was the fear of being hurt again by someone abandoning him. He had been afraid to love, afraid of rejection.

"Luke, hang on," she told him. "I'm not leaving you, and we'll talk about that later. Right now, I've got to get that cut sewn up. You're losing a lot of blood, and I need for you to be brave for me."

There would also be time later, she knew, to come to terms with the reality that Zach would never love her. But she knew now she did not want to leave Luke. He needed her. Perhaps Zach would agree to letting them stay in town, because she could not stay at the farm, could not continue their illicit relationship, and—

She heard the thundering hooves of a horse, riding in fast. Then she realized it was Zach and wondered what he was doing back from the range.

"Luke's hurt," she shouted. "He fell and cut his leg. I've got to get him to the cabin and try to sew it up."

They were almost there. Zach leaped off the horse to take Luke from her arms and run the rest of the way.

Bonnie plucked several hairs from the horse's tail, then found a mending needle.

After washing Luke's leg, she told him, needle poised, "This is going to hurt, but it has to be done. Can you be very brave and hold still for me?"

Her heart lurched when he said, "I . . . I think I can. If you won't leave me."

"I'm not going to leave you, Luke."

"I'm so sorry I told Pa lies about you." His voice trembled with guilt and pain. "I just wanted to hate you so it wouldn't hurt when you left me like my momma did."

"That's not going to happen," she said, not looking at Zach, not caring, for the moment, what he thought about any of it.

She made the first stab with the needle and glanced at Luke to see he was gritting his teeth and had squeezed his eyes shut. But he did not make a sound.

When it was over, and the wound was closed, Bonnie told him to try to take a nap. "When you wake up, I'll fix you something to eat, and we'll talk, all right?"

"All right," he said, rubbing at his nose with the back of his hand. "Just so you don't run away."

She kissed him on the cheek, then ruffled his hair and promised she would never do that.

Motioning Zach, who had stood by in amazed silence, to join her out on the porch, she minced no words. "I'm staying. I know now why Luke acted the way he did, but he'll never distrust me again, because I came back to him when he needed me the most.

"But if I am to take care of him," she rushed on, not giving Zach a chance to speak, "you're going to have to find us somewhere in town to live. I'm not going to stay here under the same conditions as before. I'll not be your whore, Zach, and that's final."

To her surprise, he smiled. "Haven't you asked me why I came back from the range like I did?"

"There hasn't been time to ask," she said, puzzled as to how he could find any humor in the situation.

"It was because I realized I couldn't let you go. I love you, Bonnie, and I was going to ask you to marry me despite Luke."

For a moment, Bonnie was too astonished to speak.

His smile faded. "I guess you don't feel the same way."

For answer, she threw her arms around him and cried, "Oh, yes, I do, Zach Pressley, and don't you think for one minute you're going to take that proposal back, because I accept."

And as his lips closed over hers in a kiss to avow their deep and abiding love, a loud cheer was heard.

Luke had managed to limp to the window to witness the happy moment and to express the joy he felt at knowing he would never again be abandoned by someone he loved.

And, their hearts bursting with happiness, Bonnie and Zach broke apart to run and join him, to fold him in the circle of their love . . . their family . . their future.